7011055?

THE ARK

THE STORY OF CLARA HAMILTON

CHAD E. HOLLINS

abbott press

Copyright © 2020 Chad E. Hollins.

All rights reserved. No part of this book may be used or reproduced by any means, graphic, electronic, or mechanical, including photocopying, recording, taping or by any information storage retrieval system without the written permission of the author except in the case of brief quotations embodied in critical articles and reviews.

This is a work of fiction. All of the characters, names, incidents, organizations, and dialogue in this novel are either the products of the author's imagination or are used fictitiously.

Abbott Press books may be ordered through booksellers or by contacting:

Abbott Press
1663 Liberty Drive
Bloomington, IN 47403
www.abbottpress.com
Phone: 1 (866) 697-5310

Because of the dynamic nature of the Internet, any web addresses or links contained in this book may have changed since publication and may no longer be valid. The views expressed in this work are solely those of the author and do not necessarily reflect the views of the publisher, and the publisher hereby disclaims any responsibility for them.

Any people depicted in stock imagery provided by Getty Images are models, and such images are being used for illustrative purposes only. Certain stock imagery © Getty Images.

Steve Wonder, Superstition lyrics © Jobete Music Co. Ltd., Johanan Vigoda Admin. Acct. Stevie Wonder Catalogue, Jobete Music Co Inc, Black-bull-music, Inc., Black Bull Music Inc, Jobete Music Co., Inc.

To contact author email t.ark17@yahoo.com
Or visithttp://www.thearkclarahamilton.com

THE HOLY BIBLE, NEW INTERNATIONAL VERSION®, NIV® Copyright © 1973, 1978, 1984, 2011 by Biblica, Inc.® Used by permission. All rights reserved worldwide

ISBN: 978-1-4582-2247-3 (sc)
ISBN: 978-1-4582-2246-6 (hc)
ISBN: 978-1-4582-2245-9 (e)

Library of Congress Control Number: 2019912850

Print information available on the last page.

Abbott Press rev. date: 8/20/2020

In Dedication

In memory of my mother,
Mattie Evelyn Hollins
(Darlene)
1945—2007
The Matriarch of our family
Someone truly to be missed

The Ark

'In Dedication

In Memory of My father,
Everette Walmsley Hollins
Unafraid to speak his truth
1936—2009
He lived his life well

The Ark

In Dedication

In memory of My Brother
Gregory Ladette Hollins
Wisdom At a young Age
1966—2017
I miss you

The Ark

I wrote this story after the passing of my mother, father, and brother. Something God put in my heart as a blessing for me and a blessing I wanted to share with you.

I hope you enjoy the story

C.H.

The Letter

Hello … it's me again. I was just checking in on you to see how you were doing and if maybe we could talk. Are you all right? I was lying here in bed, wondering if calling you would be the right thing to do or if I would be ruining things again, so I decided to write. Maybe you could write me back sometime. Or call me and talk. Maybe through all our hurt and pain, we could just take some time to talk again. Without any complications and with no one to blame, maybe just a simple hello would be good for us.

Remember when we were young, without a care in the world? Every morning you would open the window so we could both feel the soft breeze and warm sun. Remember the love letters I used to write to you? I used to come home and find you with soft music playing, our bath drawn, telling me how much my letters meant to you. I'm sorry I stopped writing you. I know you're probably thinking this is getting a little redundant, but it's four in the morning and redundancy is all I have now.

Clara, we are an old love. Yes, an old love, and we took its worth for granted, but I know better now, and the loss is too much. I know you felt like we needed some time apart so our hearts could heal, but my heart has been hurting over all this healing we've been trying to do. Clara, I'm tired. Maybe I'm not that strong. Maybe I'm not as strong as you, but I still feel like I'm strong enough to wake up in the morning with you in my arms despite all that we've been through. Someone has to find the strength and the courage to love in a hurt that might never stop hurting. Someone has to have faith we can start over again. I was just laying here in bed wondering if you and I could start again, maybe with just a simple—hello.

Love,
Me

CHAPTER

1

The Thousandth Time

I READ HIS letter for what felt like the thousandth time, wondering how he had known I was there. I had been struggling with the cards life had dealt me, and the letter was just another reminder of all I had lost. That July morning, along an Arizona mountain trail, I rested on a large rock, wanting to put it all behind me. The grip of my fingers softened as the letter escaped my hands and blew away.

The dryness of the mountain heat was unforgiving and almost too much to bear, I began running again. Drenched in sweat, my mind and body in two different worlds, I spotted the cliff I had thought of jumping off the night before. My gaze hung on it just for a moment… I pushed through the dry brush, the orange dirt swallowing my feet with every step. I picked up speed, trying to outrun the thoughts of my sorrows. The loss of a loved one is devastating, but the loss of a child is life-changing. My four-year-old son Joshua gone forever.

My chest throbbed like a ticking time bomb, yet I forced my legs to keep moving. The brush thinned as the cliff approached with a sharp edge. My mouth started trembling. My legs weakened.

Sweat blended with the warm tears forming in my eyes. I took a deep breath, stretched my arms out wide, squeezed my eyes shut, and decided to jump.

Flinging myself into the air, I pushed off on the last track of hard rock as the runway below my feet ran out and opened to a gaping landscape two thousand feet below. I had surrendered and given up all control over my life.

Tears burst out of my eyes as a calming peace fell upon me, releasing the fatigue weighing me down. Afraid of where my thoughts had taken me, and amazed at how I had let myself go to the darkest places of my life; I opened my eyes in a maze of panic. The reality of my jump was approaching a swift conclusion. *Oh no. Not like this.* I searched my vest for the handle to my ripcord but couldn't find it. After another huge breath that appeared to be my last, I pedaled my arms in the air, frantically searching my vest again. My hand fumbled across the ripcord, but it rolled away from my sweaty palms.

I grasped again. Yes, I had it. I clutched it so tight that the rope burns stripped my skin as I gave the handle a hard yank. The parachute inflated with a jolt, decreasing my speed. I clutched my stomach – shaking as I tearfully coasted the rest of the way down.

This, dear friend, is my story.

CHAPTER

2

I Thought to Speak to You

A T THE age of thirty-seven, I was a world-renowned archaeologist who had just jumped off a cliff in a bid to escape reality. Archaeology was the way I made my living, but doing extreme stunts was how I got my kicks. I had hoped jumping off that cliff would be the distraction I needed, invoking a fear far greater than the painful reality that had been wrestling in my mind. I had always enjoyed cliff diving, but, unfortunately, this was one of those days. I was having a rough time enjoying life.

The chute inflated over my head, jerking me upward, carrying me along with the rushing winds. For a few peaceful moments, I was like an eagle soaring over the rust-brown landscape of the desert, the hot wind blowing against my face. For a moment, I felt peace again. The beauty of mother earth rested below in all her glory. I could smell the delicate cactus plants in the air, giving it that distinct flavor just before it rains.

I tossed my head back, and my arms fell free. Like that, I could be anywhere. My tormented mind had lost this round again, as it had surrendered over to silence. I felt as if I were floating through heaven, tossing my head back once more. But having opened my chute so late, I had little time to relax. The ground was rushing toward me, and I could barely brace myself for a landing. A few sacred breaths were all I had.

I hit the dry ground with a hard thump, knocking the wind out of myself. I lay there for a moment, trying to recover, when I heard someone parachuting out of the sky above me yell, "Heads up!"

In a panic, I released myself from my gear and then tucked and rolled away just in time to avoid being tied up in the giant spider web that grew out of my chute.

Nearly crashing down on me was my best friend, Mike McCarty, followed by the rest of my team of helpers. They all had jumped off the same cliff I had, but me, in my cocoon of sadness, had forgotten they were all right behind me.

They hit the ground, laughing and hooting. I wiped the sweat off my brow and stood up with a groan.

"Hey, Mike, you didn't have to land near my head. You could have hurt me," I snapped at him as the pain of the landing brought me back to reality.

He laughed as he put away his chute. "And you didn't have to make your head such a pretty cushion for my fall."

I smirked. "Jerk."

"Clara, what happened? Did you forget we were behind you? I don't know why you have to be such a loner when you have such amazing friends in your life. Me, case in point." He winked. "Remember the old saying? 'Life is but a whisper; Eagle Eyes, live it out loud, you only get this one chance.' Stay focused, Clara. Stay focused."

He must have realized that my mind had wandered off again, betrayed by the blank look in my eyes. The urge to hide behind words was now stronger than ever.

"Okay, smart-aleck, but don't forget you're the one who talked me into this cliff-diving thing." I brushed off the baked dirt, shaking off the pain and hoping he would let it go.

"That's right. All in the name of living out loud," he chuckled.

I sighed with a smile, feeling accomplished. You always got an overload of encouraging words when your best friend was a self-help guru, and Mike couldn't turn that part of himself off.

My colleagues called me Dr. Clara or Dr. Clara Hamilton. But Mike called me Eagle Eyes because of my attention to detail. He knew I had a gift. With only my eyes, I could map out any landscape, territory, or mountain ridge, if given the chance. It had come in handy a few times.

Mike had been trying to help me get back to my old self for a while now.

I threw on my sunglasses to hide my distress and resumed my well-practiced façade of calm.

I wasn't going to tell him about the letter. I didn't need him treating me as if I were emotionally fragile. I just wanted to jump and be free. Those seconds of peace seemed like miles away.

I swiveled, turning away, then reeling back as he continued, "You know I only have your best interests at heart. Focus on today and the expedition." His eyes widened, trying another tactic. "We might make history today, Clara. Yes, history. So, stay focused."

My tooth bit into my lip, forming a gate on my emotions. I tried to take Mike's advice, tried to change my focus and become the Clara everyone needed me to be. I needed to do this for myself as well as for my team. I felt it would help me feel whole again, and success would be lucrative for the team. Times were tough, universities and research facilities had cut back funding. They would only give money to small digs with great potential for prestige. So, we—a team of maverick scientists working outside the system—were on a quest for just that money and fame.

My credibility was on the line. After the past four years, mostly thanks to the disruptive onset of my depression, the scientific world interpreted my absent-mindedness and tardiness at dig sites as arrogance. They took it as "blatant disrespect of my colleagues" as one supervisor put it. In truth, I was still mourning.

Sensing my colleagues had begun to doubt my work and that no one would consider me a worthy addition to their team, I had called on this unique collage of individuals—Mike, Pam, Sue, and Terry, a bunch of fellow outcasts—to help me carry out this expedition.

We were seeking to prove a new scientific theory, and I felt like we had landed in the right place to find what I believed would be one of the birthplaces of history. I had hoped all my research would prove to be accurate, because Harold, an old friend of my father's, still believed in me, but not many others did. He had funded the entire mission, so I owed it to him and to the memory of my late father to get it right. The theory, entitled, *The Origins of Mankind*. This premise would suggest that man burst out of the earth from various places around the world. If this were, in fact, true, it would mean there was not one single origin of mankind but a multitude, which would mean we were not as homogenous a species as once thought. *We are not all the same.* This notion had recently become fashionable across the scientific community, and scientists had begun scrambling all over the world to prove it. So, in the blazing heat of the Arizona desert, having jumped off a cliff, I set out to do just that.

We had landed in a narrow valley between two beautiful mountain ridges. Shading my eyes with my hand, I spotted the camouflage tarp I had ordered hidden behind the sign marking the valley.

My team of four, typically, complained about being drenched in sweat and unable to walk another step. So, I had something in store for them this time. I just hoped it would be enough to keep them off my back for a while so we could get on with the adventure. When we reached the sign, I pulled back the tarp and uncovered some new members of our team—five ATVs.

"Surprise! Guys, here are our new modes of transportation. I had these flown in a few days before we got here."

Mike whistled, letting the sound do his talking.

"Sweet set of wheels," Sue said. "Wow, you did it again."

Terry nodded in agreement.

Yet it was Pam, someone I thought to be a friend but was so jealous of me, who always had something sarcastic to say.

"Wow, I'm proud of you, Clara," she said. "We just jumped two thousand feet off a cliff, and now we're about to race through the desert on four-wheelers. Wow, what's next, horses?"

"Work with me, Pam. I think even if I got us unicorns, you'd still have something sarcastic to say."

"Yeah, Pam," Terry said. "Clara got us four-wheelers, and all you got is a big mouth that no one but you can ride."

Mike buckled over in laughter, letting out a chuckle.

Pam snorted. "Don't laugh at him, Mike."

But that's how we were—always fighting. We all found it hard to get along, but when all the chips were on the table, we fought as one. Well, at least sometimes. They didn't know how grateful I was, but we all realized our worth. Even Pam.

We got on the ATVs and drove over ten miles north to the dig site. Whether prune-faced Pam liked it or not, we were riding in style, taking on terrain and spinning tires at every opportunity we got. Being with the team lightened the air, that, or the sun was finally going to my head and tying up my brain.

We bounced over the dunes of the rugged desert, a bunch of rebels in search of a new idea. Miles of beaming sun later, we finally arrived outside the heart of a Native American burial site owned by the Hopi tribe.

The chief's second-in-command greeted us as we slowed to a stop. I collected my thoughts and put on my best face.

"Greetings, sir," I began with a smile. "Thank you for allowing us to search on your land. It's so quiet and calm, and the people seem so solemn. I admire the way you live such simple lives. Wow, this is just what I needed."

My mind clicked. My heart raced. Oh no, did I just insult him? I hoped what I had said didn't sound condescending.

The tall, slender man with the curious skin markings all over his body nodded. "Yes, it's very peaceful here. It is quite different from your way of living, but we hope you respect our loyalty to our land—"

The expression on his face urged me to stop. Maybe I was doing more harm than good.

"I'm sorry, sir. I didn't mean that in a bad way."

"Just remember our agreement," he insisted. "It's because I trust you. It's why, my friend, I thought to speak to you." He said this while looking at me with a gaze so intent it could have lasered straight through my head.

"Trust me, sir," I said a bit concerned he may not have the patience to go the distance with me. "We're not here to disrespect your culture or insult your people."

That was the problem with the black market. Reputable scientists like us often got tarred with the same brush as treasure hunters, and their lack of respect for anything but gold was a disgrace.

"I have given you free rein, yet you now have your choices." He lit his pipe, purple-gray smoke spiraling into the air.

"Sir, I've spent years researching this area. I've made charts and a map of the site. In fact, I have it here." I reached into my backpack and pulled out the map, forgetting I had wrapped my prescription pill bottle within it the night before. The bottle fell out of my backpack, out of the map, and now onto the ground.

I reached down and picked it up, but the priest grabbed my hands and opened them.

"Oh my god, no!"

We had been strictly instructed not to bring drugs onto their holy land. Not any kind. That was a part of the agreement.

His piercing eyes scared me as he snatched the bottle. Embarrassingly, he read the words on the prescription label aloud, "Zoloft!" They were my anti-depressants. "You're a foolish woman!" he yelled. "Did you forget this is our holy land?" he demanded. "Did you come intending to peddle your drugs?"

"No, I..."

"Is that why you questioned the way we live?" the chief's representative demanded.

"I-I'm s-sorry, sir." My gaze flicked back and forth between them. "It was not my intention, maybe you're overreacting." The words were out of my mouth before I could stop them. What a stupid thing to say.

The priest paid me no attention. He passed my prescription bottle to the chief so he could see the proof of my so-called deception. My heart sank even lower, so much that I was sure it rested on top of my swirling stomach. I took a tentative glance at my team, shock and confusion clear on their faces.

"Clara!" Sue tossed her hands in the air. "They warned us against bringing any kind of drugs onto their land. Not even aspirin. They don't trust anyone!"

The chief clambered onto the most prominent rock he could climb without assistance and let out a shrill whistle to command everyone's attention. "The outsiders must leave," he ruled, and his tribe nodded their assent. He threw the bottle of pills at me, landing in the dust at my feet. I quickly picked them up.

I looked up at the chief, calling for his patience, asking him to give my team a second chance.

"Please, sir, I will leave right now, but please, please, let everyone else stay."

The chief tossed a black feather to the wind, leaped down, and walked away with his tribe, ignoring my plea. The black feather whistled away into the air as a clear signal that before it had even begun, the dig was over.

CHAPTER

3

That's Life

M IKE WAS at my side in an instant. "Clara! How could you be so reckless? They told us not to bring any drugs to the burial site. How on earth could you make a mistake like that?"

I found it difficult to speak, the desert air drying my throat as much as the shame. "Mike, I forgot I'd wrapped the bottle in with my map." I swallowed, hoping to improve my rasping voice. "I honestly did not realize prescription drugs were included in the ban. Please forgive me."

Before Mike could say a word, the nasty tone of Pam came out of the background. She tore up the map I had made, the plans I had put together.

"What do you want him to say, Clara?" her venom cut in. "You've made a mockery out of us—you. How dare you bring us all the way out here and not tell us you were popping pills, knowing what's at stake. How long have you been an addict?"

"They're just antidepressants, Pam. I'm not an addict. I've been taking the pills for four years, just after my son died." My voice cracked over those last few words.

"Four years? Clara! No wonder, your reputation has fallen apart! You've been trying to resurrect your career for years, but now, with this, you're sabotaging ours."

"That's not true, Pam. Before me, you never had a career. I put this team together, not you. I would never do anything to hurt us. Believe me. I am not an addict! Please, guys, don't turn your backs on me."

"You're a liar, Clara," Pam spat. "Just a big fat liar! What else do you take we don't know about? Cocaine? Meth? Just tell us before you ruin everything, we spent years to build."

"That's a silly and baseless accusation!" I protested. "You are no one to judge. Why should I tell you anything? It's none of your business, and by the way, I built everything you've got."

"Everything I've got? Clara, you're a joke," Pam said, kicking up sand and pacing around.

"Back off, Pam. I've got crap on you too!" I shouted.

Terry raised his hands. "Wow, now the long-awaited catfight begins. Two friends at each other's throats. I bet that will solve everything."

"Shut up, Terry!" I watched Pam retort. "It's about your future too, even if you can't see it."

"Pam, stop!" Sue shouted with a clap of her hands. "We are a team. We're better than this!" Her voice of reason weakened the fight.

I walked away from the argument and out of the desert, upset and hurt, with Mike trailing behind me. All of my blood had boiled—I needed to let off that steam.

"Where do you think you're going?" he demanded, grabbing my arm.

"I can't go on like this. I'm falling apart, my life is falling apart. Didn't you hear what Pam said? Didn't you hear the chief? Just look at me, and then look at them." The words wouldn't stop falling. "The Hopi tribe is walking away, and yet I'm here having hurt the people I love the most. That's not me."

"Clara, don't go. We all came here together, so we're all leaving together. We're going back to Texas tomorrow. You'll be alright when you get back home. I promise."

Terry ran over. "Clara, you know Pam's got the hots for Mike, and she thinks you're in her way. She's just trying to run you off. Don't pay attention to her. She's jealous."

"I know, and that's so crazy." I hugged Terry as I watched Mike's eyes roll.

"Mike, I can't get on that plane and fly back to Texas with you guys. I need time to think. I don't have the strength to deal with anyone's resentment right now."

"Eagle Eyes, you're not leaving me, are you?"

I couldn't believe Mike asked me that. "Never. I'm not leaving you, but you don't understand, Mike. This is my reputation at stake, and I failed the team."

Mike's voice slowed. "You haven't failed anyone, Clara. This was just one small mishap."

"What?" Was he crazy? "A small mishap? Weren't you there? What are you talking about, Mike?"

"Clara, this is no big deal. We'll find another dig. Have you seen how big the world is?"

"Come on, Mike, even you don't believe that. And what we just lost is a big deal, and you know it." I pulled away from Terry's hug.

"Okay, but you can't keep running away," Mike insisted.

I yelled at Mike, "Running away! Is that what you think I'm doing!"

Not wanting to talk anymore, I turned away from him. Gathering my bags, I walked out of the painful conversation alone. Behind, the rest of my team grabbed their things. I could hear them muttering all the while, walking out behind me. I couldn't hear them clearly, but their sour faces said it all. Everything we had prepared for was over. Because of me.

They followed me as we left the desert and rode back to the B&B outside of Tucson. The desert dirt coated us as the ride back became another quiet moment. No one made eye contact or spoke a single word as our ATVs buzzed away. The fun of the drive there was lost. Hours later, we finally arrived back at the B&B and the rooms I'd rented for us.

I walked ahead of the group, keeping my eyes to the horrid pattern of the carpet. Pam, not far behind, was whispering with Sue, obviously still seething over the mistake I had made back in the desert.

We walked to our rooms in silence. I closed the door behind me and dropped my bags while whispering into the empty room.

"Here you are again, Clara. Another failed mission. Congratulations."

I felt so lost and empty in that quiet room that it felt big and cold, much to the contrary. I sat on the edge of my bed, gripping the rose-colored sheets only a B&B or a motel would acquire.

I then looked up, and there she was, shattering my senses. A spider, clawing her way up the walls and then to the corners. Absentmindedly, I watched her spinning her webs from side to side, trying hard not to blink in case water ran down my cheeks. As the first drop slid away, another one, and then another one, and I lost control. My tears hit the floor, sounding like raindrops against a windowpane. My head ached as I picked up my phone and left a message with my secretary, updating her on my prospective whereabouts for the next week through choked sobs.

I felt a hot shower would help me end the day, but as I looked up again, I noticed the spider was not rebuilding the old web the maids had torn down, but building a new one, this time in a higher place. Wow, what's wrong with me? Here I am sitting on the edge of a bed, thinking about a spider? Funny how after tragedy strikes, I noticed the smallest of things.

"That's it. Need to get up."

I turned on the shower, yearning to find a way out, profoundly embarrassed and humiliated. I watched that spider build and rebuild the web she called home. Maybe that was life. I wanted the web I had built. I wanted to go home. I called my secretary again and left a message saying I would be in Chicago.

I thought about my team and what they would say when they realized I was not going back to Texas with them. Terry would be cool with it—he was a laidback kind of guy and probably couldn't care less. Sue, the peacemaker, would probably be the first to call and ask to go with me just to make me feel better. Pam's reaction would, not surprisingly, be cruel at best. She could have been a nice person if she tried, but no, like a high school girl, she had a thing for Mike and was annoyed by the friendship he and I shared. If it weren't for her help with the research, I would never have invited her.

Of all of them, I knew Mike would be right there for me. He was the tough and rugged type, wild and crazy sometimes. He was that guy, always a friend. Just as I was contemplating calling him, his number lit up my phone. It was almost like he knew I was about to call.

"Hello, Eagle Eyes. Are you okay?" he asked.

Tears dropped from my eyes. "I'm fine, Mike. I just needed some time to think about everything, but I'm… okay."

"Well, that's good to hear, Clara, because you weren't fine—"

"Mike, please, I'm exhausted. I don't want to talk about all that, not right now. Okay?" I lied.

"Okay, just don't worry about Pam and the rest of the team. I'll handle it." A half-smile tugged its way onto my face.

"Mike, I couldn't wish for a better friend than you, but there's not much you can do." I sighed. "It's over, and I'm tired. I'm not flying back to Texas with you guys. I feel like going back to Chicago."

There was a pause. "Going back to Chicago? Why?"

"I don't know, Mike—it just feels right. I feel like I need to start over and try again. As I said, I'm tired."

"Are you serious? Clara, when we met, you told me you wanted a change. Together, we've made a lot of progress rebuilding your life, and now you want to go back to your past?"

"Mike, I just need some time alone. And going back home might be helpful to me."

"I just don't want you to let anything else throw you out of balance," Mike said.

"I know, and thank you so much for calling to check on me." I was about to hang up when he spoke again.

"Actually, I didn't only call to check in on you but to also tell you a Michael Godfrey's office has also been calling on you. They've been trying to reach you. Do you know what it's about? Do you know them?"

"No, I don't."

"It might be a job for us?"

"Yeah, right. They'll hire us, but then once they learn what happened to us today, they'll fire us."

He huffed. "Hey, enough of that, Clara. Enough negativity. It sounds like you need to just focus on yourself right now. Go dancing, take a break, have a few drinks. If you need a partner to help you relax, I know how to turn it up."

"Ha-ha, Mike, I don't need your two left feet stepping on my toes."

"Oh wow, Clara, some days, your cruelty knows no bounds. I am an incredibly good dancer. Thank you very much."

"Okay, Mike, whatever." The tears had stopped falling. "But my cellphone's about to die, and the hot steam from my shower is calling me, so I need to go."

"Clara, whatever you do, remember that life is but a whisper."

"Yeah, sure, Mike, whatever you say. Later." I ended the call.

With heavy eyes, I connected my phone to my charger, undressed, placed a towel on the damp tiled floor of the bathroom, and turned off the lights. I pulled the shower curtain back and stepped into what felt like a rainforest of hot water pouring all over me. It had been several days since I last had a bath, and I gladly shed the remnants of the desert's sweat and dirt off me as the steaming shower felt so relaxing.

Mike's words played in my head. Life is but a whisper? Yeah right. I turned the heat up as I cried at my whispering Life. Why so soon? But those were the cards I was dealt.

Stepping out of the shower, I walked into my hotel bedroom and raided the mini fridge. I jumped into bed, armed with several tiny bottles of alcohol. The variety of individual servings would give me enough of a buzz to dull my pain—I hoped. I drank the schnapps first, then the tequila. I rested back on the bed and tried to relax. There was more than one brand of whiskey, so I settled on Jack Daniels, enjoying the burn as it slid down my throat. Soon, each little bottle had done its duty. With my head slightly fuzzy, I listened to the pile of messages I had transferred from my office.

The first message was from Ms. Lauren Tate. *"Hello, Clara, we've already found a team for the exploration you inquired about two weeks ago. I'm sorry, Dr. Hamilton, but we will not need your assistance."*

Great.

The next was from Dr. Tom Wilson. *"Dr. Hamilton, I'm sorry, but our research is taking us in another direction. Out of professional courtesy, we are giving you a call to inform you we will be declining your assistance on our mission in Central Africa."*

What did he say? No need for my assistance? Professional courtesy? Classic.

Most of the messages were from people who had once offered me work but had since changed their minds. Word traveled fast in our community, especially if Pam was around.

I clicked the button on my phone again. The next message had a long pause, and then the words *"I miss you."* I stiffened at once as I recognized the voice. Within moments, I erased the message and nearly fell out of bed, reaching and fumbling around in my bedside drawer.

"Breathe, breathe, breathe." With every word, my chest tightened. I was looking for my spare medication or what I called my "not-now" remedy to dull my pain. Six years ago, after a hip injury, I had been prescribed Oxycodone.

That, too, I had been taking ever since.

I thought I was a strong woman, but loneliness is one hell of a beast. I had become a recluse, living inside my own head, my own heart, my own pain, so unaware of the enemy I had allowed it to grow inside of me. Day after day, hurting that enemy tearing me down, I needed to reach out for help.

I'd read all the self-help books and gone to numerous support groups, but I was so deeply in denial that I kept getting in my own way. Half of them were patronizing anyway. Years ago, shortly after Joshua died, I'd checked myself into an already crowded mental health facility and opened up to a therapist. I described my emotional state as being trapped in a dark tunnel, unable to go backward or forward, with no way out. She couldn't provide a light—only pills.

My anxiety and frequent panic attacks prompted the doctor to prescribe the antidepressants I was on. And when my hip began to hurt, the Oxycodone I was using could dull away that pain as well. With a plastered smile stretching across my face, I could hold off the world's judgment and hide the turmoil I felt each day. It was a mask handed to me on a prescription. Unscrewing the cap with a click, I shook out a few pills of each and then washed it all down with a gulp of whiskey with no concern of how toxic that cocktail could be...*Tsk!*

I had struggled each night to find rest in the deafening silence of the dark room. It created a cold backdrop, as if it knew I was unable to sleep. It was like I was locked in a haunted time machine, stuck in a loop of the tragic event that happened four years ago. The ache in my heart was so excruciating that all I could hear were the high-pitched tones of the machine's repeated beeps. Then came a message from a stranger named Michael Godfrey, which said, *"I have heard about your team. I'm familiar with your work as well, and I want to offer you an opportunity you won't want to miss."*

I stopped the tirade of messages and wondered who he was and what he wanted with me. And then, out of my repressed memories, it occurred to me. He was the same person Mike had mentioned earlier.

CHAPTER

4

Superstition ain't the way

EARLY THE next morning, I woke to water gurgling through the old hotel's pipes. My head spun, and my eyes ached after another hungover night. I lay in bed for a few more minutes, just staring at the ceiling, watching the fan go around and around. There were even more cobwebs there. Honestly, it was impressive how far across the ceiling it stretched.

I slid out from beneath the sheets with my feet hitting the floor, hearing a clink of glass. My trashed floor was covered with liquor bottles along with spilled open tubes of my pills.

What did I do? I cleaned up a bit, grabbed my things, and left the room, treading softly to avoid being heard or spotted by the team. Every footstep had me on edge.

Thankfully, I called a cab without any mishap as I quietly left Mike and the rest of my team behind. I was driven to the airport as I had asked.

When we arrived, I paid the tab and walked into the small airport. With it being such short notice, and wincing on behalf of my wallet, I paid the high price for the ticket. Three hours of waiting in the boarding area made me all too glad to finally board the plane. Stuffing my bags into the overhead and finding my seat, the tiredness hung heavy in my head.

Rushing and rumbling down the runway, we rose up and into the open skies. A gulp pushed down my throat as I swallowed, trying to take out the pain as the change in air pressure pressed against my eardrums until they gave a relieving pop. My exhaustion from the night before was finally beginning to catch up with me. I had barely slept.

Leaning back, my eyelids drooped as I tried to relax my body into the uncomfortable seat. For what felt like a few seconds, I fell asleep, slumbering in blissful forgetfulness of everything that had happened the day before. And then I was rudely awoken.

"Ladies and gentlemen," said the captain's voice, cutting through my sleep. "Welcome to O'Hare International Airport. Welcome to Chicago."

Still tired, I sat upright. Taking a deep breath, I tried to still my restless foot as I looked out the window. There it was, the city I'd tried so hard to forget, right there before me again. I wasn't sure I was ready for it, but I needed to be. I thought about another saying Mike used to tell me, "Destiny is something you will never have to search for because it's in everything you meet. You're already there. At your today's destiny."

I didn't know what he meant by that at the time, nor did I care. But for some strange reason, I remembered it, and it floated back to my mind then.

The sign overhead flashed, and I unbuckled my seatbelt, grabbed my bags, and pushed my way through the crowd of passengers and off the plane. Nobody said a word except to their own families, and that suited me fine.

The airport's scent of various foods brought a rumble to my stomach. I hadn't eaten in a while—all the haste had made me neglect myself. *I can't believe I'm back here again*, I thought, hurrying toward a Chinese food stand. Hungrily, I grabbed a handful of fortune cookies from a big jar on the counter and headed to the exit, trying to hail yet another cab.

Right outside, I spotted one. He seemed occupied as he sat on the back bumper of his tricked-out cab with a license plate that curiously read "I—Wish." He worked his way through a fistful of lottery tickets, frowning and muttering to himself.

"Wow, lost again?" he snorted at no one in particular, tossing his losing tickets on the ground. As I approached his bright yellow cab, his face broke into a smile. "Hey, pretty lady, you need a ride?"

"Wouldn't be here if I didn't. You're driving?"

"Yes, I'm your man," he responded, "I'm your man." He came over to help me with my bags. Opening his car door, he gestured inside.

"My name is Rasheed. Where to?"

"The DoubleTree Hotel, please."

"You got it."

Clambering into the cab, I couldn't help but notice all the scratched-off lottery tickets tossed about the backseat like cheap confetti. A faded picture I assumed to be of his family sat on the dashboard, smiling at me.

From his coat pocket, he pulled out a Stevie Wonder CD. He popped it in, turned up the volume, and stepped on the gas, throwing me back against the seat by the acceleration.

"Just sit back and enjoy the ride. You're in good hands with me," he said, tossing another losing ticket onto the seat next to him. "Oh, I almost forgot. Welcome to Chicago."

I sat back as I tried to relax my nervous body to the sound of Stevie's rhythmic voice flowing through the speakers. The earthy music welcomed me home again. There was a worn-out rabbit's foot hanging from the rearview mirror, swaying hypnotically with every turn we made. The cabby must have felt it would bring him the luck he was waiting for. As we got closer to the skyscrapers in the heart of the city, the sound of honking horns, the murmur of the crowd, and the pizza joints, I finally accepted—I was home again.

People scurried along the streets as gusts of cool wind rippled across the lake. The homeless in their ragged clothes huddled together to stay warm while panhandlers wandered about, begging for any loose change passersby could spare. I tossed down what I could with a jingle.

Even spare change was hard to come by. Things hadn't been this bad since the crash of 2008. Although it still seemed lively as ever, the whole city, as well as the world, was shrouded in bleakness. The crashing economy had swallowed the lives of many as it had grown so hateful and desperate, but more—so dangerous. All the people who had been laid off from their jobs and lost their homes were now on the streets or in homeless shelters. We all blamed the politicians. Yeah, the same politicians we all voted for.

I didn't know what I expected that day amidst all the upheaval as I gazed aimlessly out of the window, and yet, something caught my attention. I saw a homeless man holding a sign. In big, bold letters, it read, "And Still I Hope."

It wasn't a sign asking for food, for work, or even for money. The words didn't plead or grovel but simply affirmed that even in his condition and in these hard times, he still had hope. Perhaps sensing my wandering gaze, Rasheed turned down the music for a moment.

"Never mind him, ma'am," he said. "He's just an addict, no one like you." The music blared again. *Wow*, I thought. *No one like me*. Of course, he didn't know about all the bad decisions I had made nor the things I depended on. Yet, as if it were a message to a dead woman trying to come back to life, the words of Stevie's song moved in me. "When you believe in things you don't understand is why you suffer, superstition ain't the way." Bobbing my head to the music, the cabby sang along.

CHAPTER

5

The Encounter

T HE BRAKES screeched as the taxi pulled to an abrupt stop in front of the hotel. Stepping out, Rasheed held the door for me.

"Thank you."

"You are welcome." He smiled as I slipped the fare into his hand.

Grabbing my bags, I dragged them up to the sidewalk only to be stopped by a gaggle of fresh-faced students. Each of them gestured and spoke at the same time. Still, from their demeanor, I gathered they were admirers of mine from my alumna chapter at the University of Illinois. My secretary must have let the news go public that I had come back to Chicago. As I said, nothing stays private.

All talking over one another, the students thanked me for the foundation my father had laid for the Archeology Department. Some held out copies of my father's books for me to autograph. With a sigh, I signed my name quickly, hoping I could get through all of them and just go to my room, but the line seemed to be growing instead of shrinking.

"Listen, guys," I finally had to say, "this was great, but I've got to get going."

They scattered, and I sighed with relief, taking the stairs to the front door of the hotel. But before I could escape all of them, another pen and book were thrust into my face. This time, it was a copy of a book I had written—*Puzzled by the Past A Memoir of History*.

"Will you sign my copy?"

Without even looking up, I nodded, "Of course and thanks." I tried to get my voice to express gratitude, but something felt wrong. The hand that handed me the book didn't drawback but reached out instead, brushing against mine as I gave the book back. It took the familiar scent of his cologne for it to click in my head, bringing about the immediate sensation that someone had wrenched my heart from my chest.

Looking up, I met the eyes of someone I had been trying to get away from. Paul Hill.

I stumbled back in a clumsy attempt to escape. My feet bumped up against my bags, and I almost tripped again, trying to get away from him.

"I just wanted an autograph," he said in a painful tone, "just to see you again. Would you—"

"No!" I shouted, cutting off his plea. "Just go away!"

Spinning away, I pushed my way through the crowd, who gathered at the revolving door, and rushed into the hotel. Out of the corner of my eye, I saw him toss my book into the air and then watched it fall to the ground. The man grabbed his head in frustration, and as if it were happening in slow motion, I couldn't stop watching.

A voice snapped me out of it. "Are you okay?" asked a bellhop in the lobby. "Who was that guy? Was he following you?"

Though my heart still hammered away in my chest, I waved away his questions. "No, no. I'm fine. He was just one of my many stalkers... please, just take me to my room." I fumbled through my bags, found my credit card, and shoved it at him. With a shrug, he slid behind the desk and checked the records for my reservation.

"You're sure you are okay, ma'am?" he asked, keeping his eyes carefully lowered as he tapped away on the keyboard. "Your stalker didn't look very happy."

"My room, please," I said, trying to hold back the impatience in my voice. The bellhop was crossing a line but arguing wasn't going to get me to my room any quicker.

"Of course, ma'am. I'll keep an eye out for him. If he tries to come back, I'll have security turn him away."

Recalling how his hand felt against mine made me shudder. It was frightening. Things were different now. I hadn't seen him in a long time. I couldn't fathom how he had found me there. Then it occurred to me, my secretary. He must have called her.

The bellhop grabbed my bags and led me to my room. I gave him a tip, mostly to get him away, and he finally left me alone.

Ordering room service, I poured myself a glass of wine from the sample of bottles provided. Sitting down on the bed as thunder rumbled through the sky, dark clouds covered the sunshine outside my fifth-floor window. I felt as if I had more problems than anyone. I shot my secretary a quick text, "Keep my whereabouts private, please."

I tossed my phone aside. Curling up in my bed covers, I couldn't help shaking my head. It was unbelievable.

In times like these, the only thing offering me relief was a stiff drink. I remembered the hotel lounge.

I jumped out of my bed, key card in hand, out of my room, onto the elevator. Having pushed the button for the first floor, the doors opened. One small victory that day. Out into the lobby, the bar was just as I had remembered it. Like a jazz café with leather-strapped bar stools, flowing silk draperies, and, well, jazz. Half-finished glasses of champagne stood abandoned on the tables, their owners busy dancing the night away. People sat and sipped martinis, looking on with unreadable expressions plucking olives from their cocktail sticks.

Stepping in and taking a seat at the bar, I waited a moment for the bartender, my phone buzzed in my pocket. Sue had texted me.

Clara, what's wrong with you? she asked. *Why did you leave us like that? You never talk to me. You never talked to us?*

Reading the text over a couple of times, I considered texting back but didn't. Instead, I tucked my phone back in my pocket and waved at the bartender, a blue-eyed young woman with the name "Brittany" embroidered in hot pink letters on her tuxedo blouse.

Brittany looked bored but perked up a bit when I got her attention. She finally walked over to me, and I ordered my drink.

"A double shot of vodka with a splash of OJ."

"Gotcha!" She soon came back with a drink in her hand as I thought to have a chat with her.

"You ever have one of those days when you really just need to drown yourself in your own sorrows?" I asked her. "When you feel like life hasn't treated you, right?"

I couldn't believe I was exposing myself to a young lady like this. But sounding like an old soul, she replied. "Yes, ma'am, I have. We all have, I'm afraid."

She slid my drink to me. "Are you having one of those days?"

"Yes, I'm having one of those days today," I said, tempted to say it was one of those lives.

"I'm from here, Chicago I mean, but I just came back from a job in Arizona. I'm an archaeologist, and I was in Arizona working on a project, but it failed. It's been a tough and slow time for me. I mean an awfully bad time."

"Well, hun, don't you know it feels like that for all of us now?" Her questions quartered me.

I went on to tell her all about why I'd come back to Chicago. Of course, she'd probably heard plenty of sad tales in her line of work. Before I knew it, I was staring down at my empty glass.

"My name's Clara Hamilton," I told her. "I'm in room 526. Run me a tab."

"I'm on it," Brittany assured me. "If you don't mind, I might just have one with you." She laughed, and I nodded.

Pouring herself a quick drink, Brittany downed it in a few mouthfuls. "When this place gets as slow as it is tonight, it drives me crazy. Just when I'm ready to party too." She paused, looking around. "Weird, huh? How life takes us in circles, bringing us back to where we started. We go around and around until one day we learn to change directions."

For a moment, she seemed lost in her thoughts. Then she smiled. "Do you believe everything happens for a reason, Clara? I mean…" Shrugging her shoulders, she said, "I do."

"What do you mean?" I asked her.

"You know the old saying? If your project hadn't failed, you wouldn't have come back to Chicago. You wouldn't have completed your circle of life."

A small smile danced on her lips as she refilled my glass.

"You don't know how true that statement is."

"You seem like a pretty sharp lady, Ms. Clara, with a career and everything. Seeing people like you makes me want to up and find my new direction because this—" she waved her hands, gesturing at the bar "—sure isn't it."

Another customer called out. Brittany walked away for a moment to tend to them and then came back. "These crazy old men get so boring after a while. They're always telling me sob stories, flirting shamelessly. Sometimes I just want to let my hair down, relax, have some fun, but I have to watch out. You never know what those old geezers are up to."

"Yes, you're right," I told her.

"Keep your eye on those old guys," Brittany said.

"Brittany, don't forget, you're young. You can be anything you want. Just don't be a runaway like me."

"Come on, Ms. Clara, you shouldn't think about things like that," Brittany said, flashing me a smile. "Think about it this way, Clara, everything happens for a reason."

"You sound like my friend Mike."

Her eyes flickered toward the other end of the bar. "Remember what I said about the flirty old geezers?" she muttered, tapping the bar, and nodding at the men settling down a few chairs away. "Act cool cause that's them."

The three men looked to be in their late fifties or older, all huddled together, so focused on telling what sounded like loud jokes that I couldn't help but overhear.

"Another dive in the stock market," said one of them. "Did you hear, Charlie?"

"Yep. Heard it on the news today."

"The market may be bad, but I hear that stockbrokers are still sleeping like babies," the first man said.

"How's that?" the second man asked.

"They wake up every hour, crying!" All three of them burst out laughing. "The economy is so bad." Repeated the first man. "Not even hotcakes are selling like hotcakes!" They all expressed their amusement.

As their laughing fit died down, one of them caught Brittany and me staring and turned to us.

"I see Brittany's been telling you about us. I guess it would be rude not to introduce ourselves. My name's Earl, and this is Charlie and Sam. We're traveling salesmen."

"It's great to meet you," I said without hesitating to toss back another drink. I had a feeling I was going to need the courage that came with a buzz.

Charlie jerked his head back. "Hey, slow it down, little lady. The way you're drinking is giving me flashbacks to my ex-wife!"

"Ah shut up, Charlie," Earl said before turning to me. "Don't worry about Charlie. His ex-wife put up with his nonsense for twenty years, and after all that time, who wouldn't need a drink?"

They dissolved into laughter again, clearly beyond tipsy at that point. They seemed harmless.

The bar was nice. I liked it there.

Before the other two could recover, Charlie winked at me, a silly grin shaping his face.

"I'm taking applications for trophy wives now, sweetie. If you apply, I promise I'll give you strong consideration." He chuckled at his joke.

I leaned over, looked at him, winked, and said, "A trophy is something you have to win. Work a little harder, sport."

They all burst out in laughter at that one.

Earl slapped Charlie on the back "She sure told you, Charlie. She sure did!"

The laughter continued as they recycled what were old jokes. At first, I laughed along, but soon their voices faded into the indistinct chatter of the rest of the bar. I was alone once more. Like the seconds of the parachutes, it melted away all too quickly into loneliness.

"Brittany, keep the drinks coming," I said, looking up again. "Don't stop until I tell you to. I don't want to feel anything right now except for a cold drink in my hand. You got that?"

"Coming right up!" said Brittany, bustling over to prepare another screwdriver.

Looking up, I noticed my reflection in the mirrored wall behind the bar. Staring back at me was someone I barely recognized.

This time, I felt detached from my own body, and it wasn't just the alcohol.

I was so immersed in my thoughts that night, I didn't spot the stranger walking up behind me, nor did I notice his reflection in the mirror. I jumped in my seat when he tapped me on the shoulder.

"Excuse me, ma'am, but are you, Dr. Clara Hamilton?"

How did he know my name? After all these years, I should have been forgotten about... that's what I had hoped in this town anyway. Maybe it wasn't as big of a city as I remembered.

My alcohol-addled mind was sunk in a deep haze, so I paid him no attention. I wondered who this Clara Hamilton person might be. She sounded so distant from who I was at that moment.

"Another drink, Brittany," I said. I lip-synced to the words of the song the DJ played, feet tapping on the brass foot rail until she came back with my drink, sliding it to me along the granite bar top.

"Put that one on my tab," the man said, his voice finally rising above the mixed noise of the bar, once again grabbing the attention of my hazed mind.

At that moment, I turned to face him. His deep brown eyes met my gaze. He was a good looking, older, black gentleman, calm in his demeanor. He wore a tilted fedora hat covering his head but not his eyes. Probably in his fifties, he had salt-and-pepper hair with an earnest look in his eyes.

"Thanks," I said with a smile. "No disrespect, but I can buy my own drinks."

"I see you're a woman of means, but if you don't mind, I'd like this round to be on me," he said. Nothing about him suggested he was joking. I couldn't tell if he was flirting with me.

"Okay, whatever you want." I turned back to my drink, dismissing him with my hand.

"I apologize in advance for annoying you, but I must ask—are you an archaeologist?"

"Yes, you are annoying me, and that's a strange way of flirting with someone you've just met, don't you think?" I shrugged him away.

"Ma'am, I'm sorry, but I'm not flirting with you. I am looking for what my colleagues have called one of the greatest archaeologists in the world. Are you her? Are you Dr. Clara Hamilton?"

He put away his glasses. I perked up, holding my glass.

"One of the greatest archaeologists in the world. Really?"

"Please, I'd like to know?" He looked at me no less earnest, I wasn't wearing him down with my antics.

"Maybe I am," I admitted. "And yes, I am a woman of means, but who's asking?"

Removing his hat from his head, he slid his business card to me and said, "I work for the Makers of the Christian Institute."

I didn't take his card.

"Care to tell me why your work should matter to me, sir?"

"Because the Institute and I have been looking for you."

"You've been looking for me? Are you here to audit my taxes? I'm quite sure you've got the wrong Clara Hamilton."

He still didn't look defeated, although I saw a slight confusion crossing his face. He placed his hat on the bar, making it clear he wasn't leaving.

I stirred my drink. "Sir, have we met before?"

"No, but your reputation precedes you as one of the best researchers in this field. I've been searching for you for a while, and I almost gave up until I bumped into someone who told me I might find you here."

"Was it the bellhop? It doesn't matter either way. Whatever it is, I'm not interested," I told him.

"Ma'am," he said, leaning in with a sincere look. "I didn't ask if you were interested. I asked if you were Dr. Clara Hamilton, the archaeologist."

"Yes, sir," I said, sarcastically, making a note to myself to report the bellhop. "What can I do for you?"

"I didn't mean to alarm you in any way. As I said, I'm from the Makers of the Christian Institute and have been following your career for years. My name is Michael Godfrey. It truly is a pleasure and an honor to meet you."

The name set off bells in my head. Snatching the business card from where he left it, I brought it up to my face to read it. That's when it occurred to me.

"Oh, you're that Michael Godfrey. You're the guy who left all those messages on my answering machine."

"Indeed, I am. I'm glad you got them," he said.

"Funny to have encountered you here, Mr. Godfrey. Are you staying here?" I asked.

"No, but as I said before, I was told I could find you here," he said.

"Well, it's a pleasure, sir, but what can I do for you? Why are you looking for me?" I asked.

"I wanted to meet with you to talk about an exploration my team and I are about to embark on. We will be traveling overseas and will be looking for what is said to be the greatest architectural artifact ever built."

"Well, who's the architect, Mr. Godfrey, and what's the artifact?" I asked.

His eyes flickered to the drink in my hand. "I see you're having a drink, but it will take a sober mind to comprehend the exploration we're about to undertake. Can I meet you tomorrow?"

A sober mind? This guy had no clue what I was dealing with here, nor who I was. "Sir, to meet with you tomorrow might be a waste of my time. How can I help you today?"

"Dr. Hamilton, I'm in search of something."

"What are you in search of, sir?"

"I'm in search of the most ancient man-made relic the world has ever recorded, and I need you to help me find its remains."

"What are these remains you want me to help you find?"

"I want you to help me find the remains—of Noah's Ark."

CHAPTER

6

I Found You

MY DRINK fell out of my hand and spilled, yet, I was sure my ears must have tricked me somehow.

"Excuse me, sir, but what did you just say?"

The ice that was once in my cup slid across the bar.

"The remains of Noah's Ark."

"No offense, sir, and forgive me if I'm wrong, but are you talking about the Bible? That Noah's Ark?"

"Exactly. That Noah's Ark."

My ears were ringing. "What in the world are you talking about?"

Reaching over, I scooped the ice back into my empty glass as my mind spun. As good looking as he was, he had to be fantasizing. But the realization that he wasn't slowly crept over me. "I'm serious," he said.

This tall, courteous gentleman spoke with solitude in his mind and strength in his face—I could tell he was for real.

"Pass me a napkin, please," I asked of him. "Yes, sir, I'm sorry to tell you, but the Bible is out of my field of research. I'm a serious scientist. That means searching for facts I can unearth, not fairytales that broken and hopeless people want to believe in." The irony seemed too smart in my mouth. Broken, hopeless people—of course, I knew about that. But Mr. Godfrey seemed undeterred.

"Dr. Hamilton, what if faith were tangible, something you could feel? And belief was visible, something you could see. Would you follow God then?"

"Well, no. With all due respect, Mr. Godfrey, I'm a scientist. I don't believe in the existence of God."

"Well, I'm a scientist too, Dr. Hamilton," he said. "And with all due respect, I can't believe in an existence without Him."

"Mr. Godfrey, I believe in educated theories, proven facts, and in everything I can see, the empirical world. I cannot see God— thus, I don't believe in God." Why was I baring my faithless inner self to this stranger?

"So, what do you believe, Dr. Hamilton? That the universe created itself?"

"Yes, Mr. Godfrey, some things are random. Some things happen without reason, whether we understand it or not. Science has taught us that."

"Well, maybe random things are not random, Dr. Hamilton. Maybe we use the word random to describe the things neither you nor I understand. But don't you agree that behind every random act, there might be a reason? Maybe it is not the word random that perplexes us, but rather the word reason that keeps us so confused?"

His persistence was growing, as was my annoyance.

"Then, what is the reason, Mr. Godfrey?"

"That's why I'm here. I need your help."

"Mr. Godfrey, I appreciate your interest, but this is out of my league. I've never in my life searched for anything biblical."

"Well, your life is not over, Dr. Hamilton, and maybe now's the time to try."

"This is out of my scope of expertise."

"What, exploration is not in your scope of expertise?" he asked.

"Yes, exploration is, but fables mean nothing."

"Clara, I am no fable, and this is not Arizona."

"Wait a minute. How did you know about that? Who told you about that project?"

"Dr. Hamilton, there are over five hundred cultures around the world that have recorded the event of an enormous flood. Five hundred religions and cultures cannot be wrong."

"How could they record something that wiped out everyone?" I asked.

"You must not be familiar with the Bible if you're asking questions like that," he said.

"I refuse to argue or entertain your logic any further, Mr. Godfrey, but what makes you think you can find the remains of Noah's Ark?"

"Because I found you."

"Because you found me?"

"God has a purpose, and he has led me to the woman I was looking for. I do not believe my research is flawed. Money is no object. All I need now is you. I know this is meant to be."

"Because you found me?" I repeated, more skeptical than before.

"Yes, because I found you," he replied.

"Why?"

"Because, as I said before, Dr. Hamilton, I've been looking for you."

"Who do you think I am? You are clearly misguided if you think I would even consider anything like this."

"I need your knowledge to provide a perspective only you can give. The past has not always been kind, Dr. Hamilton, but some signs can lead the world to a better future and us to one more chance for a better life."

"So, what are you saying? That the Ark is a sign?"

"No, but the rains of war and the world's turmoil are. It's going on right now."

I rubbed my temples, feeling a rising pressure in my skull. I hoped it wasn't an early hangover. I couldn't deal with that, and this, whatever this was.

"I don't believe in signs unless they point me in the direction of hard facts. So, as you pointed out before, I'm having a drink right now. Let me consult my partner, and I will get back to you tomorrow."

"Fine, but we've only got two weeks left for your decision. I believe this will be worth your time. The door has been opened for you. All you need to do is walk through it. I would like to meet with you next Monday to tell you more about my research. Money is no object. Call me."

"I have your card, so if I decide to call you, I will," I told him.

The stranger handed Brittany money, placed his hat back on his head, and seemed to vanish from the bar. In that instant, he was gone, leaving me shocked and confused.

The chair squeaked as I spun back to the bar to gather my thoughts.

I was about to call for another drink, but Brittany was at the other end, dancing drunkenly and talking to three men. I pulled my phone from my purse and called Mike. He picked up on the third ring.

"Clara?" He sounded tired, but he'd soon wake up.

"Listen, I think I need you to do me a favor. Catch the next flight out here and meet me in Chicago."

"Whoa, what? I'm not flying all the way out there just to talk to you."

"Mike, I need you. Yes, I'm afraid, but I've got a deal in the works, and I need your opinion. Please, I'll pay for your ticket."

"Why can't you just tell me about it over the phone?"

"Mike, I know, but he... he talked about some meeting. I don't know, but if I decide to go, I might need you to attend with me."

"Clara, who in the world are you talking about, who in the world is he?"

"Michael Godfrey. The one who had been trying to contact me, remember?"

"Wow, really? You woke me up for that."

"Mike, trust me. He said there was money involved. If not, who cares, we'll have a good time together anyway. I need you to meet me tomorrow. I need your help."

Mike sighed. "Okay, Clara. Only for you. You're lucky I love to fly."

"I'm buying your ticket now, first flight out!"

"But why Clara? What's this all about?"

"Mike, I know this is going to sound crazy, but you won't believe what just happened to me."

CHAPTER

7

Life on a sunny day

"TODAY WILL be a clear and sunny day," said a cheery voice.

I cracked open an eye. My alarm clock had been ringing for the past five minutes. I'd left the TV on last night and awoke to the morning weatherman.

He ended his report by saying, "That's the weather for today. Now here's the traffic."

I crawled out of bed, wincing at the headache from my hangover.

"Wow, what happened last night?"

Hearing that it would be a sunny day lightened my mood. Wrapping myself in a bathrobe, I pushed open the door and stepped out onto the hotel balcony, trying to figure out the conversation I'd had the night before. What a beautiful day it was, the air was crisp and clear—

With a snap of the fingers, it came to me. I had spoken to someone named Michael Godfrey.

The conversation we had, the way he looked at me, the way he spoke. He talked to me about an ark. I wondered if he was for real.

I could feel the tension rising in my back as the thought of a new exploration stressed me out. I walked back inside and prepared myself a cup of coffee, trying to relax. Staring out the window at the tall buildings, I thought about an old friend, Dr. Maria Mulberry.

She was the leader of a meditation group I'd once joined to cope with my anxiety after what happened to Joshua. I picked up my phone, scrolled to Dr. Maria's name, and pressed call. She sounded thrilled to hear from me. Admittedly, it had been a long time. She invited me to the 11:00 a.m. meeting. A little jolt of anticipation ran through me as I tousled my hair, ran a bead of lip-gloss over my dry lips, and went out to buy an exercise mat, leaving the mess I'd made behind me. Maybe a session would help me clear my mind and find a way to just calm down. And stop thinking about such weird conversations.

I passed through the lobby and thought to go back to the lounge and check if my tab from the night before was covered. When I walked in, I saw Charlie at the bar having a Bloody Mary. He looked up as I entered, returning my smile.

"Hi, Charlie. How're you doing?" I said, eyeing his early morning beverage.

"How am I doing, you ask? Well let's see, it all started when I was a small boy back in Tennessee—"

"Okay, Charlie, sorry I asked," I said, shaking my head in laughter.

He chuckled as well. "It's going well, baby doll. Just sitting here, easing my way into a dazzling Sunday morning. And you?"

"Finding my way to do the same, just thought I'd stop by and make sure my tab was covered."

"Oh, last night." Charlie stroked his chin with a strange look on his face. "That guy last night, I don't know, but was he a friend of yours?"

"No, that was my first time meeting him. An interesting meeting, to say the least." I checked my watch. "Well, I'd better get moving. See you around."

"Okay, later." Charlie blew me a kiss, but then he scratched his head as if he were wondering about something.

After checking in with the new bartender, I headed out.

I rented a compact car for the week and drove to the building where the meditation group met. Still feeling a little rattled from the night before, I jabbed the button in the elevator for the top floor and then took a deep breath. I leaned back, trying to breathe evenly, preparing myself to join the group.

When the elevator doors slid open, I took a flight of stairs. They opened onto the rooftop, and Dr. Maria greeted me with hugs and squeals.

The High Relaxation classes used to be my weekend getaway, my escape. This eclectic group gathered weekly, naming themselves for this common pursuit elevated so many floors above the ground 'Relaxation,' because it was a meditation group and 'High,' because the classes were held atop a thirty-story building.

I rolled out my new exercise mat as wind wafted across the top of the building. Legs crossed, hands together fingertip to fingertip, I sat listening to the high winds rushing around my body.

The chimes rang, signaling the start of our session. We went through our exercise routine, inhaling, exhaling, chanting away the stress—together.

The sky darkened above us, threatening to prove the forecast wrong. Fortunately, the rain held off while we meditated and exercised. I felt my body unwinding, rejuvenating itself slowly throughout the session, and by the time the last chimes rang, I felt ready to face the world again.

After blowing kisses to my friends, I picked up my mat and bid everyone farewell. Waiting for the elevator, I dialed up Mike's number.

"Hey, Mike. Where are you now?"

"I was about to call you. I just made it to the coffee shop. What about you?" He sounded elated to hear from me.

"Heading to meet you now. See you!"

I tossed my bag over my shoulder and headed toward the coffee shop a block from my hotel. I still felt relaxed when I arrived. The paintings, the décor, the layout of the place—I loved everything about it. Sitting outside on the patio made it cool and refreshing, much like the rooftop I'd just been meditating on.

Mike dropped his newspaper and waved me over. He flashed me a grin as I took a seat across from him and ordered a cappuccino.

"Look at you!" he said. "All relaxed and happy. I haven't seen you looking this good since—I can't remember when actually."

"Thanks." I adjusted my seat. "I just spent an hour with my meditation group, getting in the zone."

Mike cracked his knuckles, a preoccupied look on his face, then hummed. "Well, it shows. But something's up. What is it?"

"Something beyond my wildest expectations," I told him.

"Oh?"

"Remember Michael Godfrey, the guy who kept trying to contact me?"

"Sure. Did you find out who he was?"

"He says he's from some kind of Christian Institute. I can't recall the exact name. It's not something you would've heard of."

"Okay, and—?"

"I met him at the hotel bar last night. He offered me an opportunity for a big break."

"Really! What is it?"

"Get this. Michael Godfrey's on a search for Noah's Ark."

"What?"

"Yes, really. He's a scientist in search of God. Can you believe that?"

"Barely. What does he want with you?"

"My question exactly, Mike."

"Clara, these kinds of off-the-wall projects are usually poorly thought out, to say nothing of the fact they're generally crazy in the first place. Do you think it's legit?"

"I don't know, Mike, I've never been offered anything like this."

"Yep, gotta say, it sounds like a stretch. Finding the remains of Noah's Ark from the Bible. There's no end to the problems of that whole operation. Countless people have searched Turkey and Mount Ararat for Noah's Ark, and no one has ever come up with anything."

"I don't disagree, but on the other hand, I can't help but wonder if it wouldn't hurt to try, especially if it's as well-funded as he claims."

"What? Money! Hm. You could be onto something there. But Clara, let me ask you something first—"

I held up my hand to stop him.

"Mike, I know. I don't have all the facts, but I'll get them. Don't argue with me—this is going to make good money. And isn't that what you want?"

"Who wouldn't? But listen to my question—"

I waved my hand to stop him again.

"Mike, I don't actually know much aside from a few details, so chances are, I won't know how to answer. I promise to fill you in as soon as I can, okay!"

"Clara, that wasn't my question!"

"Okay, then tell me. What's your question, Mike?"

"Tell me this. Do you believe in God?"

"Huh?" What a weird question to ask. I'd never gotten into talks of religion with anyone before, let alone with Mike.

"Do you want me to repeat the question?"

My cappuccino arrived, cutting him off for a moment. But Mike wasn't about to let me off the hook.

He spoke again as the cup settled in front of me with a clink. "I asked a simple question, and you still haven't given me an answer," he said. "Do you believe in God?"

"Why are you asking me something so ridiculous? I'm trying to believe in myself right now. I know a lot of others have looked for the Ark, but Godfrey seems convinced it's there. If he has the money to fund the search, why not at least give it a shot?" I took a sip of my cappuccino. "In fact, he said that over five hundred religions have records of this great flood in their historical documents. As he said, all five hundred can't be wrong."

Above us, the sky exploded into thunder, hard rain pouring down on our heads. Mike ran to his rental car for his umbrella as I grabbed the newspaper, shielding myself from the rain until he got back. Together, under his umbrella, we walked back to the hotel.

"As promising as this proposition sounds," Mike said, trying to speak over the rain, "I'm not sure it would be a good fit for us, seriously."

The rain grew heavier as we made it to the hotel, walking up the wet steps toward the lobby. I turned to Mike once we were inside.

"Listen, why don't you stay for a minute? Let's run a Google search on Michael Godfrey. That might make me feel more comfortable about considering his offer."

"Okay, but I'm not going up to your room."

I wasn't surprised, but I acted the part anyway. "What do you mean?"

"It's been a few years since my divorce. I just want to remain an honorable man in your eyes."

"An honorable man? Mike, come on. It wasn't your honor that landed you in divorce court but a lack of judgment." I laughed, and so did he as I gave him a playful punch. "Now get in here. We have work to do."

Shaking off the rain, we went straight for the lobby computer and booted it up to search for Godfrey. He had few solid accolades to his name, but he also had a doctorate in astrophysics. Thinking back to our meeting, I found it intriguing he hadn't introduced himself as a doctor.

Searching under Dr. Michael Godfrey led us to his bio. Many prominent scientists sang his praises, calling him one of the greatest researchers of all time, but rarely went into specifics. I just couldn't figure it out. What had he done that made him so memorable? Nobody was writing about it.

"I told you," Mike said. "He's done nothing worthy of mention. At least, not if you trust these sources."

"Mike, these people are scientists."

"So what, Clara? Scientists make mistakes too, you know."

"Now, what's that supposed to mean? Are you talking about Arizona again?"

"No, no, Clara. Not everything's about you, don't be so quick to jump to your guns. I was talking about the weather—don't you remember what the forecast was for today?"

"Yeah, right, Mike. But anyway, these people are well respected in their field of work. They wouldn't be praising him for nothing."

"Who knows why. He sounds smart, and maybe they just want to sound smart too by associating their name with his?"

"That's not how my colleagues work." I shrugged, shaking my head. There was no convincing him. "Not to change the subject, but what do you make of all this God stuff? Personally, I mean."

"I don't know," he said. "There's something keeping this crazy world spinning, but I can't figure it out."

I was quiet for a moment before I could speak again. "You know, as a scientist, I pride myself on being a risk-taker, but I don't know how I feel about this project. This whole God thing has me a little spooked, to be honest."

Mike scratched his chin. "Well, the thing is, everyone believes in something. Some of us just need to discover those things for ourselves, even if it does take a while."

"Yes, you're right. That's why I trust in science."

"Yeah, sure, Clara. Maybe a little too much."

Mike stared at the rain dribbling down the glass window, then stood up. "Looks like the rain has slowed down, Eagle Eyes. I've got to run, and, to be honest, I don't think this proposal would be good for us."

"He wants to meet with us on Monday, eight in the morning."

"Trust me, Clara, it's not for us. I'll talk to you later."

Watching him leave, I tried putting the idea out of my head. I didn't know anything about expeditions like this or if it would help my career. What I did know, though, was that I didn't want to go back to Texas with Mike, trying to patch things up with my friends. I felt it would be equally unproductive.

Without warning, thunder erupted again, making me nearly tumble out of my chair.

I clenched my teeth so hard, my jaw ached. I thought the weatherman said no rain.

8

Ms. Mattie's story

T HE RAIN stopped that evening, and I swapped one water source for another. I soaked in the warmth of my bath that night, feeling the heat down in my bones. It was such a comforting feeling after being soaked by the rain.

Relaxed, I leaned back, listening to the soft sound of bath bubbles popping around me. Water dripped from the leaky faucet, each drop echoing through the bathroom. I'd turned on some soft music to complete the mood.

What did Godfrey mean when he said he had been looking for me?

I'd never even given God, religion, or anything like that a serious thought. Frankly, religious people and all their talk of hell and condemnation annoyed me.

Godfrey had seemed different. What he'd said remained strangely in my mind—*I've been looking for you.*

I looked down to see my phone ringing. It was my secretary, Tammy.

"Hi, big mouth, I see you let the cat out of the bag." I laughed.

"I know, Clara, and I'm sorry, I didn't know you didn't want anyone to know your whereabouts."

"It's okay, my bad. So, what's up?"

"Well, Dr. Harrold, the one who funded your Arizona dig, called."

I turned the music off. "Oh no, I forgot to call him."

"I know, but he said there's no need for an apology. He just wants the best for you."

"Oh no, all that money, I could have at least called him." I slumped back into the tub. I couldn't believe I had forgotten. I really had been a mess.

"Don't worry, Clara. He seemed okay. But I know what you mean. Sometimes you've got to take your mind off yourself and pay attention to those who are trying to help."

"Shut up, Tammy, that didn't help."

"Okay, okay, but I've got more news. Guess what?"

"What?" I asked as I put her on speakerphone, getting comfortable in the water again as heat lapped around me.

"I'm getting married!" she yelled.

"Oh, great!" That statement stole my attention. "Is it Allen?"

"Yes! After four months of him asking, and I know we've had our problems, I thought to take the plunge and give us a chance. You know, Clara, I want to move on with my life. I feel like Allen is someone I can trust. I need a change."

"Well, Tammy, to be honest, I understand."

"I thought you would. Okay, I just wanted to call and let you know about the doctor's call. And I'm sending you an invitation to the wedding. Be safe."

"I will."

I hung up the phone, thinking to myself, *wow, my secretary is moving on with her life.* Why couldn't I? But I knew the answer. She had never lost a child, and my pain wasn't hers. Simply—her life was not mine. There I was, lying in a tub, contemplating a conversation I had with a stranger a days ago. Like Tammy, I wanted to move on with my life too, but she was doing it better.

My fingers and toes were starting to prune. I took another gulp of whiskey, reached over, and pulled the plug on the tub. Drying off, I walked out of the bathroom with my phone in hand and prepared to go to bed.

Maybe Tammy was right. Maybe I just needed to take my mind off myself and pay attention to those who were trying to help. I took my pills and cracked open a second bottle right before there was a knock at the door. Wrapping a towel around me, I went to look through the peephole.

The bellhop from earlier stood there, holding a package.

He knocked again. "Dr. Hamilton?"

"Just a minute!" I pulled the door open.

"Please sign here, ma'am. This is for you."

I signed for the package and closed the door, wondering what it could be and who sent it. Taking it to the table, I ripped off the wrapping. Inside was a black and gold-trimmed book and a card – from Michael Godfrey.

A bookmark was placed near the beginning. I opened the book to that page. Genesis, chapter six; the story of Noah.

A copy of the Bible.

Of course.

What else could I have expected? I walked over to the sofa. Wrapping myself in a blanket, I sat down and began to read the book, training myself to notice every detail in the story.

My glasses kept sliding down my nose, but I barely noticed. Questions teemed in my mind, the number growing with each turn of the page, emerging from the archeologist in me. How could it rain so much that water could cover the entire earth? If it had happened, where were the flood rings to prove it? Why was that guy Godfrey so convinced?

When I looked up again, my eyes tired, I had to check twice to be sure I was reading the clock correctly. "1:14 a.m.?" I muttered, "Wow, I need some rest."

Putting the book away, I set my alarm for 6:00 a.m. I needed to get up the next morning, otherwise, lying in bed all day would make me even more depressed.

I couldn't stop thinking. The Bible stories intrigued me, but as a scientist, I still found them far-fetched. How could Godfrey believe this stuff?

That was none of my business, at least for the time being. I lay there with my tired eyes open, listening to the clock ticking in my quiet room, trying to figure out my next move, but the quietness in the room scared me. Normally, I turned on the television as background noise to drown out whatever nightmares I might have, but that night, I hadn't bothered. My mind was so clouded with thoughts I could barely remember any of my normal routines.

Two a.m., and I still couldn't sleep. Crawling out of bed, I thought to go for a late-night drive. I was sick and tired of being sick and tired. It was always better to do something rather than nothing.

I put on my clothes and went down to my rental and took a late-night drive down the freeway. Rolling down my windows, I basked in the feeling of the wind whipping my hair back.

The refreshing air turned into a chill when I spotted the sign "Saint Joseph's Hospital, Next Exit."

Mike told me not to go back, that seeing those past settings would only make things worse. But the urge came over me anyway. I took the exit. I parked in front of the hospital and just sat there. I felt as empty as the parking lot.

After a while, I got out and walked into the lobby. Elevator, third floor. I already knew where I was going. As the doors opened, I could hear the breathing machine palpitating, and the alarms were going off every so often. I walked into the ICU.

It was early, barely even morning. I knew only a few nurses would be on duty at that hour.

I moved through the deserted floor, then peeked over the nurse's desk. I recognized her immediately, even though her head was lowered. She was one of the same nurses who had been with me when Joshua passed. Numbness took my fingertips.

In her hands, she held a cup of coffee. Years ago, those same hands held mine, trying to console me. Things had changed so much since then, yet somehow, I remembered every inch of the floor, and how back then, the walls had felt as if they'd been closing in around me.

The hospital was freezing. Only a few dim lights were on. Hugging myself, I rubbed my hands across my cold arms, trying to smooth down the goosebumps.

Ahead of me was a bench I knew well. I'd sat there crying for Joshua when he'd left me forever. But now there was a little old lady sitting there, her hands folded, her head bowed. In that dark hallway, a single light fixture had fallen out of its casing. It hung down and cast an awkward spotlight on her. Something about her posture, the lights, and the solemn silence brought me back to that day when I, too, had sat there.

"Is it okay if I have a seat?" I asked, my voice barely a whisper.

Without raising her head, the old woman shuffled over and made room for me. I thanked her and sat down.

Things were changing, and I wasn't strong enough to change them back. I thought I would have to carry that emptiness inside me for the rest of my life. The love I had for my son didn't shrivel. Instead, it grew, but it made the sun a little less warm, the flowers a little less colorful. Life was a little less happy. Everything had become... less. I thought that pain would last forever. Until I heard her words...

"Child, what's wrong with you? Don't you have faith?"

The elderly woman had spoken out loud. I blinked.

"Sorry?"

"Oh, I'm sorry, child. I didn't mean to disturb you," she said. "I was praying, repeating to myself what God asks me when I'm feeling down. Speaking faith aloud into my life helps me. Apologies for disturbing you. God bless you."

"Oh no, it's fine," I insisted. "I was worried I was disturbing you."

"Not at all. How are you, young lady? I'm Mattie... Mattie Johnson."

"Clara Hamilton. A pleasure to meet you." I shook her hand.

"Are you visiting a child?" asked Ms. Mattie when I let go of her hand.

"No... This is where my child lost his life," I said quietly.

"Oh, dear! I'm so sorry to hear that, do forgive me, I shouldn't have asked."

"Please, ma'am, don't say that. It's been four years. I'm gradually learning to open up about it." I took a deep breath. Ms. Mattie was watching me, her attentive eyes filled with concern. For once, I didn't feel afraid to speak. "It was cardiac arrest. The doctors couldn't save him, and he died in my arms." My breathing shortened, but I pressed on. I needed to talk about this. "I don't know why I still come here, Ms. Mattie. I guess... I guess I'm just standing in a door I'm not ready to close. I guess that's my story."

"Your story?" she asked, with a strange look on her face.

"Yep, sorry to say, my story."

"I'm so sorry," said Ms. Mattie. "When a mother loses a child, it's a pain greater than we have the words for."

A knowing look had come into her eyes again. I couldn't talk about it anymore without the lump in my throat turning into tears. So, I changed the subject. "Enough about me. Why are you here today?"

Ms. Mattie sighed. "Where do I begin? I'm here to fight for my grandbaby. He's my late daughter's son. She lost her life, so I'm here fighting for him, hoping he doesn't follow the same path."

I sat there in stunned silence. Seeming to pick up on my feelings, Ms. Mattie continued. "Ms. Clara, I pray about everything and try to worry about nothing. I can't control the unseen. But I know the one who can." She paused, letting silence fill the space between us, a name unsaid but obvious. "Ms. Clara, your hurt is human. Without love, there would be no tears. It's only natural. Just as Jesus wept because of love, so do we." Reaching out, she took my hand in hers. "Why do you still come here? Don't you have faith? Don't you believe your life might fill with joy once more?"

"...I don't know how to leave him," I told her as I fought against the sob in my throat. "I can't close that door."

Ms. Mattie locked her fingers in mine, her eyes bright with something I couldn't yet understand. "Clara," she said, "would you mind if I tell you *my* story?"

"Yes, please do, Ms. Mattie. You've got my attention. Tell me your story."

"Child, it's not about closing a door; it's about walking through a new one. My dear, I grew up in a troubled home. My father abused my mother and me, and my mother abused everything else, trying to escape it all. After it had gotten really bad, my mother sent me to my grandmother's house in the country, and after looking at the condition I was in, my grandmother said a prayer for me. That changed my life. But it didn't happen all at once. No, not at all. That change took time. I married an abusive man, repeating the same old story I'd grown up with."

I listened, letting her speak.

"I had a daughter, and at the age of fourteen, she ran away and lived on the streets. She couldn't bear it anymore. I couldn't take care of her. Well, I didn't even know how to take care of myself. She left me in that hollowed house I'd told her was home. Years later, my daughter lost her life to the streets. Everything fell apart for me. I thought I had lost it all, in spite of the fact that I still had my grandchild. I tried drugs, I tried alcohol, got with one abusive man after another. Turning to despair, I was ready to give up on life. But then God came to me. He gave me another choice. He said, 'Now that you've tried everything, try Me.' Faith—what an enormous word." She adjusted the glasses on her face as I listened.

"But it doesn't start that way. No, not at all. Faith doesn't start as a giant ready for battle, but as small as a mustard seed prepared to conquer all. But you must exercise it. Trusting God with the small things in life will help you see Him when He reveals Himself in the big ones."

She went on. "This is your season for faith. Never be afraid to step out in humility, but also with boldness. You don't have to start with a lot of faith. All you need in the beginning is a little bit, and trust God to do the rest. I'm here for my grandchild with exactly that kind of faith."

"Wow." It was all I could manage. "Ms. Mattie, that's incredible. You're such a strong woman. If only I—"

"Strong?" Ms. Mattie's voice filled with conviction cut through mine. "Let me tell you this, Clara. Throughout our lives, we will always be tested, not to make us stronger or weaker, but wiser, so that we might choose wisely. It is through our faith—or lack thereof— that God allows us to peek into the windows of our souls, to show us who we truly are."

She smiled up at me. "I may be strong, but that alone is no consolation. It's not about becoming stronger, but wiser. Because in your wisdom, there lies your strength. What I prize in life is being faithful. Day after day, I've learned to speak faith into my life, just as I speak it into the lives of all who would listen."

A doctor walked out of the double doors, exhaustion was written all over his face. "Ms. Johnson? You can come in now."

"Thank you, Doctor. I'll be right there," said Ms. Mattie. Turning to me, she gave my hands one last squeeze.

"Clara, change the way you speak to yourself. 'So, a man thinks, so a man is.' I have to leave now but remember this—when you talk to yourself, as we all do, speak victory into your life. Trust me. A life lived in the past is a life, but it ain't living. You can't live for today and prepare for tomorrow if you're still holding onto yesterday. You must look forward and live for today, knowing God has something so amazing planned for you, that you too will have a story to tell."

Slowly, holding on to her cane, she released my hand. Ms. Mattie stood up. "I'm saying a prayer for you, Clara. A prayer that your story will not be one of defeat or sadness, but of victory. A story of how you, through Jesus Christ, overcame it all. I speak victory into your life, as my grandmother did for me. *Amen.*"

"Amen," I muttered back, feeling a quiet dignity in her words.

"Ms. Johnson," the doctor prompted.

Ms. Mattie nodded her head. "Yes, yes, I'm on my way. I'm on my way."

Ms. Mattie's hands shook, yet she held firmly onto her cane. We had been strangers to one another just minutes ago.

"A life lived in the past is a life, but it ain't living," I repeated to myself. Sitting there on the bench alone, I felt I'd lost my inner strength. I sat there in that dark hallway with the light hanging out from its broken fixture, now shining awkwardly on me. I felt uncomfortable, knowing I had let Ms. Mattie see how weak I was. But was there something, *someone* out there, perhaps a God, who wanted better for me? Or was my story the end of a tale destined to be forgotten? Either way, I knew, sitting there on that bench, the next move was on me.

CHAPTER

9

Taking Some Time to Listen

I STEPPED OUT into the night again, trying to take some time to listen to my thoughts. Exhausted because I hadn't slept that night, my mind was still spinning over Ms. Mattie's words. The direction she gave me sparked my consciousness. All those feelings had been dredging up in me hours ago, but I didn't understand how to explain it, not even to myself.

A blaring honk startled me out of my thoughts. A car had almost run into me as I came back to the reality of the hospital parking lot. I'd instinctively jumped out of its path, and the driver had swerved to avoid me. He gave me another honk before driving away.

My shaking hands fumbled as I fished the keys from my purse, tapping at the buttons on the key fob.

Finally, the doors unlocked, and I climbed into the car, trying to calm my trembling body by tuning into an easy-listening station on my way back to my hotel.

Still dazed, I blinked, trying to focus on the street signs. They seemed to merge and change color from green to yellow and then back again. A warm, familiar laugh rang in my head.

Joshua.

I came to a screeching halt at the dark red hue wavering before my eyes, the same color that had painted the streets that day. He'd lain there, eyes open, but the color draining from his face, the life from his body. Tears filled my eyes. Even years later, I couldn't forget it.

I'd told Ms. Mattie, my only child had died. But that wasn't the whole story. Thinking back to her piercing eyes, I felt that she knew I had been hiding something from her even though she had opened herself up so thoroughly to me.

Thumping my hands against the steering wheel at that streetlight, I wept those regretful tears. It killed me inside and also shamed me as I admitted it to myself. The world looked at me as Dr. Clara Hamilton and saw the gifted archeologist, someone who must have had it all together. Little did they know I was a real woman, lost in her own shame, confused, trying to figure out her life.

I'd recalled my father's words after my mother died. "Clara," he'd say, leaning back into his armchair with hurt in his eyes. "There's going to be a lot of pain in life. Pain of the heart, of the mind, and the past. But if I've learned anything, it's that the worst kind of pain is the kind you are too ashamed to share with anyone else. Not only do I know what it means to hurt, but I also know what it means to hurt alone."

Back then, I didn't understand what he meant. But now, I did.

I thought about all the things I would never have the chance to do as a mother. I would never be able to help Joshua with his homework, seeing that he might be the type of kid who struggled with math. I'd never be able to hold him in my arms on the days he cried. I'd never have the chance to throw a party for him on his thirteenth birthday, watch him graduate, dance the tango with him the day he got married. But now, here, all alone, waiting for the lights to change at a crossroad, I finally understood my father's words.

The light blinked green, and I sped off into the early morning, eyes burning and bloodshot from crying. I needed a drink badly.

Yet, for some reason, Godfrey's words were stuck in my head. "What if faith was tangible, and belief was visible?" I didn't know what to make of it at that moment as I sat in my car. Wouldn't that make God real? The thought of it scared me for some reason. I had never been religious. I was a scientist, a real one. But it had never occurred to me to examine what faith was. Godfrey's words continued to echo through my mind even as I pulled into the hotel parking lot. The mere thought that faith could be tangible made me question the life I was living. I sat there in the hotel garage for a moment, reflecting over my life. For the past four years, I had been standing still, waiting for my world to change, without at least trying to take one step forward.

I couldn't help but wonder why I hadn't. I dragged my fingers through my hair, the exhaustion turning into an aching feeling behind my eyes. Searching for the remains of Noah's Ark? It sounded preposterous when I said it out loud. I got out of the car and headed back to my room.

"If there is a God," I said as I walked down the hall, pulling out my key card. "Why couldn't He just reveal these miracles Himself?"

I walked into my room and put my bags down, looked over at the table, and grabbed the Bible again. I turned the overhead lights off and jumped into bed, reading by the light of my bedside lamp. Thumbing through the book, I found a note that had fallen out from between the pages. I noticed Godfrey had separated the Bible into four sections using sticky notes to mark them out. The sections were marked: History—our past. Laws—what we use to live by. Parables—because we cannot live by bread alone. Faith—. Wow, wait a minute, what happened to faith? Why didn't he add an explanation to that word? Yet, looking down, I saw another note that must have fallen out of the book and onto the floor. I picked it up to read it.

"The Bible is not a book of fantasies, Clara," Godfrey's note read. "But rather a book of examples. Examples in stories, showing us how to grieve, how to live, how to suffer, and how to redeem joy again. Faith."

Wow, was that what this was all about?

I felt the weight of his words in my hands as I was holding onto the Bible, questioning myself. I thought about everything I had gone through, including the life I had been living. I thought about Godfrey's words and the visibility of belief. Belief! Belief in what? If it were true, could I see it in a mirror, could I see it in myself?

It felt like I was having an out of body experience. I pulled the covers off and left my bed for the bathroom as I heard the tenderness of someone crying. I could hear the hurt in someone's tears, the pain in someone's voice. When I turned the bathroom lights on and looked into the mirror, I saw that someone crying was me. Staring back at me in the mirror was a sad, broken woman with dark rings under her eyes. I'd never heard her cries before. So busy running away, trying to get away from my pain, I'd never taken the time to listen.

I opened the bath drawer, grabbed my pills, and poured myself a glass of water. Staring at the bottle clutched in my hand, I heard her voice again. *Is this going to be your life?* She asked. *Is this what you've become?* Hollow and sad, the shell of the woman you'd once been.

Only a few pills remained in the bottle. I didn't know what else to do. After a while of staring down at it, I broke down and, for the first time in a long time, looked in that mirror again and reconciled with her—I mean, me. I needed a change, and I needed to make a real decision. I called Mike.

After a few rings, his groggy voice answered. "Hello?"

"Mike, I'm sorry to call you so early, but I need to tell you about a decision I've made."

"What in the world are you talking about, Clara? It's four in the morning! Why are you calling me at these crazy hours?"

"Rise and shine, apple head!" I told him. "We've got work to do."

"At... four... a.m.... in the morning? Have you lost your mind? And what's up with your voice? It sounds like you've been crying?"

"I don't want to talk about it now, Mike. But yes, there's been a lot on my mind. Arizona may have been a failure, but I've been thinking," I told him as I paced around the bathroom floor.

"What is it?" Mike said with a deep sigh.

"Godfrey's project."

"... Are you talking about the ark?" Mike asked.

"Yeah, the ark."

"What about it?"

"Let's do it!"

"Let's do what, Clara? You mean us—you mean me?"

"Yes, of course, apple head, we're a team, aren't we?"

"Clara, we can't do this."

"I've thought about all the things I can't do, but this is something I can, or I mean, *we* can do." I corrected myself, not wanting him to feel like it was all about me.

"I thought we had made up our mind on this. So, you're telling me now you want to go to his meeting? Couldn't this have waited until morning?"

Turning on the faucet, I poured my last bottle of pills into the sink. I watched them disappear down the drain.

"Yes, let's go check it out. It won't hurt to listen."

"Clara, this is crazy," he said, I could hear him getting out of his bed.

"Crazy? Yeah, right, I'd never done a trust fall, never skydived, never jumped off a cliff until I met you! And now you want to talk about crazy?"

"There's a first time for everything!" he said.

"Yeah, you're right. We've searched for everything else. Why not this? I'm not saying for sure that it's real, or that we have to do it. We'll listen to his pitch first and see if his ideas are plausible."

"This is about you, isn't it, Clara?"

"No, Mike, it's about us!"

"Yeah, right, whatever you say."

"Now stop with the questions. I'll meet you at the Christian Institute at eight o'clock—be on time."

"Okay, but remember, your career has already taken a hit. I can't believe you're even thinking about risking it with this."

"Life is but a whisper, Mike," I reminded him, "live it out loud."

"I will—oh, I mean, we will."

10

Adding to the Conversation

I'D MADE it to the Institute early and meant to briefly rest my head but ended up falling asleep in my car. The next thing I knew, I had woken up in the parking garage. Clearing my eyes, three gray buildings loomed above everything, towering over guards, shielding the shorter building in the middle.

"The Makers of the Christians Institute," the bold letters on the middle building read.

"*Where the teachings of Christ are edified through our service to mankind.*" Wow, in this day and age, what a daring statement.

While I was still pondering, Mike arrived, pulling up along the east side of the garage. When he got out, I waved him over.

"Thanks for coming," I said as he approached.

"It's nothing," he said with a grumpy tone, "anything for you."

"Mike, you don't have to be that way, it's going to be okay."

"I know, Clara. No problem, I was kind of interested in what he was going to say anyway. I'm sort of excited."

"Me too. Let's get out of the garage and into the building."

As we walked out onto the sidewalk, I looked up and wondered what kind of place it was. It didn't look like a church, although

I spotted a small cathedral off to the side. No, it looked like an impressive research facility donning a huge fountain in its courtyard, gushing water into the air over a cross that must have stood thirty feet tall.

Other people milled about, some taking their time on the way into the building. I bumped into as few people as I could, my eyes fixated on that fountain. We made it up to the steps, and I gathered up my red hair, which was even wilder than usual, slipping a ballpoint pen through to hold it in place. We entered through a wide glass door, emerging into the vast halls of the Institute.

"What's up?" Mike asked, looking at me, "You've been acting strange ever since we arrived."

"It's kind of overwhelming, honestly," I admitted, "But I promise I'll walk away if it looks like some kind of hoax. Okay?"

He shrugged. "I can only hope for that."

We settled in the auditorium where a sizeable audience had already gathered. Reaching into my bag, I pulled out my tablet, took the pen from my hair, and got ready to take a hard look at Godfrey's claims.

At exactly 7:59 a.m., the man appeared at the side of the stage. He walked up to the podium, brushing his already impeccable dark gray suit. Adjusting the mic and looking around, at exactly 8:00 a.m., he began to speak.

"Greetings. My name is Michael Godfrey. I welcome you to the Makers of the Christian Institute, and I thank all of our honored guests for joining us today. You're about to hear about an exploration that will begin in less than two weeks, the goal of which is to discover where the biblical Ark of Noah rests." A hum dominated the crowd until he continued. "It's a mystery mankind has been trying to solve for hundreds of years, trying to confirm the validity of the story. In addition, we aim to learn more about the man who recorded Noah's tale—Moses, the author of the Book of Genesis."

Mike and I leaned forward, eager to learn more. The pause was torture. After a sip of water, Godfrey continued.

"Moses, the father of all scriptures, was raised as an Egyptian, though he was a Hebrew. While writing the first book of the Bible and describing the Ark, he used a unit of measurement called the Egyptian cubit. This is the same unit the Egyptians used when building their pyramids. Moses wrote, 'God commanded Noah to build a vessel three hundred cubits long, fifty cubits wide, and thirty cubits tall.' To give you a sense of scale, that would be one-and-a-half football fields long, half as wide, and as tall as a four-story building. This would make it the largest seaworthy vessel ever built before the 19th century."

Murmurs arose among the audience. Mike and I exchanged quick glances of skepticism. This was taking the story quite far.

"Now, you might be asking yourself how a vessel of that size, made of wood, could hold together and float? Moses tells us the Ark was built of something called gopher wood. This has been a mystery to scientists for years since we've never found any potential matches for gopher trees."

He continued. "But I have a theory. Gopher wood was a manmade wood, much like engineered plywood. The same ancient engineering processes that went into constructing gopher wood were passed down to the Egyptians from even earlier men, yet the Egyptians would go on to use it to build the pyramids. Studying the mathematics of the Egyptians, Moses must have known gopher wood would make a vessel that size strong enough to be seaworthy."

I had to give him credit, that made sense. I couldn't help but be drawn in as he went on.

"The details of how they would have constructed gopher wood are a mystery. Even with modern technology, we still can't figure out how gopher wood was made, let alone how the pyramids of Egypt were built. Based on our understanding of the pyramids, the architecture of gopher wood would also have to be equally stunning."

Godfrey paused for a moment, casting a piercing gaze around at the audience before continuing.

"Moses wrote that God told Noah to make a window and a door on the side of this vessel and to make lower second and third decks as well. It's said that God commanded the animals to board the vessel with what we believe to be the only gift he ever granted them—instinct. And so, they boarded the ark, two by two."

"By our estimates, forty-one thousand species of land animals existed at the time. If God called them in pairs, then eighty-two thousand animals would have boarded that ark. Whether we believe it or not, a vessel of that size could easily accommodate eighty-two thousand animals."

Godfrey spoke in what sounded like a recitation, his words flowing and full of passion. Even a casual listener would be able to tell he'd been thinking this over for years.

He cleared his throat. "Noah built the ark, but then he had to be patient, following God's command to wait for the promise to come to pass. The Bible tells us he was six hundred years old when the floods came."

Godfrey tapped his fingers against the podium again and said,

"My friends, imagine a rainstorm so violent that dark skies turned as bright as day with each flash of lightning. Rapid thunder would cause the earth to quake. Imagine that. The Bible states all the springs of the great deeps—the oceans themselves—burst open with water, and the floodgates of the heavens were opened. Water geysers burst out of the ocean, possibly over a hundred feet tall. This is what the earth suffered during the great flood. It happened for forty days and forty nights."

The story was well known, but it felt like he was telling it for the first time.

"Everything on dry land died. Only Noah and those onboard the Ark survived. Now, as scientists, you must be wondering, where is the proof? There are no signs of this great flood. I submit to you the possibility that earth was never completely covered by water in the way some theologians might suggest. Bear in mind, this is not a story about the destruction of this earth, but God's wrath and intolerance of evil."

A chill ran down my spine. Godfrey spoke the words with complete and utter conviction, casting his eyes around the auditorium yet again. I didn't know for sure whether he knew I was sitting there, but somehow, I felt he did.

"The Bible states that they came to rest on the mountain of Ararat. Many scientists have searched for it in Turkey and returned empty-handed. However, a closer reading of Genesis 8:4 tells us the ark came to rest not on the mountain of Ararat in Turkey, but the mountains of Ararat. Plural. Meaning many mountains. All this time, theologians and priests have been wrong. If Noah's sons traveled west and founded Babylon, they couldn't have traveled from Turkey, which is north of Babylon. In fact, the evidence suggests they never set foot in Turkey."

He continued. "The only way for them to have traveled west, as the Bible tells us, is to have come from the east. Our research shows the only mountain ridges east of Babylon are the ancient mountains of Perjure—mountains that, in Moses's day, were called the mountains of Ararat. All evidence points to this being the location of the vessel. We plan to open our search there." He gave a dramatic pause, and it was so quiet that a page could be heard turning over.

"Keep in mind, however, that the vessel I speak of is not a boat. The vessel I'm searching for was not made to sail. Rather, it was made to remain buoyant in the stormy waters that carried it. We search not for a boat made to travel, but a container meant to float. We're looking for what Moses called an 'ark'—something he himself was placed within after his birth."

All at once, the room exploded. Everyone was raising their voices and hands with questions from every direction.

"Can you prove it?"

"Are there any facts to back up your theory?"

"Mr. Godfrey, here, please—"

Godfrey raised both hands. The room grew quiet once more.

A man raised his hand, and Godfrey pointed at him and nodded. Taking a microphone offered to him by an assistant, he spoke up.

"Mr. Godfrey, if we find this ark, will you also be trying to learn how gopher wood was made?"

"Yes. That will be one of the questions we address."

The crowd muttered amongst themselves. I could stay silent no longer. Standing up, I raised my voice loud enough that even without the microphone, my voice reached every corner of the room.

"Sir, it sounds like you're trying to prove the existence of God. With all due respect, isn't that impossible to prove?"

Everyone in the room turned their eyes on me, stares penetrating my back, but I stood tall. Some muttered with indignation, others with agreement. Godfrey met my gaze. For a moment, something that could have been a smile flitted across his face.

"That's true. It can't be proven. But I'm not trying to convince anyone of the existence of the One who created me and everyone here. For me, we are proof of His existence. I'm not trying to prove His existence to anyone. All I'm trying to do is add to the conversation of why we're here. Will you assist me?"

Hushed whispers swept the room as I raised my voice again.

"To do what? Find God?"

"No," Godfrey said, his voice calm as ever. "Add to the conversation."

His words sank into me. "Add to the conversation."

From behind me, someone else spoke out. "Mr. Godfrey, where will we find the Ark? Could you repeat where you said we were searching?"

I sank down in my seat as Godfrey took to his mic again. "I'm glad you asked. We'll be going to a nation whose attitude toward us has been volatile at best, where threats of war abound, and

Americans have been beheaded. We're going to the mountains of Perjure—or what is known today as the mountains of West Iran."

"Iran?" Mike exclaimed, looking at me, "You never said this would be dangerous! I'm out."

I kept my mouth shut, but I had to agree with Mike. How could we risk our lives for something we weren't even sure existed?

Staring right at me as if there was nobody else in the room, Godfrey spoke again. "I understand your fear. But, Dr. Hamilton, I ask this of you—will you trust God and assist me on this journey? Are you in or out?"

Bowing my head, I thought hard about how life had not been treating me well. All the hurt, all the pain, all the *why Me's*. I was tired of going through it. I reached down and scribbled a few words on my tablet. After a moment of thought, I raised it over my head for all to see.

"I'm In!"

Mike's jaw dropped so hard, I practically heard it clatter on the floor.

"You're in?" he mouthed as he read the tablet. "Clara, you can't be serious!"

I knew Mike wouldn't like it, and seeing the cocktail of emotion on his face, I could only sigh.

"You must have lost your mind..."

"I need a change, Mike. I need a change."

CHAPTER

11

I Need a Change

"WHAT'S GOTTEN into you?" Mike demanded. "Why would you ever agree to something like this?" The surprise in his voice only got louder as he wrung his hands. "You promised me you'd never intentionally hurt yourself. Well, this just might do it."

"Mike, have faith."

"Faith? What in the hell are you talking about? This is not about faith. It's about going into the mountains of some country we might not come back from."

"We will make it back. I trust Godfrey."

"Clara, you're out here searching for God?"

"No, I'm searching for my truth. Our truth."

"This is crazy."

Reaching out, I took his hands in mine and summoned up the most heartfelt look I had.

"Trust me on this, just this once. I have a feeling this might be the answer to everything. Please, call the team and let them know the plan."

"Are you kidding?" Mike drew his hands back. "They're not going to listen to us. They won't follow you on some wild mission like this."

He opened his mouth like he wanted to say more but turned away. Trying to convince him any more now wouldn't help the situation. I turned to find Godfrey instead.

Godfrey was mingling and chatting with various audience members near the podium. I moved through the auditorium, making my way next to him. As the crowd began to fade, I finally got a chance to speak to him.

"Dr. Godfrey, it's a pleasure to see you again."

"And to you as well. Thank you for coming."

"I have four other members on my team," I told him, not that they had agreed yet.

"I understand," he said. "I'll make provisions for them as well."

Running my hands through my hair, I let out a long sigh along with the rest of my concerns.

"To be honest, this does sound kind of crazy. But if it's true, it seems like a game-changer."

"Yes, Clara, but keep in mind, something of this magnitude won't come without risk."

"I'm willing to take the risk if you are willing to take a chance on me."

He offered me his hand, "Well, the devotion of one's risk can only be honored with the commitment of another. I give you my hand not only with a commitment of finding the Ark, but also to bring you and your team home safely."

With that, we shook hands.

"Thank you for that, Dr. Godfrey. It's what we all wanted to know."

Ending my conversation with him, I looked over to see Mike standing in the hall, lost in thought. I walked through the squandering crowd toward him, easing my hand under his folded arms and resting my head on his shoulder. He looked at me without saying a word as we both walked out to the parking lot.

I grasped his hand. "I trust Godfrey, but if you feel like this guy can't be trusted, then let's walk away. But if not, we're going to need our team. If anyone can bring us together, it's you. Please, Mike. Call them for me."

His hand twitched like he wanted to withdraw it, but instead, he closed it around mine.

"I'll try. But can you blame them if they don't want to do something so dangerous? Are you even ready to do this?"

"Yes, I am!"

"Clara, I always thought you were a woman with many layers, but this layer might be the icing on the cake."

"You want to hear something a friend once told me?"

"No! Clara, I don't want to hear the old 'life's just whispering' thing anymore."

"Come on, please?"

"Okay, but I hope that you're right this time."

"This time?"

"You know what I mean."

"Yeah, I know what you mean."

After our goodbyes, I left him standing in the parking lot. All I could do was hope he could bring together the people I had trusted in the past.

The days after the meeting flew by. Our departure was soon, so I took the time to study, preparing body and mind. My anticipation was building as the day of our journey approached until I could hardly stay in one place for more than five minutes.

That day began just like any other, the early morning sunlight waking me up with its warm rays. Bolting out of bed, I felt fresh and alert. After a quick shower and some light packing, I grabbed the Bible and hurried to hail a cab to the airport.

Godfrey was already waiting in the boarding area along with other members of the crew he had assembled. He came up and gave me a warm hug. "I'm glad you could make it, Clara. It's great to see you here."

"Thanks Godfrey, and they are?"

"Oh, this is the rest of the team that will be assisting us." We all shook hands introducing ourselves.

Pam and Sue, along with the guy's walked up to us, their expressions tense.

"You know, none of us would be here if it wasn't for Mike," Pam said with all of her usual spite.

"I'm just glad you agreed to come." Turning to Sue, I asked, "And what about you?"

She tilted her head, studying my face. "I'm in. But to be honest, I'm not sure I'd be here if I didn't need the money."

I gave her a quick wink. "In any case, I'm happy you decided to join us. Welcome back to the team."

She cracked a small smile, then leaned forward, and pulled me into a hug. Having the whole team there made me feel ready, but the fact that Sue was joining me gave me the most strength.

Releasing Sue, I turned to Terry. "Don't think I've forgotten you. I'm so happy you're here."

"How could I not be?" He laughed. "I'm just as addicted to taking a gamble as you are, and this is just about the biggest long shot I could ever dream up. I'm with you all the way."

Coming forward, he pulled me into a bear hug. I laughed, "Okay, enough said."

We chatted until it was time to board the plane, filing in, and taking our seats. I strapped on my seat belt, and soon after, our plane rose above the clouds.

I turned to Dr. Godfrey.

"I'm honored to be here. Truth be told, I did some prior research on your work before I attended your lecture."

"Of course," he said, a sparkle in his eye. "You called me *Dr. Godfrey* that day. I never told you my title when we first met."

He's observant. "Well, I was wondering what type of scientist you are."

Godfrey exhaled. "It's a long story."

"We have a long flight ahead of us, sir."

"You're not wrong about that." He settled into his seat. "But before I say, tell me a little about you and your team."

"Well, my full name is Dr. Clara Eugene, Hamilton. I got my middle name from my father. I guess my mother thought it was cute. After moving to Texas four years ago, I started working at Texas Tech, that's where I met Sue. She introduced me to Pam and Terry. I met Mike at a conference he was holding."

"Wow, okay, and that's how you guys formed a team?" Godfrey asked.

"No, that's how I formed the team."

He smiled and then launched into his own background. "Twenty years ago, I started the Christian Institute. It was an organization of scientists who dared to ponder aloud the possibilities of changing science. 'What if?' we asked the establishment. What if thinking something different could change our hearts? What if doing something different could change our lives? For years, scientists told us the universe started from a singular meteoric collision—the big bang theory."

"Right," I nodded.

"But the Bible tells us God created the universe from nothing. And now, some five thousand years after the Bible was written, most scientists agree that the big bang theory may be wrong. The universe was created from nothing, which ancient men told us in the Bible thousands of years ago. So, over the last billion years, something has never been created from nothing, because we are living in the seventh day, and God is resting."

"But, Godfrey," I said, "mankind is over forty thousand years old, not seven thousand years old like the Bible says. The science points to it."

"I hope you'll forgive me if I beg to differ. On the sixth day, after creating light, earth, water, and animals, God created mankind, both male and female. Moses called their names Adam and Eve. God made them perfect and pure, with the intention that they would live forever. For all we know from the Bible, both may have lived in the Garden of Eden for millions of years before being cast out. Even before there was a devil."

"Interesting."

"But they were not the only people God created. According to the Bible, Cain, son of Adam, left his father and married a woman in a faraway land after sadly slaying his brother, Abel. Who was this woman he married if Adam, Eve, and their sons were the only people on Earth? God created others, and it must have happened during the time Adam reigned over the Garden of Eden."

"That proves my point!" I said, nearly jumping up in excitement. "Mankind came from the earth, from many different places. Why did you say the idea was a fable at the bar?"

"I never said the idea was a fable. I said this is no fable. God created Adam and Eve first, and after them, God created others. In fact, I believe there were people all over the earth, but they were all washed away in the flood. The only people who survived were those on the Ark, the descendants of Noah, the ninth-generation child of Adam. Yes, people lived on earth for thousands of years as Adam and Eve lived in the Garden. The Bible doesn't start recording until the fall of man, when Adam and Eve fell into sin, losing their dominion over the Garden."

"But, Godfrey, if other people lived on earth, then why doesn't God mention them?"

"He does. Again, who was the woman Cain married? God spoke about them, but they were ultimately rendered irrelevant when the flood destroyed the world. The only ones who survived were the descendants of Noah, who himself was the grandchild of Methuselah, the oldest man that has ever lived. Methuselah was descended from Enoch, who, throughout the generations, was descended from Seth, the third son of Adam."

"Wow, that's some lineage."

"Yes, that it is. Since Abel was killed and Cain's descendants got washed away in the flood, it would be Adam's third son, Seth, who would be honored to become the ancestor of all mankind. For it was Seth's children, by way of Noah, who repopulated the earth. What if God is right, and all who doubt Him are wrong?"

Godfrey stopped and took a deep breath, his face flushed with emotion. But he leaned into me, catching my gaze, and asked, "What if, Clara? Have you ever considered it?"

"But you're talking about faith now," I told Godfrey.

"What if I am? Would you step aboard an ark in faith, even if you saw no rain?"

I squirmed, trying to escape his piercing gaze. "Dr. Godfrey, you're a brilliant man, but sometimes you speak in riddles. I don't believe in your God. Sometimes it's hard to understand what you mean."

"Then let's focus on the mission at hand. In due time, we'll find out if we're right or wrong."

Godfrey became quiet. Even in his silence, I saw his eyes darting, searching for new thoughts. It astonished me, seeing a man like him in action.

After eighteen long hours, the flight attendant announced we would be landing shortly. It was early evening when the plane touched down in Tabriz, Iran. Relieved to be free of the tiny seats, we hurried out, only to be greeted with a long, drawn-out, grilling in customs. It was almost an hour before they gave us the final clearance and let us go to take the bus to our hotel.

Godfrey went to the front desk to get us checked in, while the rest of us hauled our bags into the lobby. Leaning on my suitcase, I took in the beauty of the artwork hanging on the hotel walls.

I'd never been to Iran before, but the fact that it was one of the oldest cultures in the world made my heart quicken and my eyes scan the sights at speed.

"Heads up, Clara."

I looked just in time to catch the room keys Godfrey tossed to me.

"We'll meet back here at eight tonight to go over the itinerary," he said, tapping his watch.

"Great, I'll be there," I told him. Stiffness made a home in my back, and my nerves were rattled from the turbulence on the plane. Truthfully, I just felt like unwinding with a chilled glass of Merlot and settling down for the evening. But Godfrey was eager, and I could hear it in his voice, although I wasn't fully listening to everything he said.

I wanted to walk over to the bar but chose not to go. Godfrey was standing there, and I already knew how his deep talk could ruin a perfectly good drink. It didn't matter. I had already checked with the concierge. There were mini-bars in the rooms. I was already back to my old habits. What could be the harm in having a quick drink to recharge? Just a little one.

CHAPTER

12

If There Is A God?

A FTER GOING upstairs to my room, I rewarded myself with one drink, then another. Two turned into four, and eventually, everything turned to a familiar haze.

I woke the next morning to a loud banging on my door. Sitting up with a pounding headache, I glanced at the mini-bar. It was empty.

"Clara!" Mike called my name again.

Wincing, I dragged myself to my feet, leaning against the wall. "Hold on, guys. I'll be right there."

"Is Clara the archeologist in there?" Mike yelled sarcastically. "What's she doing still asleep?"

"Give me ten minutes, Mike! I promise... I'll meet you down in the lobby."

"You'd better hurry," Mike said. "We've got work to do!"

Their footsteps trailed off. I rushed to get ready, combing my hair together into a bun in an attempt to look presentable, more than I felt.

Reaching the lobby, Godfrey gave me a cool look as I approached. "I'm glad you could join us today, Dr. Hamilton, but we have no time for slackers."

"I'm terribly sorry, sir," I said, lowering my eyes, "I promise this will never happen again."

He waved his hand. "Do you know the itinerary for today?"

I opened my mouth, then closed it.

"Of course, you don't. You missed the dinner meeting last night, and now you're lagging behind the rest of the team. I'll do my best to catch you up on the way there, but going forward, it's imperative you attend all our meetings. I don't have time to waste."

"Yes, sir."

"Good. Everyone needs to stay focused. We're headed out south of the Osku Kandaven Caves today. Our tour guide will be one of the locals there."

As Godfrey walked away, Mike nudged me in the back. "You need to get it together."

As the day broke, the entire crew boarded the bus heading out of the hotel. I rushed ahead so I could grab the single seat in the back, needing some time alone with my thoughts as much as for my sore head.

We left the city behind, turning onto a dusty road, and headed out and into the country. For a while, the beauty of the natural landscape put me at ease, reminding me of more peaceful times.

The smell of the open fields and the solitude of the ride gave me an opportunity to reflect. I thought about the letter I'd gotten back in Arizona and how I needed to respond. Writing had always been therapeutic for me, and with so many doors left cracked open, I thought it may be time to close a few. I reached into my bag, took out my pad and pen, and decided to free write what was in my heart.

"Hi… I'm sorry I haven't called. I know it's been a while since we talked, but the last time we heard from one another, we didn't talk at all. I can't lie and say I've been too busy or intended to write sooner.

The truth is, I didn't know what to say. Maybe we were given to each other for a season, maybe for the hurt? I can't help but wonder where we would be if all this had never happened to us. I feel—"

The bus rocked, distracting me. As our vehicle shuddered over the terrain, I put away my journal and hung on tight, feeling the open winds of the countryside gusting through the window. I would have to finish the letter another time, but the words hung on.

Where would I be if my life had taken a different path? I was in a foreign country, on a bus, driving into what may as well have been another world. The lush valley was filled with farmland and small huts, and the nomadic inhabitants standing in the fields looked up as we passed.

Godfrey turned to me. "Muslim fundamentalists lead the tribes in this area," he said. "They're incredibly strict in their religion and dangerously bloodthirsty. They have no tolerance for anyone who defies their traditions and threatens their way of life. We must be careful."

A chill ran down my back as I looked at the people in the fields with new eyes. Later that evening, the bus shuddered to a stop, and we disembarked.

"We'll be climbing this mountain range," Godfrey said. "Be prepared."

Night fell, and my crew went for the secret bottles of whiskey they had smuggled from their hotel rooms. I watched them drink, feeling guilt settle in my heart for missing the meeting. It stayed in my mind even as we prepared to sleep.

When the light dawned the next morning, I couldn't help but be amazed by the vast mountain range. The broad valley stretched before us, an intimidating journey to be conquered before we could ever hope to reach the base.

Our guide arrived soon afterward, shaking each of our hands and flashing us a smile. "My name is Ashkan Muhammad. I hope to be of help on your expedition."

"His great-grandfather claimed to have discovered where the Ark was located," Godfrey told me when Muhammad turned away, "but no one believed him. From all of my studies, I'm sure we can verify the claim."

Loading up the caravan, we set out. Muhammad led us toward the first base camp at the foot of the mountain range. Over the next three hours, the path became progressively rougher until it was no longer passable by caravan. Everyone got out of the bus, and I followed, tucking away my thoughts like the half-written letter.

The forest rose up to meet us. Taking machetes from our bags, we hacked at the thick brush. Gradually, it thinned out to grasslands, which soon eroded into a valley filled with flowers waving in the wind. I took a deep breath, drinking in the fresh scent of the air and the beauty of the scenery.

Muhammad walked ahead, leading us on. Eventually, he and Mike walked side-by-side, and they began to talk.

"So, how did you come to God?" Mike asked.

Muhammad smiled. "In the beginning, I was not seeking God. But in His everlasting mercy, He sought me. I am humbled to be His servant now. He shows me life as I'd never imagined it before. Yet even today, I don't understand why He wanted me, such a lowly man."

His smile lingered as the two of them walked ahead. Fragments of their conversation drifted back to me, but I stopped trying to listen. I had my own questions to ask. Watching Godfrey walk with a studied look on his face, I wanted to approach him, but he seemed so absorbed in the mission.

Eventually, the questions burning in my heart won over. The fires erupted. While the rest of the crew trudged along, focused only on getting to our next destination, I caught up with the man who had brought us there.

"Dr. Godfrey, I was thinking about the Bible you gave me."

"Yes. What about it?"

"I have a question about this road to heaven I've read about."

"And what is your question, Clara?"

"If there truly is a God, and if God wants everyone to go to heaven, why does He make the road so difficult to travel?"

"Difficult to travel?" Godfrey chuckled. "God wants everyone in heaven, but the road to heaven is one the world hardly looks at. God never said the road was hard or difficult. He said it was the one 'seldom traveled.'"

I had never thought about it that way. I thought faith was always a difficult task. Every time Godfrey spoke, it amazed me how much wisdom he had.

"You believe in your God, don't you, Dr. Godfrey?"

"Indeed, I do. He's always been there for me."

"Perhaps He has. But it seems like He hasn't been there for many others," I told him.

Godfrey glanced at me, tilting his head. "Why would you say that?"

"Well, I mean, if there truly is a God, and He is so good, why does He allow all those poor children in Africa to starve?"

For a while, Godfrey walked without saying anything. I could tell he was thinking, so I kept silent. When he finally spoke, his words came without hesitation.

"There is an endless amount of fresh water on this Earth—enough fresh water to nurture every man, woman, and child in the world. In America alone, we throw away over forty million tons of food every year. That's enough food to feed every starving child on the planet. The Bible tells us the Lord has provided. But because of man's wars and his selfishness, poor children have been driven so far out into the desert that they can't access the supplies God has for them and the rest of the world. Clara, the question is not why God allows poor children to starve to death. The real question is, why do we?" Everything he said was like a gem of uncovered wonder, yet I had more digging to do.

"Well, why would your God—a God of mercy, a God of love—allow bad things to happen to good people?"

Godfrey paused, just for a moment, and said, "I don't know, Clara, maybe it's to show us how good people handle bad things."

I nearly tripped as my feet got tangled in the weeds along the valley path. Even as I struggled to free myself, I couldn't help but frown at his answer.

Someone yelled in the distance.

"Dr. Godfrey," his voice echoed throughout the valley. "Over here!"

It was Chuy, Dr. Godfrey's right-hand man. He had left ahead of the rest of the expedition and was now on a tractor, along with a small group, clearing brush and beckoning us toward him.

Straining my neck, I gaped in awe as we crossed the expanse, standing at the base of the mountain ridge. Each curve, cliff, and peak struck dramatic contrast against the sky. The mountains rose into the heavens, appearing to brush against the sleeping stars. Ararat, as the Bible called it.

I was finally able to look away, joining my teammates in pitching our tents and building a fire. It was springtime in the valley, but those mountains looked cold. Muhammad gave us a quick overview of what he thought was the safest route, his finger outlining a stark path in the looming mountains.

"We must be careful," he said, lifting his head and taking a deep breath. "I can smell it in the air. There's a storm on the way."

"I'll keep that in mind," Godfrey nodded. I studied him but couldn't read fear or any kind of frustration. He looked as calm as ever as he sat down next to the campfire, rubbing his hands together.

The fire's warmth and the sound of its crackling drew me in too. When I sat next to Godfrey, he greeted me with a warm hug, then gestured to Chuy.

"Without him, planning all of this would have been difficult."

"Dr. Godfrey exaggerates," said Chuy, a mild smile on his face. He sat across from us, drawing a cigar from his pocket.

"How'd the two of you meet?"

Chuy smiled and said, "It's quite the story. I used to be a man of the world, living life as if I'd never die. My days were filled with mindless pleasures. But one night, I walked into a bar, already drunk, and I wanted only to lose myself even more. I ordered another drink there. A man sitting next to me was making a lot of noise, yet I paid him no attention until he got out of control. Before I knew it, he came over and bashed me across the head with a beer bottle." His hand flitted to the right side of his head, and in the flickering firelight, I saw the scar where his hair no longer grew. He continued.

"It turned into a full-on brawl. I had a chair in my hands and was just about to return the favor when I heard a voice."

"Did your life flash before your eyes?" I asked. Godfrey gave me a pointed look, apparently not amused by the flippant question.

Chuy leaned down to light his cigar in the fire.

"No. It wasn't my life that I saw, but his. And I saw that he had brought his young daughter into the bar. She couldn't have been older than seven, and she dropped to her knees and begged me not to hurt her daddy. I can still hear her voice today... My hands shook, and instead of smashing the chair over his head, I cracked it over his legs."

The end of the cigar gleamed, hot like the smoldering embers in the fire, but Chuy didn't draw back. He seemed lost in another time; the leaping flames reflected in his eyes.

"Go on."

"When it was all over, they still convicted me of assault and battery, and I had to spend several years in prison. The hell I went through there..." He paused, wrestling with his own memories. "God didn't allow me to go through hell to give me a warning about life but to give me a lesson on how to live it. It took my prison sentence to make me stop and listen to Him, to understand that not every battle needs to be fought. Life is so much bigger than that."

He lifted the cigar away from the flames, staring at the smoldering end, glowing with a dim light.

He added, "My ears are so close to the mouth of God now, so close that He can guide me with a whisper. And it all started in prison. In my cell, I listened in on the ministry team nearby. They spoke about redemption. I was moved and went to listen when I got the chance. When I walked into that room, I bumped into the leader of the ministry team. It was none other than Dr. Godfrey."

A small smile played across Godfrey's face. "And what a meeting that was. Do you remember the first thing I asked you, Chuy?"

"I'll remember it forever. You asked me 'Can we put the past behind us?' There I was, facing this man who didn't know me or what I had done, but knew I had work to do. I've been with him ever since, and now here we are, on the greatest journey of our lives." Chuy put his cigar to his lips and took a puff. The smoke curled, masking his eyes, but I felt them on me.

"May I turn the tables on you for a moment?" he finally asked. "I would like to hear about your story as well. What brought you here?"

I folded my arms, a little overwhelmed by his request. Neither Chuy nor Godfrey rushed me, giving me time to find my voice.

"My father was Dr. Henry Hamilton, who established the School of Archaeology at Chicago Tech. He raised me after my mother died when I was ten. To help me cope with the loss, he taught me to observe the beauty that could be found on Earth. He asked me to imagine the earth as a living, breathing entity, fully alive, and self-aware."

I paused to lick my lips. "It was a tough time for us, but my father was tougher. I remember what he used to tell me, 'She's gone now, but hers is a love you keep, tucked away in your heart.' Sure, he was hard on me sometimes, and he was prone to a good knuckle-rapping when I got things wrong." I rubbed my knuckles, remembering those lessons. "Archaeology felt amazing. I knew it was something I wanted to do for the rest of my life. I worked with my father on some of his explorations and eventually began unearthing things on my own. I became the lead archaeologist and the department head at Chicago Tech years later."

Chuy made an impressed sound. I took a deep breath, preparing myself to formulate the story that followed, words hanging heavy.

"I had a child named Joshua. As all mothers do, I made a promise to him and myself that I would always be there for him anytime he needed me, you know, the best mom in the world. I wanted to give him more love than I had ever experienced."

I took a moment. "But life didn't allow that to happen for us. One day, I came home to relieve his babysitter. As she left, I noticed Joshua was persistent in his pleas to go outside and play as he was tossing his ball all over the house. Exhausted that day, I did something that ordinarily would have been against my better judgment. Reclining on my sofa, I told him he could go outside and play again. I felt uneasy, allowing him to go out unsupervised, so I got up and went outside to watch him. Joshua took off like a rocket and chased that ball as it bounced out of the driveway and into the street. Not noticing the oncoming traffic, and before I could yell anything... my child ran out into the middle of the street and was hit by a car. The whole thing happened right before my eyes."

They looked on, quietly letting me gather myself.

"I rushed out after him, of course, screaming and in shock. I pulled him out from underneath the car's bumper, screaming, 'Open your eyes, Joshua. Please open your eyes.' Kneeling on the street, pulling my child from underneath that car, I screamed again, 'Please Joshua, please, just open your eyes for momma.' He never did. The doctors did their best, but they couldn't save him. I don't remember much from then on."

Crushing his cigar, Chuy leaned in and hugged me around the shoulders. "I'm so sorry for what you went through," he said.

"I'm... I'm okay," I said, gulping down the sobs forming in my throat. "It's been painful, but I've been trying to move on. Mike's been a big help."

"I'm sorry if this is intrusive," Godfrey said, "but are you two an item? You've yet to explain his role on your team."

I blinked, caught off-guard. "I... well, if you ask me like that, I'll have to tell you. We're not an item, and Mike's not in the business. In fact, he's not a scientist at all."

"He's not?" Godfrey asked, a new wrinkle in his brow.

"Nope, not at all. He's my life coach. My personal self-help guru. It's strangely embarrassing to say out loud, but I needed one after what happened to my child. I hired him a few years ago. We've become working partners, but also best friends."

"Is that why he's always giving you some kind of pep talk?" Chuy asked.

"Yeah. Honestly, I have to credit him with helping me keep much of my sanity."

"Well, we all need somebody," Godfrey said, nodding.

I breathed a quick sigh of relief, glad Godfrey didn't turn judgmental or preachy on me, so I went on.

"I met Mike when I left Chicago and moved to Texas. There's this phrase he used a lot from the very start, 'Life is but a whisper, so live it out loud.' So, he and I came up with the idea that before starting a new dig, we'd do something extreme, like jumping out of a plane onto the dig site, parasailing, maybe bungee jumping." The memories of cliff diving in Arizona last time made me smile, although it faded quickly. "All of this in the name of living out loud," I continued. "I'm not sure how to explain this, but the loss of a child is not something a mother can ever get over. It's a lonely pain a lot of the time, and that makes it worse than any other kind."

"Clara," Godfrey said. "The storms God allows to come your way are storms worthy of your faith."

"Maybe you're right," I said, feeling frustration rise in my chest. "I can't help but wonder, Dr. Godfrey. When do those storms wash away? I mean if there truly is... a God."

CHAPTER

13

Knock Away the Ice

WE SPENT the rest of the night talking. Godfrey answered my questions without fail. Before then, no one on the team except Mike had known the details of Joshua's passing. No one knew the toll it had taken on me, not only as his mother but also as a witness to his passing. No one had ever asked, and I never brought up the subject. I felt invisible, emotionally unseen. How could the world just go on without coming to my rescue? Yes, I had to admit—I had grown withdrawn and cold. But now, speaking frankly with Godfrey, I was glad to break the silence. It was refreshing, despite the ache I felt swelling within me.

Again, and again, we returned to the subject of God. Godfrey talked about faith and how it stood in relation to catastrophe. He talked about how faith in God was no illusion. Despite his patient explanations, I could not quite work through my thoughts on the subject. But for the first time in my life, I truly felt curious. Even when Godfrey finally stood and advised me to rest, I could barely keep my eyes closed.

The next day was the first of a few days spent scouting the mountains. We assured ourselves we were on the right track. We even thought we had found the trail a few times, but they all led to dead ends.

While going through all the motions of preparation, including the scouting, I was still thinking about the conversation I'd had with Chuy and Godfrey. At least now they knew why I left Chicago. I had needed to get out of there, away from it all.

Days passed, and we all felt like we had been searching for nothing. Up the mountain, down the mountain—and for what? Things looked bleak.

I was tired. We all were. Yet we were determined to see this crazy adventure through. We had all promised to keep our negative thoughts at bay, as hard as that was.

We set up another camp miles away from where we had started, hoping to find the trail we were searching for. That morning, a brisk wind whipped across my face through the opening in my tent. I put on layer after layer of clothing to protect myself from the bitter cold waiting ahead. Unfortunately, this was the only time the Iranian government would allow us to search. They knew the harsh weather would limit our travels, helping them keep an eye on us. Leaving my tent to check the sky again, I encountered Godfrey standing in the distance. Sleet pelted his jacket as the wind blew sideways. His smile was strained, his eyes fixed above. I smirked and shook my head as I looked up to the overcast sky. For once, I felt glad not to be in the lead—I wouldn't have to worry about letting anyone down.

I brushed the sleet off my shoulders, stuffed my freezing hands into my pockets, and made my way to the fire. I wasn't exactly sure of things myself. My stomach was doing flips, but the freedom of being out there and exploring made me crave more. Now fully awake, I felt the cold assault my body. The nervousness in the pit of my gut burned even more. I bent over and vomited. *Maybe I could use a little less of this freedom,*

I thought, kicking ice and dirt over the mess. What a way to start the day.

I found myself wiping my mouth before last night's dinner could freeze around it. Standing near the fire reminded me I was here to stay grounded.

Chuy was making coffee for the team. The scent brought a tinge of pleasant normality to my morning.

"Good morning, Clara. Coffee? It's mountain-grown," he said jokingly.

"Sounds good to me, as long as it gets me going," I replied.

Godfrey walked over, pointed to a log nearby, and nodded at the fire. "Sit down there and warm up before you turn to ice. I'll grab the coffee."

The air above the fire shimmered with heat. When Godfrey came to hand me a mug, I already felt less frigid as the warmth of the campfire blazed away, penetrating the layers until it reached my skin. His smile faded again as he eyed the horizon and the weather. The sun had just risen and broken through the clouds. Against the brightening sky, the silhouette of the mountain ranges we were going to climb looked massive.

"What's that look about?" I asked. "Aren't you the one who is so sure we're on the right path?"

Godfrey took a sip of his coffee and said, "I can assure you this morning—I have full-hearted faith we are."

He sounded confident enough. Maybe I needed to stop worrying about so many things.

"Clara, I have decided we're going to need your eyes to assist us and lead the way from here," Godfrey said.

"Lead the way? I thought I was just here to help."

"No, not anymore," he replied. "We need your eyes. I have complete confidence in you. Stay focused on the task, and together we will make it. Don't overthink it."

"Don't overthink it? Well, that's a quick turn of the tables, wouldn't you say, Godfrey?"

"I know, but that's life."

That's life? Wow, what a way to start a morning. I sat there with my cup of coffee in my hand, wondering, yet not saying a word. All I could do was think. I had not come out here for that. I traced the sleet on the ground to avoid making eye contact. I couldn't believe it. I hadn't come here to lead anything, but to fade into the background, unseen and unknown.

Before long, the rest of the team joined us.

"Good morning, everyone!" Mike announced as all the others stalked the coffee pot, grumbling under their breaths with the icy morning blues.

Godfrey left the group and wandered a short distance up the hill, looking around the rough terrain and snowcapped mountains. I knew just as well as he did that our time was limited. There looked to be a storm heading our way. With his expression unreadable, he briskly walked down the wet hill back to where we were. He tossed the remains of his coffee onto the dying embers, which went out with an aromatic hiss.

Running across the rough terrain a few hundred feet away was Muhammad, waving his hand in the air. Once he got closer, I could hear him say, "I found the trail. The one on the map my grandfather made."

Godfrey looked at us and said, "We need to get moving. We don't want to get caught in a storm. There's not much time left."

Everyone grumbled but picked up the pace.

Although my heart pounded in my chest and doubt dampened my excitement, I pushed myself to think positively, fighting back the negative thoughts trying to crawl into my mind. No matter what, I had to stay hopeful.

The cold wind lashed at me, but I stood strong. After all, what was this to someone used to being knocked off her feet?

Godfrey, stepping in front of the team, announced, "It's time to head out. Muhammad, along with Dr. Hamilton, will lead us and scout out the way."

"I'm ready, Dr. Godfrey," Muhammad replied as he put on his backpack. His eyes, full of conviction, cut through the haze in the path we were to take. I could tell he was no amateur by the way his eyes flickered and how steady he stood.

Something about his courage flipped a switch in me. My messy thoughts came to order. It was now or never. There I was, on a journey searching for something I wasn't even sure existed—something biblical, an item built by nothing other than faith—Noah's Ark. Wow, what a morning.

I strapped on my gear just before the skies started turning gray. It looked like it was about to start snowing, and felt like it too. We had no choice but to move on. Muhammad handed me his map. According to him, today was our last day of the journey.

Under the cloudy skies, Pam and Sue came over and gave me a big hug. They were going to stay back and assist two of the seven members of Godfrey's team in keeping track of our whereabouts. The others went with us. Concern danced in the eyes of Pam and Sue.

"Don't worry about me, guys. I'll be okay."

Muhammad waved one hand in the air as a signal, and we got started. Walking ahead of the team, Muhammad never wavered, even when the overgrown trail faded in and out of existence under our feet. I followed close by his side, casting my eyes ahead.

The higher we climbed, the more the winds punished our team. Sleet pelted against our faces. Some turned back, unwilling to go on. The core members of the team, along with a few others, continued undeterred.

A few hours later, we finally found a spot to set up the second camp. Chuy and Terry assisted the last small group of Godfrey's team in setting up the location as a radio contact spot. At that altitude, Chuy and Terry were the only ones Godfrey and I trusted to man the contact camp if anything went wrong. That left the four of us—Mike, Godfrey, Muhammad, and me. We prepared ourselves to climb the snowy trail up to what the elders called "the Old Bridge." It was the link to another mountain—the one said to hold what we were looking for. This fifty-foot rope bridge was built during the British invasion. Now it would serve us as well, granting us access to the most remote sections of the distant mountain. Weird how a century-old decision could impact the world in ways nobody could have ever seen coming.

While we sorted and repacked our gear, I took every precaution I could think of, visually plotting our journey through the binoculars. I wasn't going to slack off. Letting everyone down again wasn't an option.

"Hard at work, I see," Godfrey said. He was already finished repacking.

"It's only natural for an expedition of this size," I said.

Godfrey picked up his gear. "I'm glad you're here."

The four of us strapped on locators in case of separation and then headed down our chosen route. It was unfamiliar to all of us, but it was the way the elder tribesmen believed Muhammad's great-grandfather had gone when he discovered the Ark's remains. Muhammad led us through a forest and into a valley that rose into the mountains, all of it stretching on for what seemed like an infinite distance. Standing in that valley, we had all gotten disorientated, it felt as if we were lost. I pulled out the ragged and torn map Muhammad handed me before, studying it for a moment, my eyes made out our direction.

Looking through my binoculars, I pointed. "Those are the mountains we'll be climbing."

The winds rushed at our chapped faces, but it was nothing compared to what we would face at higher altitudes.

Worried, Mike asked, "Clara, are you sure?

Looking over that map again, I told him, "I'm sure."

I put that map away, although like Mike, I was afraid. But it was in the encouraging words of Godfrey, when he said,

"Eagle eyes, lead the way." I got moving.

There was only a short window before the weather became unbearable. We fought the wind, continuing onward and upward.

"Is this even safe?" Mike worried aloud.

I couldn't respond. What little courage that had swelled in my chest earlier faded as the winds picked up. A dry lump formed in my throat, and that's when the "what-ifs" crowded my mind.

What if we got lost? What if we couldn't find it? What if we froze to death out here? What if I threw up again? My resolve began to waver as I stopped in my tracks, thinking about all the things that could go wrong.

"No, Clara, not now!" Godfrey yelled.

He must have seen it in my eyes, but it was too late. My nerves got to my stomach, and just as I predicted... I'd thrown up again.

Over the high winds, Godfrey asked, "Clara, are you okay?"

"Yes, it'll only take me a second to get myself together, but let's keep moving." I forced myself, chest aching.

"Okay, let's keep moving. You know we need you!"

Regaining my composure, we continued the hike. Godfrey tried to keep me encouraged. He talked to me about conquering mountains, giving me scriptures and God's word. But it seemed like the further we hiked, the taller those mountains loomed. *Don't overthink it, Clara, don't overthink it.* Every fiber of my being screamed for me to stay still and go no further. Yet, even as I stood rooted to the spot, I felt something dark closing around us as our clock ticked down.

"Where in the world is that bridge?" I near cried.

Turning around, Godfrey faced me. "We're in this together," he said. "Don't quit on me now!"

I looked back. Ice covered Mike's terrified face. He shuddered—eyes wide. Everything about this seemed like too bold of a journey and too big of a step for Mike and me to have taken. A fresh gust of snow hit my bare face, leaving it aching. Forcing my legs to move again, I continued without choice. The trail grew so steep, we were forced to take out our ice picks and plow our way upward. After several hundred feet of this grueling exercise, I nearly stumbled when the ground flattened out. The hardest part of our journey was behind us. Despite my frozen face, I cracked a small smile. Off and into the horizon, I saw it. We found the bridge.

The snowfall began to ease up. As we sat there, panting and gathering our thoughts, my scattered impressions started coming together and making sense again.

Without resting, Muhammad walked ahead to scout out the bridge. I trudged over to Mike and sat down next to him with a flop.

"I'm so sorry I asked you to come. This is much harder than I anticipated."

"Well, there's no turning back now," Mike said, hugging his coat and giving me a shivering thumbs up. "I'm glad to be here with you, just so you're not alone."

With exhaustion clearly etched on his face, he gave me a few words that improved my mood. Before we could talk much more, Muhammad came back, struggling through the deep snow, the corners of his mouth downturned.

"We face a new obstacle ahead."

"Is the bridge out?" Godfrey asked.

"No, sir, it looks strong—but it's covered in ice and snow."

Godfrey's eyebrows shot up. "If we can't get through that way, how will we pass over?"

Mike and I exchanged glances. Seeing his disappointed face only drained me of whatever warmth I'd gained in our travel.

"These mountains are too dangerous to find another route," Muhammad said. "There's no other way. Either we turn back now, or we knock away the ice and cross the bridge."

I couldn't believe my ears. "Knock away the ice? Muhammad, that can't be the only way."

"There isn't any other way. We need to clear off the ice to cross the bridge."

Even as Muhammad spoke, his voice trailed off into a weak whisper. The lack of confidence certainly didn't inspire the rest of us with much hope.

Godfrey, seeming exhausted, pulled himself off the ground and said, "Well, were here now and I don't know. But wrestling with our fears want change anything. I am not going to be afraid to try. I will go out there and knock away the ice."

"Godfrey no!" I said. "It's to dangerous!"

Out from nowhere, Mike yelled.

"Not without me!" as he dropped the bags that might have weighed him down.

"No, Mike, you don't know what you are doing, this is way too risky!"

Pulling out his hammer, Godfrey began to knock away the ice. My heart panicked, when I saw Mike follow him.

I watched, those two men, taking each step with care, over a derelict, swaying bridge. Striking their hammers on those old wooden slats, breaking away the encrusted ice. A single slip-up on any one of them would be their last. With worn ropes as handrails, we would have to walk across the frayed bridge like acrobats. I'd done some questionable and dangerous things in my life, but this one might have been the worst. Although my mind screamed at me to turn back, I stood my ground against my mind and fears. If I was to keep going, I had to find away. I had to find my way, to knock away the ice and fears that had frozen over my heart.

In front of me, Mike and Godfrey began to move out. One board at a time, the two men took small steps, holding their axes sideways to scrape off the ice. The bridge swayed precariously over the abyss.

As I watched them, I felt my limbs quivering at the mere thought that Mike could slip and fall off the bridge. He had no business being there beyond me. He was neither a researcher nor an adventurer of any kind. But there he was, risking his life for me. He was there for me, and if anything happened to him...

Despite the treacherous conditions, Mike and Godfrey managed to clear the whole length of the bridge. With a few final steps, they made it onto the ground on the other side. Mike looked back and waved me forward, his voice rebounding off the walls of the mountain.

"Come on, Clara! Come on!" Despite the distance, I heard his voice crack with urgency.

"Go ahead," Muhammad said as a friend, standing behind me. "I will hold the bridge as best I can for you."

Shivering equally from cold and fear, looking over that bridge into the eyes of Mike and Godfrey, I raised my boot from the solid ground, gingerly taking my first step onto the weakening boards of the rickety bridge. Then the next, and the next. It didn't get easier. I heard water rushing hundreds of feet below me. There was a yawning abyss and snowflakes swiveling around some lost and cold river.

At least if I fell, I might die before I ever hit the ground.

I heard boards, creaking beneath my boots as I tried to cross the bridge. That hard bridge of change. Yet, there I was. The winds whipped at my back. Forcing the fear out of my mind, I kept moving. I tried to be cautious, but my boot cracked through one of the ice-encrusted boards. I grabbed a hanging rope, reaching out in a panic. I barely felt the hand rope through my glove when I heard Mike shouting on the other side, "Don't look down. Keep going, keep going—"

Shaking, I slipped again. I didn't want to die out there, not like that. Planks began to snap, trapping my foot. Stuck between boards, the sharp edges pressed into my ankle, cutting off my circulation.

A strong hand grabbed at my flailing arm. It was Mike. He had crossed the bridge from the other side to meet me halfway.

"Don't move, Clara, I've got you." He reached down to adjust the boards and freed my foot, pulling me up. With one arm around him, I made it across the last few feet and fell onto the snow-covered ground. The bridge seemed to drain the life out of me, the wind robbing me of my breath.

Looking back, a wave of relief washed over me. I pulled myself out of Mike's embrace, looked up, and saw Muhammad sprinting across the bridge, one leap at a time. Within seconds, he landed on the steady earth again. Standing up, he dusted the snow from his coat. He'd made it look easy.

"We made it!" he announced, throwing up his arms. "This is the place my great-grandfather claimed to have found the Ark. Now that we've gotten so far, we can't fail now."

Struggling to my feet, I finally managed to regain my balance. "I'm ready, guys. Let's get moving."

We took our time but traveled ahead. Only Muhammad seemed able to bound forward with confident steps. Miles later, and at that altitude, finding it hard to catch my breath, the trail narrowed along the side of the mountain. I held on to the rocky side of it, trying not to fall off of the steep cliff that our pathway hugged. My feet shook in my boots as they began to slip with every other step. Once again, I was walking on thin ice. The wind blew up from underneath me, lifting me off the trail, tossing me against the side of the mountain, and tried to pull me off the cliff. But I landed back on the thin ice, that same ice Godfrey had just walked over.

"Godfrey!" I yelled, my voice brittle as I realized what was happening with the ice.

"What's wrong?"

"The ice is cracking, and it's about to give way!"

The fractures crept through the ice, faster and faster, stretching in every direction along the walkway.

"Just hold on!" Godfrey shouted. "I'm following Muhammad's footsteps, so you can just follow mine!"

It was too late for strategies. Before I could react, the ice had shattered, and I plummeted down again.

Falling through the ice, I grabbed onto part of the remaining walkway, dangling there as rocks fell away. My mouth wanted to call for help, but all I could manage were incomprehensible crying screams.

I tried to lift myself while holding onto that piece as tightly as I could. Godfrey, with fear in his eyes, secured himself to a rope and jumped down off that cliff and toward me, straining his arms around my waist. His hands intensely tightening as he held on to me. Hanging upside down, and over that cliff, I looked down and saw the breathless void over what we helplessly hung.

Frantically, I closed my arms tightly around Godfrey's shoulders although I felt the rope starting to slip. I grabbed again. Pulling myself up the rope, scrambling over Godfrey's arms, I felt him push me to safer grounds.

Collapsing against the wall of the mountain, I wept, the tears all but freezing on my face.

I heard a faint voice shouting my name from beneath. "Clara. Clara! Are you okay?" In my panic, I had all but forgotten about Godfrey.

"Yes! Yes, I'm okay."

"Then, will you help Muhammad pull me up?"

Before I could respond, Mike moved forward. He and Muhammad acted quickly, fastening a rope around Mike's waist. Slowly but steadily, he lowered himself over the edge of the cliff, extending a hand toward Godfrey. Muhammad held the other end of the rope, veins popping on the backs of his hands.

"Hold on," said Mike. Grabbing hold of the rope, he began to attach it to Godfrey. Finishing, he turned back and signaled to Muhammad that he was ready. Steadily as always, Muhammad pulled the two back up. They emerged over the edge, collapsing onto the solid ground just as I had.

I didn't know what to say. My body still trembled from the whole ordeal as I pressed myself into the cliff wall, trying to regain the feeling in my body. Nothing around me seemed safe anymore. I turned away as I had always done in my life. Staring into the distance as my teammates approached me. I should have turned around and shown some relief with them, but I had no cheer left in me. I didn't want any part in this so-called "adventure" anymore.

Pulling out my homing device, I readied myself to push the panic button that would send out a distress signal for help. Mike, Muhammad, and Godfrey were too preoccupied with gathering their own wits to notice me. Even the usual calm on Godfrey's face had gone blank. How many more scares before these mountains ended up killing us?

I needed to put an end to it, right then, right there.

Just as I looked back at Godfrey for a signal to press the button, I noticed something strange in the sky beyond him. With one final howl that shook me to my core, the turmoil of the winds finally disappeared into a dissipating silence...

The snow settled, and the air cleared. Off in the distance appeared to be an enormous platform coated in snow. It was outlining the side of the mountain's wall. The surface was unusually flat, whereas all the terrain around it was rocky.

Mike slid down beside me.

"Clara, please. Whatever you're going through, whatever's going on in your mind, please, don't lose it out here."

My eyes outlined the mountain as my breath caught in my throat. The snow seemed to fall off the side of that area, cradled between the mountain's walls.

"Look at me," Mike yelled out. "Look at me. Where are you right now?"

I couldn't utter a word. Not one. My eyes were fixed on what appeared to be a gaping field, extending beyond the edge of the cliff. The ridges of the mountain dug into my back. I put the locator back into my pocket and felt for my hammer, pushing myself away from the rock-covered wall and onto my feet again. I started walking along the cliff toward what looked to be a huge snow-covered area.

I could hear Mike calling my name in the distance, but I paid him no mind. That terrain was calling me. The hairs on my neck stood up as each step I took felt odd, unbalanced. What was I standing on? My heart began to race as I pulled out my hammer.

My walk turned into a jog, and my jog turned into a sprint. Adrenaline rushed through my body as I raced over the snow-covered terrain, jumped into the air, and swung my hammer down, striking at what the ice was hiding. Bang!

A reverberating *boom* rang through the cold air.

The ice cracked. I swung my hammer again and again. *Boom! Boom! Boom!* My heart was in total shock, as I looked back at the others and saw my own confusion reflected in their eyes. The strange feeling in my stomach and heart was validated. With one last swing, I broke through, creating an opening in the ice. The hammer slipped out of my hand and down the hole I had just made. A few seconds passed before the ring of my hammer hitting the bottom sounded back up to me. A wind rose from the hollow hole, blowing right into my face. Wincing, I thought I had broken into some sort of cavern. This couldn't be what I thought it was. I shook as I took the flashlight from my pocket and turned it on. Shakily, I stuck the butt end of it into my mouth and poked my head through the hole, trying to see something, anything. It seemed to be a vast void, or a cavern hidden underneath the rocks and snow.

Then, slowly, my eyesight adjusted and began to make out how deep the hole was. My eyes traced left, and I saw a gigantic tar-covered wall. Toward the top of that old wall, I saw what looked like the imprint of feathers, like a bird's wings had brushed up against it during flight or while escaping captivity after that wall was patched with pitch.

I angled the light so I could get a better look. Protruding from the walls were what appeared to be weakened floors; one-story collapsed on top of another. With a few of the floors intact, it allowed me to see clear down to the bottom. I spotted my hammer in the remnants of some sort of cage.

Oh wow, is that—? No, this can't be what I think it is.

There was more I could not believe. There were several other cages and what looked like several other rooms that might have held—

I flinched when I felt someone grab my shoulder, pulling my head out of the hole.

"No!" I screamed, frustrated, unable to articulate my thoughts, or convey what my eyes had seen. In my panic, the flashlight fell out of my mouth and sailed down into the pit, illuminating the insides. I heard it hit the bottom as I huffed out an annoyed breath and reached up to wrangle the hand that still had a hold of me.

"Clara!" It was Mike. Pale and with his eyes wide, he released my hair.

"I thought we'd lost you! I was calling your name, but you weren't moving! I thought you were suffocating down there. What is wrong with you?"

I was trying to unscramble things myself as it all came flooding back to me. Shocked and amazed, I had forgotten all about the team who waited for a word from me or for my return. I must have appeared to be in distress because Mike grabbed me and hauled me to my feet, shaking me roughly. I was overwhelmed with emotion. No wonder Mike had become more concerned.

"I saw… a huge, gaping wall. There were the remnants of what looked like three broken floors. I'm sorry if I'm not making sense, but Mike…there was a tattered cage at the bottom. And there were these small areas that looked like they had been sectioned off, and—"

"Clara." Mike stopped me. "You saw a cage?"

"Yes, Mike, I saw a cage."

"Are you saying what I think you're saying?"

The look of shock ran over his face, and his reaction didn't surprise me—I would never have believed those words if I hadn't been the one saying them.

"Mike, get on the radio and call for the helicopter!"

"What for, a rescue?"

"No, for a recovery!"

"A recovery?"

"Yes, Mike, yes!" I cried out. "The ground you thought you were standing on is not the ground at all. It's the remains we've been looking for! We are standing on the remains of Noah's Ark!"

"Clara, no!"

"Mike!" I screamed, cutting him off. "We found it!"

His eyes widened as he swayed from side to side, barely able to keep his balance.

Rushing toward us, Muhammad and Godfrey looked like mirrors, their expressions reflecting the same astonishment I felt. They must've heard me screaming and recognized the surprised shock in my voice. Rays from the rising sun burst through the clouds, shining upon the ancient ruins, revealing more of its mystique. No bow, no stern, just a box-like structure perched aside a mountain's cliff. The shape of the hull and its solid wooden walls were unmistakable. Godfrey reached for my hand and squeezed it as he broke more of the ice away.

"It's gopher wood."

It was real.

Mike yelled into his radio. "Three-three-two-six, can you read me? Come in, three-three-two-six, over!"

"Three-three-two-six here. We read you loud and clear, over."

"Well, pop the champagne and pull out the cigars. We found it, my man, we found it!" Mike's voice trembled as he took a deep breath. "We've found the remains of Noah's Ark!"

I could hear the thrill in Chuy's voice over the radio when he yelled back to the rest of the team. "They found it, they found it! Oh my God, they found it! Mike, we've noted your location and are on the way!"

We couldn't believe it ourselves. Our voices, awash with emotion, echoed over the radio waves. The four of us were amazed and elated as we laid our eyes on the miracle. It was humanity's greatest discovery in over two thousand years. I dropped to my knees and covered my face with my hands, gasping in utter disbelief over the joy that had begun to fill up in me. I watched the men strike their hammers with renewed strength, the fatigue of the journey stripped away.

Chunk after chunk, piece after piece, we knocked the ice away, revealing more and more of the petrified wooden platform on which we stood.

We had dismantled the landscape by the time Chuy and the rest made it there, our hands aching but pushed on by an invisible force.

Chuy ran ahead of the rest of everyone else, leaping into the air and pumping his fist in triumph. With his bare hands, he broke off a large piece of ice and tossed it off the cliff. Closing his eyes, he sank to his knees, thanking God for showing mercy and love to the group.

"Some storms are sent by God not to hurt us, but to change us," Godfrey exclaimed. "You said you wanted a life-changer, Clara? Well, here it is, and all you had to do was knock away the ice!"

Easy laughter echoed off the craggy mountain walls. In a short time, we made considerable headway breaking away the ice and debris that had masked the structure for so long. Extending his long arm into the opening, Chuy broke off a small piece of wood with his hammer. He kissed it and tossed it into the air.

I opened my eyes, flicking them upward, and the piece landed in my hands.

My heart stopped for a moment. In my hands was a twisted, bound substance, what Godfrey had estimated to be gopher wood. I pondered the unthinkable events I believed God had conspired to get me to this place. It was no less than remarkable.

Mike worked on widening the hole I had found. "Grab the ropes because I'm going in first!" he yelled.

"Not if I beat you to it!" Chuy countered.

Tears of humility ran down Godfrey's face, yet he beamed.

"Clara, what if faith was tangible and belief was visible; would you follow God then?" he asked, looking me in the eyes.

"With all of my heart, Godfrey," I said. "With all of my heart!"

Our hands passed around the chunk of ancient gopher wood, a crystallized piece of Godfrey's question now verified.

Faith was now tangible because I could feel it, and belief was now visible because I was holding it right there in the palms of my hands.

CHAPTER

14

Eyes Wide Open

MY TENT shook. *What the heck?* "Wake up, apple head! We've got work to do." *Of course, it's Mike.*

"Yes, sir, I'm up, and we got work to do." I still couldn't believe it.

A few days had passed, but we had gotten the extension for exploring the inside of the vessel from the Iranian government. Only because they were sending their own scientist our way. That morning, we lowered ourselves by rope into the hole I had made. Chuy beat Mike down, and, in fact, Mike was the last to enter, just after Godfrey. We walked along the massive hull of the vessel, flashlights attached to our helmets like miners searching for gold.

What seemed like decks made of bamboo-like straw, possibly reeds separated the vessel into three unique stories. They were all built the same way but changed depending on the angle at which they were viewed. Not much of the vessel was left intact due to decay and time, but the walls that remained were massive. Hieroglyphics coated them in dense layers—whether they told the story or something else, we didn't yet know.

I guess even back then, someone had a lot to say, I thought, trying to follow the clustered symbols. Maybe it was the only way to pass the time with a storm raging outside, drowning the world. I couldn't imagine how lonely it would have been, how frightening. I took pictures of them.

We marveled at the faith it must have taken for Noah and his family to build the Ark. The construction of the vessel seemed so complex, I didn't believe they could've built it in a few months, not even a few years. A decade seemed plausible, maybe. Maybe a century had passed by before it reached its completion. The Bible said Noah lived to be more than nine hundred years old, so ten decades might have been nothing for him.

I thought the vessel would be made of wooden planks stuck side by side, or something like plywood, as Godfrey had described. No, not this vessel. Gopher wood was not wooded planks or anything like plywood. We pulled ourselves out of the hull and onto the deck again. I cast my eyes over it once more. Not even Leonardo da Vinci or the greatest engineers of the world could have imagined it. There were no interlocking wooden planks in a row. No two-by-fours side-by-side as one might have expected. No, it was a work of art. It snaked out east and west and then forward beyond the cliff. It was one gigantic deck of interwoven bamboo-like wood, braided together and covered with tar. Most of the vessel was built that way—gopher wood tried and true. As we gazed over it, we were all overwhelmed. This was what made it buoyant, and the tar they covered it with was what made it waterproof. Studying every inch of the vessel sent shivers down my spine.

I lived and breathed the Ark during those days. When I closed my eyes at night, I imagined the waves crashing around me, rain pounding against the wooden hulls. It felt so close.

Excitement kept us running without sleep, as well as an excess of coffee. Reluctantly, after a few days, we decided to return to base camp for some real rest. But my eyes snapped open well before the alarm rang at 5:00 a.m. before Mike even had the chance to shake my tent. I had barely slept a wink that night, so thrilled to jump back into the action.

I still couldn't quite fathom it. The petrified gopher wood I'd held in my hands that day, the massive surface beneath me when I descended into the hole—it all seemed to prove the impossible. Godfrey had been right. It would have taken nothing short of a miracle to craft this, nothing short of the work of God Himself.

I was baffled by what I had seen, as I'd taken our exploration for granted. The faithful had searched for hundreds, even thousands of years without finding what I, a skeptical, downtrodden scientist, had discovered in a matter of days. If the old saying was true, that everything happened for a reason, then what was the reason, and why me?

Pushing those whirlwinds of thoughts out of my mind, I got dressed. By 5:07, I stood outside the food tent, waiting for the first steaming cup of coffee.

Chuy had hired a small helicopter to assist us up and down the mountain once we realized it would require several days just to chip away the ice coating the vessel. The sun had yet to rise, but the day was already warming up. The winds died down, so we had the chance to examine our haul more closely with our helmet lights.

Our second task of the expedition began that day. Our awe notwithstanding, we still needed proof to show the public and other scientists. Without carbon dating results, we wouldn't be able to prove anything regarding this being Noah's Ark. Besides that, I needed to prove I was still on my game.

Pulling aside the flap to the kitchen tent, I gaped at the towering figure hunched underneath. At this hour, I didn't expect anyone other than Mike and myself to be awake. "Chuy, is that you?"

With a smile, Chuy handed me my coffee mug. "I couldn't sleep. I've already called ahead to the Iranian government. We're requesting more assistance in extracting the Ark from the ice."

Chuy poured three sugar packets into his coffee and stirred it for a while before lifting the steaming cup for a careful sip.

"It's going to be an interesting challenge to get that huge thing off the mountain," he said. "That is—if it can be done at all."

Before I could open my mouth, Mike came into the tent with a grin on his face. He poked me in the ribs and grabbed Chuy, starting a wrestling match that knocked over all of the Styrofoam cups. I couldn't help but laugh.

Clearly, Chuy and I weren't the only ones excited that day.

I couldn't wait. This would be the best rebuttal to everyone who thought I was washed up.

"I'll show them," I muttered, without realizing Mike and Chuy had already settled down.

"Clara," Mike must had heard what I said. "We're all excited, but we have to keep in mind this is about something bigger than ourselves, got it?"

"Do I get it? Do you get it! You guys are the ones in here horse playing and clowning around."

Biting back a smile at the thought that my name would be attached to this whole thing, I had to keep a straight face. I refilled my coffee mug as Chuy, perhaps trying to break the awkward silence, began to detail what Godfrey had planned for the day.

"Godfrey wants to start cutting the wood, so he can get a reasonably sized sample to take back to the States with us for testing. He's out right now waiting on the Iranians."

He had barely finished his sentence when the tent flap opened. In walked Godfrey, followed by a strange sound that shook the whole tent, whipping the walls back and forth as if we were in a bad storm.

"Don't panic," Godfrey said with a sly smile. "We've got help. You'll see."

Following him, we stepped outside and saw two American Chinook helicopters hovering over the camp and blowing the soft, new snow into a flurry around the campsite.

Two copters. I could barely believe it—Godfrey had worked his magic. With these, we'd get whatever parts of the vessel we needed out of there in no time.

The engines thundered above us as the helicopters dropped, coming to rest at the base on the north side of the mountain. People poured out of them, more than I imagined could fit inside. Godfrey introduced them to us as Captain Amado Justus and an Iranian military pilot, leading forty engineers, a mix of American and Iranian. Finally, we had reinforcements.

"It turns out, the only way the Christian Institute could get into Iran is with the assistance and under the approval of the Iranian government," Godfrey told us in a deadpan voice. "As you can imagine, the Iranians wanted pilots here to keep an eye on us. It's as much a part of their history as it is the history of believers everywhere." Behind his serious expression, I spotted a sparkle in his eye, the same excitement we all felt.

Stepping forward, he cleared his throat, addressing the newcomers. "We're about 40,000 feet away from where the artifact is at the moment. We'll guide you there."

With that, he started handing us our assignments. He, Mike, Chuy, and I would all board the choppers. Terry, Pam, Sue, along with others, would join us later.

We flew for a while in the cold skies, catching the magnificent views which took our breaths away as much as the weather, then landed atop the vessel. Godfrey stepped forward to introduce me.

"This is Dr. Hamilton, she's one of our team leaders. She helped lead this expedition to recover the vessel."

Taking a step forward, I met their eyes with confidence and shook their hands. "Pleasure to meet you. We were thinking of cutting pieces off the ship and then flying them down the mountain to our base camp." I began explaining more about how we planned to lift the gigantic vessel off the mountain. I had begun working out the plan myself. But the Iranian pilot raised his hand.

"It is nice to meet you, madam, and I have heard mention of your name, but I will speak with Dr. Godfrey from here on out."

Stunned, I took a stumbling step back but collected my thoughts quickly. "What did you just say to me?"

Mike squeezed my shoulder from behind. "Choose your battles wisely," he whispered.

"Sorry, sir, she gets a little feisty sometimes," he chuckled. Seeing him trying to calm the unamused helicopter pilot only made me seethe even more. The choice words I'd prepared melted in my mouth. As always, Mike was right. I couldn't let things get too heated. This was too important.

"Where do we start?" Godfrey was eager to change the subject and get the team moving in the right direction.

Walking over the hardened platform, the pilot grumbled aloud.

"We were told that your team might be stranded up here. We've come all this way to rescue you and help you with your artifact. You need help to bring your discovery down the mountain? Well, where is it?"

Mike clapped the newcomer on the back and pointed at the ground. "You're standing on it!"

The pilot looked down, dumbfounded, at the deck of the Ark beneath his feet. From high in the air, the deck seemed like a solid covering of rock and ice, but upon closer inspection, the entwined petrified wood united and made one staggering image.

"What is this?" he asked in his amazement.

My sarcastic voice came echoing out of the distance. "Didn't you hear him? You are standing on the remains of Noah's Ark."

The man shook his head and looked again.

"You're kidding!" Coming to grips with the reality of the situation, he finally ordered the team to get to work.

The second chopper arrived, and they rushed in excitement, tossing equipment from the helicopters. I watched as they unloaded powerful saws and other cutting instruments. They got to work immediately. That fateful morning, forty men and their saws were hard at work. The noise was deafening, but I stayed as close as I could without getting in the way.

Although the gopher wood was incredibly dense and difficult to cut, those engineers took their chance and got busy. Eventually, they cut off the first, forty-foot section of the vessel that was not covered by ice and prepared it to be airlifted off the mountain. I had never seen anything like it. My heart raced in anticipation. The job was almost complete.

Mike appeared beside me but had to shout to be heard over the equipment. "Clara, you go with Godfrey while I stay to help with the air-transfer."

"You're in over your head. Let the more experienced workers do that," I told him, blowing off his suggestion. Unease washed over me, and I had to stop from biting the inside of my cheek. Mike looked at me in concern until I released my breath.

"Clara, I've got this. I'll fly down with the pilot and see you at the bottom. Now get out of here."

I didn't know why, but just the thought of Mike staying behind and then riding on the helicopter with the giant piece of gopher wood gave me a bad feeling. I shook it off, attributing it to nerves. "Whatever you say, Mike. See you there."

Unearthing the Ark from the mountain would be dangerous, but Mike was fine with it. I just hoped nothing would happen to either him or the artifact. Using heavy metal chains and tightening them to ensure safety, the engineers worked well together. Great care was taken in securing the piece in such a way that the holds would prevent any damage. None of them wanted anything to mar the sole proof that the events of the Bible were real and true. In faith, there was unity.

It had taken many hours of work, but the moment finally arrived for the helicopter to lift the first section. Godfrey and I were flown down to the camp in the valley to ensure the section was handled correctly upon its arrival. We met the rest of the team there and watched Terry smile and give high-fives to everyone.

"We have the thumbs-up," Mike yelled over the radio. Every few minutes, he kept us informed of what was happening. "The air's a little thin up here, so we're having some difficulty taking off... We're in the air now... The piece is still on the ground, though... The piece is airborne. We are on our way to you."

Down in the valley, Godfrey and I had been looking up at the cloud-covered sky, unable to see the action play out. The wait was making me anxious. Every so often, I would find myself biting my nails.

I put my hands down at my sides, but as the minutes passed, I started biting again. The air was unusually calm, but the stillness only increased my nerves. After everything we'd been through, I was cautiously optimistic—something I hadn't felt in a long time.

The clouds covering the sky were still until suddenly we heard an odd noise from above us. At first, it sounded like a small explosion, then a swarm of bees coming our way, but soon it amplified into a thunderous moan, forcing us to cover our ears and duck.

I looked up and stared in shock as the copter fell out of the sky, black smoke billowing out of the rear engines as it spun around in the air, overwhelmed by the weight of the artifact. My heart dropped to my stomach as I watched the chopper spiral out of control.

"Mike!" I screamed. "No!"

My voice was drowned out by the sound of the roaring engines. I rushed forward as if I could do something to help. I looked up and stopped.

From out of the sky, the massive chunk of the Ark hit the ground, and then, in horrific slow motion, the chopper crashed, blades first, into the foot of the mountain. The explosion was deafening. Everything went dark, with smoke and dirt flying in every direction. I stood paralyzed.

Godfrey pulled his coat over his nose and mouth, then pulled my scarf over mine, stealing me away. We ducked behind a large rock, waiting on the black smoke to clear and the flames to die down. All I could feel was my heart pounding in my chest, beating so hard I was afraid it would leap from my throat.

Panic came into Godfrey's eyes for a split second, then faded into his usual calm demeanor. I couldn't understand how he did it. My whole body shook, even though I could barely feel the cold. Tears stung my eyes.

"Mike was on that chopper!" I cried, my voice hoarse and faltering, "Help—"

Godfrey swept me into a hug.

"That pilot might be a hard-head, but he's highly trained for situations like these." He held me closer as if maybe he wasn't sure.

Flames licked at the metal and the gopher wood. The helicopter let out a final groan and exploded in the intense heat. My ears rang again. I could hear footsteps approaching us from behind. When I looked up, the other half of the team approached, Terry and the rest, their eyes wide and in shock. They didn't even look down to see us. All they looked at were the flames swallowing up what was left of the crash. Wobbling to my feet, I stood up, turning to see what they were looking at.

A familiar figure appeared through the smoke, growing closer and closer until he emerged into the open. It was Chuy, carrying a man across his shoulders. He coughed and choked but didn't lower the man to the ground until they were a safe distance from the fire.

Even though his face was black from smoke and ash, I recognized the man he was carrying. It was Mike. His chest rose and fell, still breathing, although it came in wheezes. I let out a cry of relief, stumbling closer as Chuy collapsed beside him.

The medics wasted no time rushing to assess their injuries. I heard their words without really comprehending them. "Alive, serious inhalation burns, needs immediate medical attention."

Clambering over the ground, I reached Mike and hugged him, ignoring the soot coating his whole body.

"Hey, Eagle Eyes," he said in a raspy voice. "Is everyone okay?" With his weakened limbs, he was trying to get up.

"Lie still, Mike! I can't believe you're alive, and yes, everyone's okay." I could barely speak as I held on to him.

Mike shook his head. "Don't worry about me. There's the man you should be thanking."

He lifted his finger in a weak attempt to point at Chuy, who had already regained his feet, as if unaffected by his injuries.

Before I could get in another word, the medics pushed me aside, grabbing Mike and loading him onto a stretcher. In their jumbled explanations, I understood they were taking him to the same ship meant to take us and the Ark's fragment back to the States.

"I'm not going," Chuy said, waving away the medics and looking straight at Mike. "I'll make sure nothing happens to Ms. Clara. Don't worry about anything and just focus on recovering."

A weak smile spread across Mike's face. He raised his hand slightly before the medics rushed him off to the waiting helicopter. I waved back until the chopper had risen into the air, and he couldn't possibly see me. The wind of the rising choppers dried my tears quickly enough, as I was now even more focused on what we had to do.

After Mike was gone, Godfrey gathered the team and surveyed the scene. He may have been as determined than ever to deliver on his promise, but the rest of the team was exhausted, myself included.

We needed fresh recruits to dig up the rest of the Ark and divide it into movable pieces. Godfrey and I walked closer to the crash site and stared at the section we had cut out. It had plummeted into the ground, stuck upright. It towered twenty feet above our heads and was forty feet long. I couldn't even imagine breaking it into sections. Would we even have the time to organize a whole new mission with the resources we had? Time, recruits, and money were running out by the day.

Choking smoke wafted from the scene of the crash, stark against the white-capped mountains. It was drawing attention. Initially, only a few locals approached, evidently curious enough about the source of the fire to complete the five-mile trek from the nearby village. But as the hours passed, more and more villagers turned up, gazing at the dying embers of the burning aircraft. Women pressed their children to their sides. Perhaps they thought it was a military jet, marking out the beginning of more war and unrest.

Smoke began to dissipate, revealing that even more villagers had gathered around. Muhammad stood on a boulder, trying to take control of the people. Later he would tell me what he said, but that day he spoke eloquently to the crowd.

"My friends, please do not fear. Let me show you what our mountain has been hiding for so long." With the usual bounce in his feet, he jumped off the rock, setting down the path to the relic. The villagers swarmed after him, some carrying their children in their arms, others helping the elderly along the path.

Godfrey stood near the crash site, scanning to see through the smoke.

"I don't know how we're going to get it out of here in time," he mumbled as I approached. "The extension we were granted will run out at nightfall, so we need to do something fast," he added.

I looked around, trying to be as much help as I could, and then I saw it. A short distance up the hill was a second piece that must had broken off as well. It looked to be a twelve-by-eighteen-foot smaller section. I tapped Godfrey's shoulder.

"Dr. Godfrey, look. There's a piece of what looks like gopher wood over there. It must have come off the larger one when it crashed."

He squinted and looked where I pointed. I could tell he was having trouble seeing what I saw. He shook his head, closed his eyes, then looked again. A smile spread over his face.

"Clara, you've done it again. That larger piece can stay where it is. We can handle a piece of that size." Wasting no time, Godfrey pulled out his radio and called the engineers, issuing orders to salvage the small piece. He radioed back to Chuy to bring the tractor-trailer we left back at the base camp.

Behind us, a curious crowd had gathered. All eyes were fixed behind me. A gust of wind cleared away the last of the smoke, revealing the fallen artifact looming over us.

Even though I'd seen it before, seeing it again took my breath away. To think this was only part of the larger vessel.

The villagers didn't look frightened or angry like I had expected. Instead, they drew closer, drinking in the sight of this massive thing that had crushed the peace of their valley.

The clicking of the Iranian soldier's radio broke the silence. An elderly man took up his staff, standing before the crowd. He closed his eyes, seeming to reach deep into himself.

"Is that the village chief?" Godfrey asked. Muhammad, who had perched on a rock nearby, nodded in affirmation.

"I'll translate," he said, coming closer to us and whispering when the man finally spoke, his words flowing over the villagers like a gushing river.

"My fellow villagers, we have suffered long enough. Our children cry out because we have little food to give them. They have grown up believing poverty to be the way of the world. I am done offering myself to the gods of poverty, fear, weakness, and despair. I am tired of this wretched way of life and will no longer live in the dark without hoping for anything more than survival." He took a moment and then continued.

"God has been with us all this time. We asked for many things but never expected Him to come through for us like he did today. He has borne witness to the hurt and pain in our lives, and He has finally acted. This is a divine artifact, from the sky, here as a message from the heavens."

The villagers gasped. The chief brandished his staff, a fire blazing in his eyes.

He continued. "No more will we fear what the guards may do to us. God has shown us He is real. We failed to pray in the past. But today, our hearts open to Him once more."

The crowd erupted into cheers. Three women ran past me, yelling, chasing a child as he ran toward the entrenched wooden artifact. "Stop, child, stop!" One of the women yelled.

The miracle overwhelmed me, and I sank to my knees. It was so humbling unlike anything I'd ever felt. My eyes were finally open, my heart receptive to the change I was so desperate for.

I had come so far, nearly lost my best friend, nearly died myself. But looking over the crowd, I realized this was about something greater than I had ever imagined. I had asked God for a breakthrough, and He had given it to me.

The crowd advanced toward the Ark. I could barely hear anything, could barely even think. All I heard at that moment was the sound of that woman's voice again, rising above even the commotion of the crowd, calling her child's name. "Tumar!"

15

Only the Yellow Ones

The Story of Tumar
(narrated by the author)

THE IMPACT of the helicopter crash left the people reeling as if the entire countryside was under attack. Thick black smoke filled the air, blinding them. The acrid smell of white-hot metal and burning rubber poured into the air on an otherwise quiet day.

The sound of the crash echoed throughout the valley. One young woman by the name of Quitarre was working in the field with her eight-year-old son, Tumar, and her two sisters when the crash occurred. The three Arab women lunged to grab the child as they fell to the ground, fearing it was a military strike, but soon, they saw other villagers running toward the smoke, taking cover for what they still thought was an attack.

The women soon realized it was not an assault at all, but some type of accident. They, too, were curious to find out what had happened. Smoke billowed from the location, and following the rest of the crowd, Quitarre's child, Tumar, had run ahead of her as if an invisible force were tugging at him.

Desperate to catch her son, Quitarre shouted at Tumar, "Stop! You must not go that way."

Quitarre had taught her child life, love, and poetry. She was also protective of him, sheltering him from the world as much as possible, for not only was he small in stature, but he was also born blind. Quitarre did all she could to protect him. Tumar refused to heed his mother's warnings. Instead, he followed an invisible attraction toward the warmth of an unseen crash. From a distance, his mother and sisters noticed a red-haired American woman standing there with a tall, black gentleman.

"Tumar, stop, please stop! Those are Americans up there. They might harm you."

But he didn't listen. He kept running up the hill, ever farther out of his mother's reach, and passed the Americans after nearly running into them.

Struggling to get to him before he hurt himself, Quitarre called out, "Wait! Come back, Tumar. Please!"

But he continued to run in his darkness, putting his hands out in front of him, as if to find his way to avoid any obstructions. Then, at that moment, he ran into it. His hands walloped as he hit the fallen portion of the Ark sitting massively over him.

He stood for a minute and then rubbed his fingers along its rugged surface. Intuitively, he placed one hand on his forehead and the other on the wood. A surge of warmth radiated through his body as the wind blew hard against his back. He didn't realize it at first, but the film that had covered his eyes from birth started to fade away. Tumar turned his head upward, and the stunning color of the blue sky appeared to him as it never had before. Finally, he could see.

He shouted, "Mama! Where are you? Where are you?" Rubbing his hands over the wood again, he cried, "Mama, where are you?"

Quitarre and her sisters caught up with him. "Child, what is wrong with you?"

Tumar said, "Mama, I can see."

His mother hadn't heard what he'd said when she bent down and scolded him. "Why did you run away from us? This place is filled with Americans, and they are dangerous people, so we must leave right now."

Tumar stood up and faced his mother and repeated, "Mama, did you hear what I said? Mama, I touched that thing, and now I can see!"

His mother instantly dismissed his claim. "Come away from there."

"When I touched it, I felt the heat go through me, and then I could see the light."

"What light, child? You've been blind since birth."

Remembering the soft and gentle way his mother used to describe herself to him, a child who was without sight, now seeing the light, fell to his knees. "Mother, you taught me about the light, but the light I now see is in your eyes. I'm telling you the truth—I don't know how, but somehow, someway, I can see!"

"Tumar! Stop, you are scaring me, child!"

But the child continued, remembering the muse his mother had described herself to be.

"Mother, you once told me your hair was bronze, but you never told me bronze would make me feel so strong." The child pleaded at his mother, finally seeing the beauty in her long hair. She remembered the passion and strength she'd wanted to share with him. "Mother, you once told me your eyes were dark brown, but you never told me your dark brown eyes could comfort me."

Quitarre covered her mouth in shock, and tears welled up in her eyes. Her pain now felt like hope.

"Mother, I have imagined this day since I first heard your voice. The warmth I feel must be what it feels like to be in heaven."

Quitarre's heart trembled, her hands covering her mouth again. She could not believe what her child was telling her.

"Mother!" Tumar yelled.

With tears now rolling down her frightened face—so afraid of what he might tell her next—she dropped her hand away from her trembling lips. "Yes, child?"

"You once told me to have faith, but how do you have faith and bear no witness?"

"I've got faith, child, but I am a realist."

Tumar got off his knees, dusted himself off, tossed his hands into the air, looked Quitarre right in the face, and asked, "Mother, can I tell you something?"

"Yes, child, you can tell me whatever you want."

"I can see, I can see, I can see!"

"Oh, my God!" Quitarre screamed. Everything she had in her hands hit the ground as the joy beamed from her child's soul and out of his mouth.

"Mommy, I can see, I can see!" he shouted again.

Quitarre got off her knees, still in shock when she ran down the hill, screaming, "My child can see! He can see!"

She ran down to join her sisters and told them what had happened. She looked over to see her once-blind child standing in a rainbow of colorful flowers. The three women ran over to the fallen portion, dropped to their knees, and placed their hands on the holy vessel, no doubt hoping to receive what Tumar had received. Healing.

A supernatural power radiated from the side of the large relic, and the fire of faith overwhelmed them. Quitarre was knocked back and ended up sitting on the ground. She looked around for Tumar, only to see him running up the hillside, jumping and yelling, waving his hands in the air. "I can see! I can see! I can see! Thanks be to God! I can see!"

In the end, what was thought to be a tragic crash and a damaged relic would turn out to be a blessing. For if it had not been for the smoke-filled skies from the afternoon's crash, Tumar might never have been healed. Quitarre gazed at her son standing in a rainbow of beautiful flowers, and yet he was only picking the yellow ones.

>—⊕—<

16

The Blessed One

THE OVERCAST skies pitched a misty gray tone over the site, but the mood of the local people who had come to see it was as bright as a midsummer's day. I took note of the fact that more and more locals had come to the site, and now many of them had walked up the hill to where we were, although we were rushing to get out.

I'd heard a child's voice earlier that day and saw him running through the field, but I couldn't understand what he was saying, as he'd spoken in broken English. Yet his voice had cut through the air, drawing my attention as we had walked up the hill. But now, hunched over and working feverishly on the smaller section, it was getting late in the day—hours had passed. It had taken much longer than expected.

We had almost finished when a commotion broke out in the valley. A crowd had formed around the larger section of the relic.

Police trucks had pulled up. A group of uniformed men got out and walked toward us. As soon as they were up the hill, one of them grabbed me, sharply twisting my arm so hard I couldn't help but cry out. It was the Iranian guard.

"By order of the government, you must come with me." His gruff voice startled me almost as much as how roughly he handled my arm.

"This artifact cannot be removed from here. You don't have the permission."

His fellow guards joined him, looking at me with hard eyes.

"All we want is a small piece," I argued, trying to get his hands off me. "Just enough to determine its age."

One of the guards came forward and spat on the ground in front of me. "Shut up," he snarled.

I slammed my hands against the truck, my blood boiling.

"This is not something that belongs to anyone," Godfrey shouted. "It belongs to the world!"

From behind the officers, a well-dressed man in uniform stepped out. His eyes were stern, and he spoke English well, yet his voice sounded suspicious.

"You are right, Dr. Godfrey. But you must understand that I'm losing patience with you, my friend."

"Godfrey, do you know this man?" I asked. Godfrey turned to me, about to answer, when the man cut him off.

"I am Ambassador Shahryar. We got news this morning about a collision or some sort of crash. I can see the burned-out helicopter from here. Two of my pilots were killed, while one of your people escaped?" The ambassador studied us, his eyes darting. "Why did they die?"

"Well, sir, there was a miscalculation—"

"A miscalculation? Never mind your explanation," he said, cutting Godfrey off again.

"I already know what your answer will be."

He surveyed the valley using binoculars, pacing the ground steadily.

"Two days ago, the news of your find reached many tribal men and women, and, yes, indeed, our capital city. They are calling this a miracle."

"I know nothing about that," Godfrey said. "The only thing I know is that we had a deal with your office. They gave us permission to extract a small section of the artifact to take back with us for testing."

"A small section." He laughed, as did the rest of the guards, following his lead.

"My comrades," he chuckled, turning toward his guards, "can you see that massive structure over there in the valley. You must admit—that's far from small, right. You Americans, yes—you are so funny."

"Oh, no sir," Godfrey said, "You are mistaken. That's not the section we wanted to test, but this smaller portion over here." There seemed hope.

He walked over to the smaller section and nodded, "Are you sure—this is all you wanted?" His eyes narrowed to slits.

"Yes, sir, that piece will do."

"Well, my friend," he said with a clap of his hands, "You have my permission to take it, but only it."

"Thank you for being so kind, Mr. Ambassador."

"No need for that," he chuckled again, shaking his head. "Just do as I said. News travels fast."

Godfrey nodded in agreeance, showing we understood. With a final brisk nod, the ambassador yelled something in Arabic to his men, and they piled back into their vehicles and drove away.

Finally, Chuy, along with one of the engineers, arrived, speeding past the ambassador's convoy. He drove the tractor truck and a trailer down through the valley and up the hill to us. Unhooking the trailer, he drove the truck around to help with the lifting. The trailer had the materials on it along with a winch to assist us in elevating the twelve-by-eighteen-foot portion of the Ark out of the mud. While it was not quite professional-grade, the winch would have to serve the job. The area was too remote to bring in any other type of heavy equipment in the short time we had. Metal chains were wrapped around the sides of the artifact and tightened.

Once they were all in place, we tossed the chains over the winch and connected them to the truck for it to start lifting. Its engine revved in an effort to lift the piece of wood just four feet above the ground so the crew could then pull the artifact onto the trailer, but the mud did its best to keep it stuck. The truck roared again, pulling the chains, yet the artifact hardly budged. The locals noticed the truck was struggling, so they tied ropes around the front end of the tractor and started to pull.

"Pull!" Chuy yelled out.

The tires churned, yet the tractor still struggled to lift the petrified portion off the ground. Chuy yelled again.

"Pull!"

Finally, it moved. The chains tightened, tensed, and strained as they slowly lifted the heavy portion.

"Pull!"

Once again, the portion rose up, inch by inch, then foot by foot. The stress on the chains was increasing, and the winch began to warp as the underestimated weight of the petrified gopher wood was overbearing, making this even more dangerous.

"Pull!" Chuy yelled once more.

By now, everyone in the vicinity had jumped in to help, throwing ropes over their shoulders to assist in helping to raise the artifact. With all their hearts and minds, the crowd joined in and pushed the strength of the winch even further, but out of that struggle, suddenly, one of the chains *snapped*. A huge buckle swung loose and headed toward the heads of the helpers.

"Look out!" yelled Chuy. The buckle swung around, missed the helpers, and slammed into the side of the tractor Chuy was in, barely missing him as well. My chest was pounding.

The tension grew even more as the crash of the buckle into the side of the truck made a booming sound across the valley, putting a ripple of panic through everyone.

Some people scrambled and gave up, but Chuy called out, "Get your heads back into this work! Wrap those chains around it again and pull!"

Godfrey grabbed hold of the ropes and told his team and the villagers, "On one, we all pull together!" Godfrey counted down to one, and everyone pulled again. With our last bit of strength, we pulled, up and over, pushing the wooden artifact over as it came crashing down onto the trailer. The huge piece hit the flatbed with such weight that the trailer began to sag. Chuy connected the truck to the trailer again, jumped back in, and floored it. The wheels of the tractor spun in place as it dug into the soft ground. Eventually, it caught some traction and started to slowly make its way up to the valley.

While the wheels of the truck were spinning, Godfrey, Muhammed, and I jumped onto the back of the trailer as the rest of the team rode in a minivan. The locals trailed us as Chuy drove up the hill and into the valley.

The smaller piece that had fallen was all we needed, and now we had it. Godfrey let out a long sigh of relief, rubbing his temples.

Placing my hand on Godfrey's shoulder, I flashed him a wide smile for the first time in what felt like forever. "Let's go home."

In the valley, a crowd had gathered around the larger, embedded segment of the Ark. Their voices rose in unison, a chant of complete adoration filled with a tone of wonder.

Then, they saw us as we rode by. A roar went up through the crowd as people broke away, running, cheering, and chanting. I looked at Godfrey, and his bewildered face emulated the way I felt.

"You are the blessed one," one woman said, reaching out to touch my feet. "Oh, blessed one!"

The phrase rang through my mind. "The blessed one? What are they talking about?"

The women and children began throwing flower petals at us, while the men stomped their feet, singing in Arabic.

"They're calling us the blessed ones because they believe we brought forth a sacred object, bringing healing to their people," Muhammad translated.

"What? Why?" I said, more to myself than to him. It all just seemed so surreal.

Even when we had jumped onto the trailer, starting down to the valley, I couldn't help but feel like I was living in a dream.

"Godfrey, what have we gotten ourselves into?"

"I don't know." Godfrey mopped his brow with a handkerchief. "Muhammad told me the artifact we brought down healed some children. I may be wrong, but I think these people are their parents."

Looking back at the crowd, I shook my head. "Wow, what a day, right?"

I looked over at Godfrey and saw he was exhausted as well, probably barely understanding what I had said. We had uncovered nothing less than a miracle, and now we were about to travel cross-country, accompanying it all the way to the Mediterranean Sea, and then to the States. I had expected a homecoming, but nothing like this.

Gazing out the window, the locals were cheering in the valley below, and then something strange happened. The crowd gave way as a young man followed by a camera crew emerged. A red and white logo emblazoned across their gear, seared itself into my vision.

"Is that an American news team?" I gasped, pressing my face to the window to see better. An American news team… I wondered how they'd known what had gone on. They must have been in Tabriz covering the news there and had heard about the crash. As the ambassador had said, news traveled fast.

I'd hoped all would be okay as we were leaving that day. The madness was over, and we had gotten what we came for. A cause that began as a mission of faith and hope was unfurling and was now becoming a reality.

We finally hit the main road, and a shower of relief came over me. I reflected on all we had been through. The decisions we had made, the chances we'd taken, the loss we almost suffered, and the journey we were still on. There we were, in a foreign land, trusting in a God we could not see, knowing we had put it all on the line. I felt triumphant as I waved goodbye to all those who walked alongside the road headed toward the valley. I was elated, knowing that after all these years, and all those tiers, my colleagues would undeniably know that I—Clara Hamilton—was back!

CHAPTER

17

The Ripples in the Waters

I POPPED THE cork off the champagne, laughing as the
bubbles overflowed onto the deck.

"Watch out," Godfrey said with a smile. "You don't want
this celebration to get messy."

"Is it really a party if we don't get messy, though?" I joked,
striking a dramatic pose.

The artifact had been safely loaded onto the large freighter,
secured in place on top of the deck. Now, all we had to do was
enjoy the trip as we sailed for U.S. soil.

It all felt like a movie with the whole team there, united
onboard after overcoming all of the mountains and hurdles that
led to our success.

Yet even as I laughed, I felt a soft pang in my heart. If only
Joshua was there to see me. Perhaps he was watching from beyond,
like a guardian angel shining down on me with the same love a
parent has for their child.

Mike was also onboard but staying below deck in a room
outfitted to serve as an infirmary for the voyage. His injuries had
begun to heal, but he still needed a better-equipped treatment

room in a real hospital. As great as the cruise experience was, I desperately wanted to arrive at the mainland so he could get the care he needed.

After a few sips of champagne, I couldn't stay there celebrating without knowing how he was doing. I went below deck and began to wander through the confusing corridors. It took me forever, but I finally found the infirmary.

The door was ajar, but instead of walking in, I decided to look through the crack. I saw Pam kneeling next to Mike, holding his hand in hers. He looked back at her, his smile bright as always, perhaps even brighter as he brought their entwined fingers over his heart.

I wanted to chat with him and ask him how he was, but I resisted the urge to walk in. After the past four years of Mike's efforts to keep me going, I owed him much more than I could give back. The best I could do was let him live his life without constantly worrying about me. I, of all people, knew how fragile love could be.

I closed the door and silently wished them luck, but that didn't last. Pam soon emerged.

"Clara, from this day on, leave Mike alone." She walked up to me, gritting her teeth.

"Pam, I don't want Mike, he's just my friend."

"Well, he's mine now, so go away."

"Pam, you have no reason for this. Mike and I are friends, and that will never change."

She smirked. "He's not yours anymore."

"He was never mine. I know how fragile love can be. I would never come between you two. Trust me, I'm trying to find my way back to my own love, and it's not Mike."

"Then leave us alone."

I walked down the hallway, away from her, shooting her the finger.

"Back at you, Clara," she said. "Back at you."

I couldn't believe I had to go through that again. Making my way back to the top of the freighter, I realized Pam's insecurity had not ceded but was as strong as ever.

I walked up the steps and onto the deck, annoyed and wondering why, after all we had gone through, she would still be jealous of me. Mike was my friend and only a friend. I grabbed another bottle of champagne out of the ice bucket and walked over to the bow of the ship. The fresh salt-sprayed air came from the sea and blew over the deck as I left Pam and her problems behind me.

Life's too short to do all that worrying—I never understood why she did it. Looking over the rail at the ocean glimmering in the moonlight, a profound sense of peace settled over me. I looked back over the deck and saw Terry was also helping himself to a bottle of champagne as Godfrey and Chuy smoked their celebratory cigars. In two swigs, I downed what was left of my drink and thought about my life as the misty winds blew through my hair. Was all this suffering and heartache worth it if you had no one to share it with?

I grabbed the champagne bottle by the neck and flung it over the side of the ship and into the ocean. A splash, and then ripples spread across the silver surface as the bottle sank, carrying with it my old regrets, the hurt and pain and all of the anger I had once bottled up inside. It all faded away along the midnight blue waters of the sea.

But from out of nowhere, there was a new noise that disturbed the silence, one I could not believe. Bursting out of the ocean as if they were dancing in the moonlight were whales, dolphins, and other large fish. They were leaping above the surface, the bodies of sharks shimmering as they glided past the ship's bow. I watched them, not really believing my eyes, yet feeling something new was happening in the world. Something larger than life, yet with humble beginnings, and I was a part of it.

That night, I watched the dolphins play and guide our vessel through the ocean. With blue finfish and whales chasing alongside dolphins, leaping over them and back into the sea, none of us could believe what was happening. It was as if they had a sense of the precious cargo we had aboard. I spent my mornings recording the events of the journey, jotting down notes about the artifact, and peering through my binoculars, watching those animals spring out of the sea, following us the entire journey.

I looked on in awe at the enormous, biblical artifact we carried across the ocean. It was captivating. Just think, if it were not for Mike, my self-help guru, I might not have ever seen that day. Yet there I was, a witness to it all. It was something, with all my years of research, I could have never imagined.

We were set to arrive back in the States the following morning, and I had already let it get late in the evening. I walked down to the cabins again, two doors past Mike's room and peered in. It was Godfrey at his desk with his back to me, typing away at his computer. I looked at the title of the paper he was writing, *"What If?"* He was completing his notes, preparing himself for the speech he was going to give. I fell against the hallway walls as the weight of the announcement we were about to make flooded my heart. The gravity of it all, how heavy it was, was no longer farfetched. It was etched in my mind, and I needed to prepare as well. For the first time in our relationship, I understood Godfrey.

He was a man engulfed with his studies, enriched in his mind, and always careful with his words. I watched him intensely preparing for the press conference we would have and the changing words we would use in two days. It would be at the University of Chicago where we would announce to the world, we may have found tangible proof for the existence of God.

CHAPTER

— 18 —

What If

THE NEXT morning, I woke to the joyful cries of Sue and Terry.

"Clara, get up. Get up here now!"

Wrapping a blanket around my shoulders, I dashed out of my cabin and onto the deck. To my delight, I saw the Statue of Liberty on the horizon. A warm feeling of pride washed over me, subduing the chill in the air. We were home again.

"Liberty Enlightening the World," the engraving on the statue read. As amazing as the statue was to behold, the discovery of the Ark trumped it, and anything else I could imagine.

Hello, America! Things are about to change! I wanted to shout it to the shore. I couldn't wait to see people's reactions. There would be some backlash, no doubt, but that was just part of our journey. Taking steps forward in our line of work meant facing obstacles, but I already knew that all too well to be afraid of any pushback.

Godfrey seemed equally confident, yet I sensed the unspoken questions we shared. Finding the Ark was only the first step in discovering the truth. And the second one—why were we here?

The explanation of life's meaning and to what purpose it served. Why all the heartache, struggles, and guilt? So many questions, and yet not enough answers.

We cruised through New York harbor on a cool yet sunny day. I noticed a host of sea creatures clustered behind us as we were pulled in and anchored against the port deck. Terry shouted to the shore men, "This will be a heavy one, so be careful!"

Seagulls poured out of the sky, flooding the shipyard as men came running from all over the port, gawking at the marine life swarming our freighter. Their mouths fell open when they saw the lofty section of the Ark, tied down atop the liner, roaring into the seaport. No doubt they'd heard about our discovery but seeing it was something completely different. They muttered to one another as if they were trying to figure out how to unload it.

A crisp breeze blew off the shore and over the shipyard as the crew leader started conducting several groups of men in unloading the weighty thing.

It was so unnatural to see something so ancient, so treasured, being lifted off a freighter. But there it was—sturdy and proud, strong enough to save the world.

Walking off the liner, Godfrey paced around the busy shipyard. He spoke into a small microphone, noting his experiences and recording our exchange. The delivery of the artifact and the effort it was taking to unload and reload was enormous. The crew must have heard how much Godfrey valued the relic, as they took every safeguard to ensure its integrity.

Smoke seeped from the crane's engine as it lifted the relatively small portion of the Ark and placed it carefully on the flatbed of a wide semi-truck.

Once the section landed safely on the flatbed trailer, I heard Terry yell out, "Bingo, baby, now that's what I'm talking about!"

Chains, braces, and cables stretched from one side to another, securing the artifact into place.

Several port emergency vehicles pulled out front and behind the semi-truck, turning on their caution lights. NYPD's finest would lead the way.

Revving up the engine, pulling the whistle of the semi's horns, the truck pulled out with smoke pouring out of its pipes, scattering the seagulls away.

Sue stood next to me, we looked on in awe and concern as the artifact was hauled out of the shipyard.

Men of the port crew removed their hard hats in honor of this startling piece of history.

The artifact would be trucked more than a thousand miles, from New York to Colorado. Following that, it would be held at a research facility and then tested. Now that we found the ark, we had to prove it was what we claimed.

A medic emerged from the crowd of onlookers, pushing Mike along in a wheelchair. Running over to him, I knelt and gave him a big hug.

"I'm so glad you're okay." It had been a while since we had last spoken.

"Yeah, it was a close call. I can't believe I'm still mostly intact. Oh yeah, by the way, Eagle Eyes, why didn't you come down to visit me—you didn't forget I was down there, did you?"

Before I could say anything, he abruptly cut me off.

"Ah, never mind," he said as he spotted Pam walking toward us. "I think I know why now. Listen, I'll see you back in Texas. I don't want you to worry, Pam will take good care of me."

Just before he was wheeled away, he winked at me and grinned. At least I knew his humor was still intact. I was glad to see him in such good spirits.

"If it weren't for you, who knows where I would be," I yelled as the medic rolled him away.

"You go get them, girlfriend!" he shouted, giving me the thumbs up.

"Don't worry, Mike, I'm on it. I'll make you proud!"

We were all scheduled to board a plane from LaGuardia Airport and fly back to Chicago, but after Mike's injury, my team decided to fly back to Texas. Godfrey and I went on to fly back to Chicago to prepare for a press conference the Institute had arranged.

A sleek, black limousine pulled up, sent from the university. I certainly hadn't expected this.

"A limo? Can you believe it? I guess the university's taking us seriously."

"Us? No, Clara, not us, but God." After that, all I got was Godfrey's kind smile as we were driven to the airport.

Hours later, we arrived in Chicago, where yet another limo waited outside the airport to drop me off at my hotel, and Godfrey back to the Institute. We had rested for much of the ride but eventually started talking over our plans for the next day.

"Tomorrow, we'll meet with the scrutiny of the scientific community," Godfrey said. "There's going to be a lot of press there, Clara. We need to keep things short and to the point. At the moment, we don't have enough facts to fill in all the blanks."

"Short and simple. I got it," I assured Godfrey, stepping out of the limousine. We had arrived at my hotel.

Godfrey waved, "See you tomorrow, Clara."

The limousine pulled away. Tomorrow seemed so close already.

I was a little nervous knowing this might be the most important press conference of my life.

Entering the hotel lobby, I spotted the mail carrier collecting the mail, which reminded me of the letter I had yet to finish.

I had so much on my mind that day, but I promised myself that as soon as this press conference was over, I would write. The elevator doors opened, and I pressed the fifth-floor button again, taking the ride up. Out of the elevator and into my room, I pulled out all the notes I had and immediately sat down to prepare. It was important for me to be ready for questions about where we found the vessel, how we conducted the research, and our mistake—underestimating the weight of the relic.

At a small oak table in the corner of my room, I pored over photos of the hieroglyphics we'd brought back. Photos that the media had never seen. Picture by picture, frame after frame, I downloaded them all and emailed them to Dr. Langley, an old colleague of mine who was an expert in ancient symbols, languages, and other encryptions. He would be able to decipher the photos and give me more insight about the vessel's history.

Thinking about it made my head spin, and a break was what I needed. Pushing away from the table, I thought to make a pot of coffee, hoping it would help clear my mind. I turned on the television, and BBN News was on.

"In other news, an American Chinook helicopter crashed in Iran, taking with it the life of two of its pilots."

"Wait a minute." I turned the water off and put the coffee pot aside. "What did she just say?" Walking back over to the television, I sat on the corner of the bed, leaning in closer to listen as the anchor continued.

"Let's join reporter Christopher Elliot at the scene of the crash."

A fresh-faced reporter appeared at the site of where we were, the site of the Ark. I couldn't believe it. I listened as Christopher began his report.

"Christopher Elliot here, bringing you breaking news. I am currently at the crash site of an American helicopter. It appears the helicopter, with three people on board, was attempting to bring down a portion of an ancient artifact they found suspended alongside a cliff, some two thousand feet above. It seems that the crew underestimated the weight of the artifact, leaving the helicopter overloaded, and plummeting into the valley below."

The reporter continued.

"Two people on board the helicopter died at the site, while a third, archeologist Mike McCarty, was rescued but seriously injured. The helicopter's remains have been removed, and now all that remains is a portion of that artifact standing upright, perched into the ground, allowing us this full view of its ancient history. There are local women walking around the site, some of them even kneeling and placing the palms of their hands on the side of it, saying what sounds like prayers."

Debra, the news anchor, broke into the report from the BBN studio.

"Christopher, what is it that the people who are praying are saying this artifact is exactly?"

"Debra, I'm glad you asked. It seems that archeologists and the locals here have found what they believe to be the remains of Noah's Ark."

"Wow, Christopher, my grandmother is going to love this one," Debra responded sarcastically. "What a remarkable piece of news you got there. Please keep us posted?"

"I'll keep you and the rest of our audience up-to-date as the events continue to unfold. This is Christopher Elliot with BBN News," He ended his report,

"Now back to you."

CHAPTER

19

Shake the hand of an honest man

O H WOW, we made the news. I couldn't believe it. Flipping the coffee maker on, the thought rushed over me. They got some of the facts wrong, though, like Mike being an archeologist. "He's not!" I laughed at the mistake the reporter made. But it didn't matter, it didn't matter at all, as long as we got the press. Wow, this was going to be big, and by all means, I had to get it right.

Kicking off my sneakers and turning the heater up a bit, I took a quick shower and jumped into something more comfortable before returning to my work.

The heat warmed my cold body as the pot of coffee filled the room with the smell of coffee, Mocha brew.

Making myself a cup, I felt a deeper meaning for my life. The world had to know what had gone on out there, and I was going to be the one to tell them.

Writing throughout the night, one cup of coffee after another, making point after point, I noticed the hours ticking away.

I dozed off for minutes at a time but often woke with something else I had remembered to write.

A knock at the door woke me from my last nap. Lifting my head off the table, I cracked open my eyes and saw the sun peeking through the curtains. Morning already? My room was a tattered mess with my notes scattered everywhere, the coffee pot stained and empty.

I stood and stretched my stiff limbs, wincing at the ache in my back, I heard a knock again. I looked through the peephole and saw it was Godfrey with a fresh face.

"Shake the hand of an honest man," he said when I opened the door.

"And you would have shaken a hand indeed," I said, remembering a quote he taught me when we were back in the valley.

"Good morning, Dr. Godfrey."

"Good morning," he said, "looks like you've been up all night?"

"You're early, and yes, I have. I've been reviewing our work to prepare for the conference today, and I didn't realize how long I had been working until I saw the sun come up. Oh, did you see we made the news? It's exciting, right."

"Yes, I did, it's a delight to hear. It's why I arrived earlier than expected. I don't mean to rush you, but the limo is waiting for us—we don't want to keep the world waiting any longer."

"Sorry," I yawned, rubbing my eyes. "I need a moment, you go ahead. I'll meet you in the car."

A little later, I strolled out of the hotel, dressed in a dark blue suit, wearing an oversized hat, hoping my makeup was perfect. With my coat tossed over my arm, I donned a pair of sunshades to cover my still tired eyes.

Godfrey suppressed a smile as he opened the door to the limo for me.

"What's wrong?" I struck a pose. "The hat too much for you?"

"Not at all," he chuckled, "but sometimes you are."

"Okay, I'm the flashy type. But trust me, Godfrey, I have a pure heart."

"I know you do, Clara, but you're not wearing that hat and glasses into the press conference, are you?"

"No, of course not, I just did it to get a rise out of you."

"Well, that you did. Now please, take that off, and let's get moving."

Giggling at his lack of a sense of humor, I took the hat and glasses off, feeling Godfrey must have thought I'd lost my mind. But I hadn't, just a little too excited about the big news. I yawned and let out a dramatic sigh.

"I'm exhausted."

"I know, this can be a lot of work," he said, handing me a cup of coffee. "But don't think your hard work is not appreciated."

"Do you think the conference will be long?"

"Not if we do as I suggested and keep it short and to the point."

As we drove off, I noticed Chuy was in the driver's seat.

"Hi, Ms. Clara. Get buckled in, it's going to be a great day today. Yep. A great day indeed."

It took us about forty-five minutes to reach the University of Chicago Research Center, where the press conference would be held. My heels clicked against the pavement as I stepped out. We fixed our eyes on the Myers Building, which housed the Department of Archaeology, our destination.

The pressroom we were scheduled to be in had some power issues, so the conference was rescheduled, and we were rerouted to an auditorium. The media had yet to set up their equipment, so we got an extra half hour to finish up our notes and prepare for questions. Casting my eyes through the auditorium door, I felt my heart begin to pound intensely. That large oval-shaped room could easily seat a thousand, but we weren't expecting nearly that many. The high ceiling and red carpet were impressive, but it was the oak trimmed stage that gave the hall its elegance. I was ready for it all, excited to get the conference started.

Thirty minutes later, a relatively small group of press members filed in, while Dr. Clarence Long, president of the Christian Institute, called us into a side room that led to the stage we would be sitting on. He thanked us for coming and then began coaching us on what to say. *Remember, guys, don't say this—say more of that.* Godfrey seemed as uncomfortable as I did. We had done the work, why wouldn't he just introduce us and let us take it from there?

Taking off his hat, Dr. Long apologized and said, "I don't mean to sound condescending, but those reporters can be a little harsh. I heard them talking earlier outside."

"No worries, Dr. Long," Godfrey assured him, "We'll let you lead the way."

After a long wait backstage, we finally heard the announcement.

"It is with great pride that I introduce to you our honored guests, Dr. Michael Godfrey, and his distinguished colleague, Dr. Clara Hamilton."

The room erupted into applause. The curtains were pulled back, and we walked out on stage.

"The Christian Institute sponsored their expedition to the mountains of Iran. Their efforts have proved as fruitful and rewarding as we were expecting. I'm thrilled to announce that they have unearthed what we believe to be the remains of Noah's Ark."

Applause roared throughout the room again, and with each flash of the cameras, my stomach seemed to jolt as I remembered the horrifying journey we had all gone through.

Dr. Long took a seat and waited for them to settle down again before speaking. Godfrey and I sat on either side of him in front of the microphones.

"Their team endured an incredibly treacherous journey and finally found the vessel perched on a mountain ledge, covered in a thick layer of ice.

These two daring scientists are here today to answer any questions you may have."

Hands shot up, and people shouted questions all at once from all corners of the room. Dr. Long called on one of the reporters, and being handed a microphone, the reporter stood and asked,

"When will you know for sure that this is the biblical Noah's Ark?"

Godfrey cleared his throat.

"Good morning to you all. As we speak, a portion of the vessel is being trucked across the United States to a research facility where it will undergo careful analysis. We will use carbon dating to determine the age of that section. Within six weeks, we will have the results for sure."

"Who will be doing the testing?"

Dr. Long spoke up, "The renowned Dr. Benjamin Baines, of the Baines Institute."

By the look on Godfrey's face, I could tell he recognized the name.

"Dr. Baines is one of the most prominent researchers in the field of Classical Archeology," Long said, "and will be overseeing the testing process."

The crowd began to clamor once again. Covering his mic, Godfrey leaned closer to me.

"I wonder why he didn't look for someone else to test the specimen."

"Maybe there was no one else available," I whispered back. "Why, is this man a problem?"

"I'll explain later. For now, let's focus on this."

I nodded, though his concern unsettled me.

"Dr. Hamilton, aren't you the daughter of the famous Dr. Henry Hamilton?" Another reporter asked from out of the crowd. He looked oddly familiar, though I couldn't place him at that moment.

"Yes, I am."

Holding onto the mic, he held up his hand to halt any questions the other reporters had. "Wait a minute, wait a minute!" His voice boomed throughout the hall.

"Aren't you the same Dr. Clara Hamilton who recently took a team to search for the consecrated remains of a so-called 'ancient woman' in Arizona?"

That's when it hit me. It was Peter Prestwick, the critic who'd been chasing after me for the past few years. I didn't know what bone he had to pick with me, but he'd been giving me all kinds of negative press, both true and false, all of it unflattering. I resisted the urge to stand up and shout him down as he continued speaking.

"How can you claim to have found something that scholars have been seeking fruitlessly for years? Can you say with certainty that this isn't another failed attempt to convince people you've found a 'true relic' of some kind? And would you mind commenting on how you feel about tarnishing your father's legacy with the unproven claims you've been churning out for years now?"

"How dare you talk like that about my father?" I yelled.

"Sure, but Dr. Hamilton, if I'm not mistaken, didn't you just check yourself out of rehab some months ago? Your critics have all concluded that you're unstable and unfit for such technical work. Shouldn't you have just stayed on the sidelines to work on your personal problems first?"

Oh wow, my heart sank, and I felt my cheeks flush as this was getting far more personal than it should have been. I couldn't even respond as I found myself incensed with the questioning.

Dr. Long leaned over to me and whispered, "I told you, this might get a little nasty..."

"Dr. Hamilton has been a great help to us," Godfrey interrupted, trying to clear things up. "We have every confidence in our find and in her."

The other reporters fought for attention, but Prestwick spoke up again, ever eager to hog the microphone.

"I sure hope you're right, Dr. Godfrey. You know, I've been following Dr. Hamilton for years now, and when she's wrong, she'll say anything to protect her name and reputation. Who knows, she may have fooled you as well."

"That's a dirty lie!" I shouted into the microphone.

Godfrey held up his hand once more, reassuring the audience of our expertise.

"Dr. Hamilton and I both have years of academic experience, research, and fieldwork under our belts. We are among the most qualified individuals in the world to tackle this challenge. To determine the age and source of the artifact we procured, testing must be completed. In six weeks, we will hold another conference to give you the results. Now, if there are no questions regarding our findings or the expedition, I'm going to end this discussion. Thank you for coming."

As usual, Godfrey relieved me, yet I was still seething at the reporters for turning the press conference into a witch-hunt.

Staring at Godfrey, with his head bowed toward the table, watching him collect his things, I wondered if he would view me differently now having heard about my troubled private life.

Walking outside of the pressroom, Godfrey walked out behind me, calling my name.

"Clara, Clara!"

I turned to face him as I could hear the tone in his voice growing stronger.

"Why didn't you tell me that you might have critics among the reporters today who knew you personally?" he asked. "We could have prepared and been ready for them."

"I don't need your protection. I don't need you speaking up for me, got it!"

"That's not what I asked you," Godfrey said. "I'm not sure what happened in there. But out of courtesy, you should have told me you had issues with the press. We can't allow the media to dismiss this finding. It's simply far too important."

"I had every intention of keeping my personal life private, but apparently, they found a way to rip me apart."

Godfrey shook his head. "It doesn't matter what they think of you. Just keep true to yourself and keep committed to our research."

There I was, with my career on the line, being mocked by people who couldn't see past their own judgment. I couldn't just let it go like that.

"We have to think bigger than those reporters out there, bigger than ourselves."

"They were out for blood, Godfrey. I need to sort this out and clear my name."

"Clear your name? Clara, there is a time and place for everything—this isn't it. God will clear your name, and He will do it in His appointed time."

I shrugged. "I have no clue what that means, and God's not really helping right now."

"Then pray about it, Clara, and let it go."

"Pray? Really. Godfrey, that's something you do. I mean, I don't even know the words to say. I don't even know how."

"It doesn't matter what you say, or how you say it, but pray with sincerity, and in time, God will answer you. Give God your full attention, Clara, and not those reporters. I'll see you in six weeks with the results. Then, whatever doubts may remain will be laid to rest." Godfrey turned away to collect his things.

I grabbed my bags and strode out ahead of him, still feeling incredibly embarrassed.

First Pam and now this? It was as if in spite of all we had done, people hadn't changed. And now my reputation had just gone down in flames. Was I now part of that group of scientists who no longer mattered?

I tried to connect with Godfrey's words, "Let it go for God to handle."

That was a new one for me, letting my thoughts and fears go for a God to handle? The thought of that had never before crossed my mind, as I was someone who liked to be in control.

Yes, knowing myself all too well, I knew the praying about it part would be easy, but it was the letting it go part that would be tougher for me. But why not try and trust God... After all, I had gone through all the mistakes I'd made, all the wrong roads I had taken, and all the failures that burned me. Why not? I had tried everything else in life, so why not Him?

The sky filled with clouds that day, and the chilling winds blew in with a mist of rain. Wrapping my coat around me, I could still feel the sting of humiliation as I walked out of the building and down the drizzly sidewalk. Looking up, I saw Chuy standing on the wet curb beside the car with his arms out. I approached him with a plastered smile on my face and held on to his embrace.

"What happened in there, Ms. Clara? What's wrong?"

"We'll have to wait six weeks for the test results, so we have to be patient."

He scoffed. "Wait! Why? Didn't you guys tell them we found it?"

"Well, that's not how the press conference ended, and I don't want to talk about it now."

Chuy tossed his hands up in a fit of frustration. Godfrey, putting away his cellphone, walked up to Chuy and said, "She's right, my man, but while we wait with nothing else to do, I have something to keep our hands full. I know a woman who runs a homeless shelter down on the south side. She'll appreciate our assistance, and it'll take our minds off ourselves and problems as well."

"But what about the Ark?" Chuy asked.

"Not to worry. I, too, have been praying, and I'm convinced everything will work out. For now, let's just get down to the shelter."

I felt a little guilty for allowing myself to get sidetracked. Unlike Godfrey, I was more concerned with clearing my name and feeling better, forgetting why I was there, and how precious that moment was—how valuable and how irreplaceable the artifact we recovered might be and what it would mean to the world. It was bigger than whatever problems I had, and I couldn't risk being distracted by what the reporters had to say.

Godfrey's phone dinged as soon as we got on the road. Reading out loud, he told us the relic had arrived safely and was now at the Baines Institute.

"Awesome," Chuy said as he drove us to the shelter Godfrey had insisted we go to. The weather was cool that day, but my heart was warm. Hearing the relic had arrived safely meant the testing would begin soon, and hopefully, that would shut those reporters up. Until then, going down to the shelter sounded like a good idea, something to help me take my mind off things, as Godfrey said. A recharge was what I needed, and helping others was always a way to do that. Who else, other than me, would need to hear a kind word, see a hopeful smile, or to hold a helpful hand? Who else needed someone to speak victory into their lives, someone to let them know a change was on the way.

20

Faith without work

Ms. Jenkins story

C
HUY DROVE off into the cloudy weather as we headed to our destination. The tone of our surroundings was changing as we had been traveling south through the Windy City streets. Poverty was showing its face in the wake of abandoned buildings, looming on every corner. As we drove, we came upon a sign reading, "And Still I Hope," rising above a dilapidated lot. Next to it appeared to be a worn-down former church building, but was now a food shelter, yet still invoking the respect and character of what it once was. Chuy didn't seem bothered by the uneasy feeling some get when they enter such a neighborhood when we drove into the parking lot. He looked eager to get started until he saw the long feeding lines of homeless people were wrapped around the building, and there seemed to be no end.

Some seemed to recognize that we were volunteers. A few quietly thanked us, while others shouted, "What took you so long!"

The shelter was a tough place, but more protective than the streets. Hot meals were served there, maybe even a cot or two to sleep on, and blankets for when temperatures plummeted.

Before we could enter the building, a short soapbox preacher by the name of Timmy sternly preached the word of God. With the worn red brick building as his backdrop, he stood near the entrance and proclaimed, *"God is good!* Amen, brothers and sisters," with a Bible in his hand.

"Yes, He is, yes He is," the homeless responded. Boosting the Bible high above his head, the preacher shouted in a stirring tone, "For God is the author of our lives, the maker of our faith, the joy in our hope. Yes, my friends, He is an awesome God! The world may call you a victim, but I call you a victor. The world might call you weak, but your suffering will become your strength if only you call upon the name of the Lord for salvation! The world might condemn the downtrodden, but in the name of Jesus, let us stop focusing on what the world might say and through Christ become redeemed! Once we do so, no sin can hold us back!"

The doors to the shelter opened. One of the staff members emerged and directed us to the mess hall. Other volunteers lining the cafeteria walls greeted us as the homeless flooded in with equal warmth.

"Most of us were once street people ourselves," one of the volunteers told me. "It's not just the food that draws people here, but the love that's shared does as well. We try to make people feel as welcome as possible. They don't have a home, so we welcome them home. We welcome them to this one."

Smiles spread across the volunteers' faces as they tended to each of the homeless, treating them warmly as guests.

A chant broke out from around the room, "Anything is possible! Anything is possible! Anything is possible!" The volunteers sang and clapped their hands.

One of the men sitting at one of the tables caught my eye. Shuffling through the crowd, I made my way to him.

"Hey there," I said. "Aren't you the guy who stands on the corner downtown, holding up that, 'And still I hope' sign?"

He smiled and reached out to shake my hand. "That's me. My name's Kenneth Keys. I bet you thought I was homeless. Well, I was, but not anymore. I hold that sign to get donations for the shelter, to give back to the people who helped me."

"That's a great heart you have," I said, sitting down next to him.

"Oh, yes. I really enjoy helping Ms. Jenkins feed the people. Back when I was on the streets, I came here for services, and she offered me a home-cooked meal, a good word, and a job. I couldn't say no to that. It's an honor to get to spread hope throughout the city, to tell people it's not as bad as it seems, you know?"

I looked on at the hall, transfixed. Pots and pans clattered together, heat surged from the oven, and a delicious scent emanated from Ms. Jenkins's kitchen, welcoming the hungry to come and eat.

"Ms. Jenkins!" Godfrey called. "Is that you?"

Out from behind the hot kitchen, an older, gray-haired woman wearing a hairnet and a wide smile exited.

"Is it me? Who else could it be!" she said sweetly, "Michael, baby, is that you?" She took a hard look at him and answered herself before he could. "It is! Child, why do you bother me? I'm cooking." She smiled with joy.

"I know!" Godfrey said. "I don't want to keep you, but my friends and I came to volunteer. Could you use some help?"

"Of course! There's always room for more here," Ms. Jenkins said with a twinkle in her eye.

Taking up a position behind the steam tables, I stood next to Ms. Jenkins with a spoon in hand, ready to serve the mac and cheese. Chuy and Godfrey stood over pots of steaming pinto beans and pans of fried chicken. Kenneth filled mugs with coffee from a massive metal coffeemaker.

"How're you doing?" Godfrey asked. "You've certainly got a dynamic preacher out front."

"I'm doing great, Michael," Ms. Jenkins said. "But I didn't put that preacher out there. He's there of his own free will, spreading the Gospel. Such a sweet boy, too. I remember when he was ten years old, he asked me if he could stand there and preach the Word of God to the hopeless. Three years later, he's still at it. To think, he's now only a thirteen-year-old child, but he can preach with the passion of a wise, old man. Miracles will never cease."

"That's pretty impressive," Godfrey said. "Oh, by the way, I would like to introduce you to my friends. Ms. Jenkins, this man on our left is Chuy, the woman next to you is Clara. Guys, this is Ms. Emma Jenkins. She taught me some of my first lessons when I joined the ministry. She alone built this shelter."

"No, Godfrey, God did. Remember the words I told you to always remember?"

"Faith without works is dead," Ms. Jenkins and Godfrey said at once. She looked back at him in annoyance.

"Service is the best way to exercise it," Godfrey added.

"Of course, of course," Ms. Jenkins said with a roll of her eyes. "Now shovel some food, big guy!" Her voice carried throughout the cafeteria, drawing laughter from guests and volunteers alike. Then she looked over at me. "Yes, service." She filled a pan of peas and then walked over to me. "Sometimes, by helping others, you help yourself. Come here, child, and taste some of these peas."

I took a spoonful. "Wow, Ms. Jenkins, that's good." I nodded in appreciation.

"I know. Now that you got food in your belly, take this pan and get on the line. Some of those people ain't ate in days."

I walked back to the line with a full pan with what tasted like home-cooked peas, ready to serve. Chuy and I started doing our duty, attending the line and filling plates. The atmosphere was cheery, as the volunteers served with a compassion I hadn't seen anywhere else. These were people helping others without expecting anything in return. Seeing how hard they worked encouraged me to work even harder, as I was determined to serve the hundreds lined up outside, even if it took hours. If they could do it, so could I.

The time passed in a whirlwind of laughter, the steam warming my cheeks, and the companionship doing the same to my heart. When the day ended, and we had served the last person in line, Ms. Jenkins appeared in line after him, shaking the hands of all those who'd helped. "Thank you. Thank you all so much! We appreciated your help, we really did."

"I don't know how you do it," Chuy said, slumping in a chair, mopping the sweat from his forehead.

She sighed. "Some mornings, I ask myself the same thing. I've been doing this for twenty years. All I can do is thank God for the opportunity."

Wiping her hands on her apron, she looked at them. "Two hundred pieces of chicken, forty big pans of cornbread, plus sides every day. All on a dime. I didn't grow up learning to make a meal—I grew up learning how to stretch one." She gestured to the kitchen. "Come and help me do dishes, or we'll be here all night."

"Have you ever thought about quitting?" Chuy asked as we headed in.

"Faith without work is dead, so the Bible tells us. I got faith in me, and I choose to live."

She handed us aprons, and we paused to tie them before plunging into the mountains of pots and pans along with the rest of the volunteers, letting her speak.

"Sometimes, pulling myself out of bed at five can be rough," she said, scrubbing a huge pot crusted with beans, "but I love these people, and so many of them would have nothing to eat if I quit. So many shelters out there feed these people but treat them like nobodies. I try to treat them like I'm feeding God himself because He's the one I see when I look at them."

Soap bubbles crept up my arm. I flicked them away, focusing on Ms. Jenkins as she continued.

"Christ once said, 'Whatever you do for the least of these, you do for me,' and I believe that. How can anyone say they love God if they refuse to feed those He loves? Someone must serve them, and I am that someone."

"But doesn't it get hard," I asked, "for you, or for anyone who sets out to help?"

Ms. Jenkins nodded. "Everyone faces hard times at some point. But what better way is there to heal than to focus on meeting the needs of others? We give these people a generous helping of food and treat them with respect. They leave here full and encouraged. Even if it's just a small way to spread the word, 'Still, I hope.'"

A quiet smile spread across her face when she spoke those last three words. Judging by how much pride she took in making people's lives better, I could tell her shelter was a genuine mission of hope and service.

"Your dedication is amazing," Chuy said, still elbow-deep in soapy water.

Ms. Jenkins shook her head. "My dedication is because I understand the hardship in these people's lives. Some of them have suffered incredible tragedy, moments we can't even begin to imagine."

Incredible tragedy. My fingers stiffened around the plate in my hand. I didn't have to imagine it. I had been there.

"But we tell them," Ms. Jenkins said, "no matter how hard things have been, it's crucial that they keep hope in their hearts. Only hope will bring about the better days that God will use to write the story of their lives. They tell me they can feel the warmth in this room, and I tell them that they're feeling what love and service built. Faith without work is dead. Sometimes you've just got to get off your backside, stop moping around, and do something for yourself. It can be incredibly difficult, but you must try with all your spirit. That's the only way you'll ever see change."

"Amazing," I murmured.

Rinsing off the last pan, she wiped her hands on her apron. "Well, I hope you enjoyed listening to an old lady," she joked. "With help from all of you, the dishes stood no chance."

"Well, Ms. Jenkins, you are a strong person," Chuy said.

"Strong? Child, please. Samson was strong until Delilah cut his hair off." She sat down on a chair. "What a fall from grace."

"Ms. Jenkins, may I ask, what brought you to God? What's your story?" I couldn't help but want to hear more. Every word she had said so far spoke to my soul, and I had a strange feeling that there was some great mystery I was about to solve.

"Well, Clara, let me start with this. Yes, I will tell you my story, but I'm not going to tell you my whole story because my whole story is not for you to know. But I will tell you what's important."

She then, looked me in the eyes.

"I know you may know a little about faith, but I'm going to tell you about faith through work. I very well might have been one of those people in the mess hall waiting to eat, losing my life. But now I'm here, praising the name of Jesus. My life was difficult, and my spirit suffered even more than my body. For years upon years, I sat around, begging God to rescue me from the heartache I was in. But there was one morning when I woke up, decided to get out of my bed, and thought to cook something for myself. Walking into my kitchen, turning on the stove, I put a fire under the pan and started cooking. I forgot to turn the lights on, and so there I was, cooking in the dark. Then, a voice spoke to me and said, 'Turn the lights on.'"

I couldn't help the reaction that flickered across my face.

"I told that voice, 'I don't want to turn the light on,'" Ms. Jenkins continued. "Yet again, that voice spoke to me and said,

'Emma, if you don't turn the lights on, you will forever be cooking in the dark.' And with that message, I hit the switch. The lights came on, as did that voice flick on a switch in my heart. I went to the bathroom and washed my body in His mercy. I washed my face and patted around the pain I had woken up with that morning. It was when I started acting on my own behalf that I realized He was trying, with His word, to rescue me. *Hallelujah.* But without working from faith, I couldn't possibly have recognized that."

"Why not?" asked Chuy, leaning in to soak up the story.

"I was dead. Physically, I moved through the world, ate, talked, slept, but I had buried myself in a pit on the inside. So, I prayed and asked God for strength, and not just any old kind of strength, but the kind of strength I could step out on. I still remember so clearly reading the scriptures God gave me. They were about service. It felt like an answer to the question I didn't even know had been plaguing me. The only way to get rid of my sadness was to serve." She paused for breath.

"I pushed back against it for so many years because I couldn't see the truth. I thought I was the only one hurting. I found out there's a whole lot of people out there in the world, hurting just like me. But everyone has their own pain."

Her eyes glanced around as she spoke. I had the strangest feeling she was lingering on me, reading my very thoughts as I urged her to go on.

"Other shelters work to feed people. But for me, it's my God-given labor of love. I'm so in love with this place that I couldn't stop if I wanted to. That is what keeps me getting up, morning after morning, coming back again and again even when it's hard. We've fed over 20,000 people, and my work has only just started. We live within our means. Never once have our lights been shut off, or have we faced the threat of eviction or closure. But, most importantly, no one has ever missed a meal." She wiped her forehead with her apron. "I don't mean to be rude or cut things off, but I'm positively bushed. I'll be heading home soon. It's right down the block."

"Can we give you a ride?" Godfrey asked. "I would hate to see you walk home with your donation money in your bag. It's dangerous if nothing else."

"Dangerous!" She chuckled. "Child don't worry about me. I'm going to be all right. I carry the Word of God in my heart because I love the Lord. And a pistol in my pocket for those who love the devil. Ha!"

We all burst into laughter as the mental image rested in our minds.

As the evening ended, our small group walked out of the shelter. Little Timmy was finishing the last of his sermon. He spoke at the top of his voice, preaching the words God had given him.

"Saints, turn your light on, put on the full armor of God, for the armor is Christ because Christ is the light, and the light is in you. You must stand up and fight the good fight. No one or nothing will ever separate you from the love of God. When your days grow hard, your mind gets weak, and when you feel tempted to give up, you must do as Jesus did and tell temptation, 'Get thee behind me, Satan.' With hope in your heart, you've got to shine the light of God's Word into your darkness. You've got to walk with that light held firmly in your heart and praise God's name. Saints, no matter how bad things get, no matter how dark the days grow, you can be the light that walks out of that darkness! I don't know why some marriages end in divorce and some don't. I don't know why tragedy may strike your home but not the next family. I don't know why life gave you a hard situation and not the next man, but what I do know is this, 'All things work together, all things work together, all things work together for those who love the Lord,' Romans 8:28."

He got off his soapbox, handed all the people in the crowd little tiny flashlights, and then climbed back up. "Now turn them on!" he yelled. "Saints, turn the light on. Turn your light on and allow God to show you the way. All you have to do is turn your light on, and He will show you the way."

He stood and held the Bible in the air with his right hand. "Can I get an amen, brothers, and sisters, can I get an amen!"

The homeless yelled in a single voice, "Amen, brother, amen."

As the crowd walked away, little Timmy jumped down and grabbed his soapbox.

He placed his Bible in the box, took Ms. Jenkins by the hand, and walked her home. Godfrey, Chuy, and I now walking over to our car, could hear Timmy from a distance, preaching the 23rd Psalm: "The Lord is my shepherd, I shall not want." Timmy spoke the Words of God into the darkness, as the homeless walked away, shining their tiny flashlights into the night.

CHAPTER

—21—

Feel the Breeze

C HUY DROVE us back to my hotel, conversing
lightly, merging into the downtown traffic. When the
conversation stalled, I used the time to think about the
day and how badly the press conference went. *Maybe I should leave
Chicago,* I thought. I could return when the testing was done.

It was a viable option, but one that had the aftertaste of me
running away from my problems again. I didn't want to give the
reporters the satisfaction, because I knew they would take it as
a win.

It was really encouraging to see Ms. Jenkins and to hear about
her plight in life. Service. It was what seemed to keep her strong
and grounded, unbent and unbroken by the old winds of her
past. She put a lot of dedication toward her work, and it seemed
to have paid off. *Two hundred pieces of chicken plus sides and no
one has missed a meal.* It's ironic that she began her ministry in
an abandoned church building, and after all those years, she was
still going.

I needed her strength to be able to deal with the pressures of
my crazy life and the hounding press as well. I regretted a lot of

the things I'd done, the pit I had fallen in, and I felt ashamed. I should have never checked myself into that clinic. What an embarrassment it all turned out to be...

Godfrey had advised me to put things in a better perspective, and I was trying. I hoped I hadn't lost his confidence, as I thought about the look on his face earlier that day.

My mind sputtered as the car slowed to a stop in front of the traffic lights. Rolling down the window, I noticed the streets downtown were unusually quiet, whereas this place was typically home to a discord of voices, car horns, and many other sounds, that didn't make sense. The only sounds I heard that night were the click-clacking of horse's hooves, amplified by the stillness that shrouded the streets.

I turned to the source and saw a coachman directing a pair of white horses, pulling an empty carriage. They pulled over and stopped at the entrance of a park as the coachmen got down from the box seat to brush and care for them. Seeing the smile on his face, the peace in the horses' stride and the comfort the coachman took in caring for them made me want to abandon the sound of the car's engine, the mindless chatter my friends and I were having, and join them. A blissful ride down the city streets after all that I had gone through sounded like a good idea. I loved horses after all, and this was my opportunity to feel like a tourist, even if it was just for the evening.

"Oh, Chuy, please pull over," I said. "Do you see the white horses? I want to get out over there."

"What? Clara, we're nowhere near your place."

"Yes, I know, but seriously, for me."

After a moment of dithering, Chuy eased out of the traffic and slid to a stop at the edge of the pavement. I blew Chuy and Godfrey a kiss and walked toward the park's entrance.

I didn't have to wait long before the empty white carriage rolled up to where I stood. "Hey, Mister," I hailed the coachman. "Can I have a ride? Is this carriage available for hire?"

The coachman, wearing a top hat and white suit, waved me over to come aboard. I climbed into the carriage, feeling like a princess.

"This carriage ride will take us through the park," the coachman said.

"Great, just what I was looking for." I smiled, making myself comfortable.

The carriage jolted once he slapped the horses on their hides to get us rolling. Into the park and onto its cobbled stone walkway, his old hands guided the horses down the winding path.

I relaxed, melting into the soft carriage seats, thinking about my better days, remembering back to when I was a young girl, the time my father and I shared when we used to ride the carriage every so often. He allowed me to ride upfront so I could be near the horses and feel the breeze. He taught me not to be afraid of the horses, as they were regal and noble.

I remember a poem he wrote to me, a poem of contentment and legitimate happiness.

"No far-off stars, nor glowing moon,
Nor endless ocean need I consume.
No paradise, nor islands, I need not see,
Lest I forget the winds that travel with me.
For it is the gentleness of those winds that set me free,
The gentleness of the breeze that carries me..."

Oh, wow, I knew there was more to it, but I had forgotten it. I rattled through my mind once more, trying to remember. It had escaped me for the moment, it was one I really liked. Yet, there was one thing I didn't forget, and that was how we had sat in the box seat of the carriage. Leaning forward, I tugged on the coachman's sleeve. "Excuse me, sir, I have a request to make."

"What's that, ma'am?"

"If it wouldn't bother you too much, I'd like to climb up there and sit next to you."

He pulled the carriage to the side of the road.

"If I'm not overstepping myself, ma'am, do you mind if I ask why?"

"When my father was alive, we would go on these carriage rides, and we would both sit up front, kick back, and enjoy the breeze. I would like to enjoy the breeze again, I mean, if you wouldn't mind?"

"Well, sure thing, ma'am. Come up here and sit next to me."

One leg at a time, I climbed over the front seat of the carriage and plopped down with a smile on my face.

The coachman was taken off guard, but not completely surprised. "I didn't think you would climb up like that," he said offhandedly.

Apart from him, one or two other people on the sidewalk noticed it, but I didn't care. My father wasn't there anymore to feel the soft winds, but the coachman and I were. Making myself comfortable again, I nuzzled up next to him and began to reminisce,

"I remember when I was a little girl, riding down Michigan Avenue, I was so afraid of the horses that I would hold onto my father for dear life."

"It's okay, you can hold on to me, ma'am." He gave me his arm. "Don't worry, I won't let these horses bother you. An old man like me has been around them for years, so they've got no issues with me."

"Don't worry," I said, giving him a smile. "I used to spend the summers at my grandmother's ranch, I've learned a fondness for them as well."

The coachman grabbed the reins and slapped the horses on the backside once more. They pulled away, and the cool air streamed across my face, taking me back to a simpler time. I tried talking to the horses for a moment as if I could get them to whinny back to me, but they paid me no attention. Well, I guess it was something that only worked when I was a girl.

I chuckled lightly, knowing the coachmen heard me and my playful antics.

Thinking back to when I was a kid growing up in Chicago, and after my mother passed away, I remembered the kids used to call me Ginger, like Ginger from Gilligan's Island. They'd say, 'you think you're pretty because of your long red hair.' But when my hair fell out after a bad perm, they all laughed at me and called me far less imaginative names.

I didn't have a mother to do my hair back then, all I had was my father, and yes, he was a scientist, but when it came to my hair, he had no idea.

It was terrible how people could be, not caring what they said or who they hurt. Always trying to tear someone else down. Never taking the time to find the joy in their own lives.

Looking into the night sky, I took a deep breath and exhaled, watching the coachman do the same as his eyes followed my gaze.

"It's a disappointment, isn't it," he said, leaning over to me. "It's a shame how the bright city lights dim the stars. No matter the night, no matter the hour, dimming the stars is what *they* do."

If he only knew, I was still a little upset with those reporters' attitudes. I felt as if *they* were the city lights, dimming my star.

He continued, pulling his attention away from the sky.

"It's why I like riding through the park."

"Why is that sir?"

"Because there's no city lights, only a glowing pathway to guide us through."

"I guess you're right, the stars are much clearer out here at night."

"Yes ma'am, it puts you at ease when you've had a rough day."

"I know what you mean, I know all about that. I had a press conference earlier today, and it was really rough."

"Oh, are you some kind of reporter?"

"No." I snorted. "Not at all. I'm actually a scientist."

"I knew I could sense brains in you," he hummed. "You must be pretty smart."

"Yeah, sometimes," I smiled wryly. "But those reporters were hell-bent on ruining my career. They said the most awful things about me."

A baffled look came across his face. "Little lady, you have no business caring about what *they* say." He hugged me comfortingly. "Let me tell you something I've learned in my many years. *They* will always talk about you. *They* will always have something to say. *They* are always living in the past, hoping one day to bring you down with them. In fact, do you know the only thing *they* will ever forget?"

"No, sir, what could that be?"

"There's a God in Heaven, and He is greater than *them*."

"Well, I guess you're right again, sir." We both laughed. He must have experienced that foolishness in his day as well. But now, he had what sounded like joy in his laughter, appreciating the stars, the horses, and maybe even life.

It seemed I had made myself three new friends traveling down the glistening path of the park that evening. The coachman who guided the carriage, and those two beautiful, majestic horses. I needed that more than anything. A break, some space, and time to disconnect from the world. Some time to admire the sky and appreciate the stars. Some time to just live in the moment—some time just to feel.

Oh, and then I remembered it. It came to me in a whim, the rest of my father's poem.

"For what good is a man, nestled in mindless greed,
Pursuant to the world's mindless needs.
The treasure he gained, has all gone in vain,
diminished in value, the collector proclaimed.
Because it's all in the leaves, that dance in the trees,
blowing over the waters that romanced the seas.
Woe is a man who does not partake in these,
woe is the man, who's never felt the breeze."

CHAPTER

22

Emptying my Thoughts

THE RIDE through the park gave me time to reflect on how far I'd come and how fast my life was changing. How strong I really was, even if I didn't notice it at the time. I was glad I stood up for myself earlier at that press conference, even if things didn't go my way.

As the walkway began to run out, we found ourselves on the city streets again, heading toward my hotel just a few blocks away.

The clicking of the horses' hooves and the sound of people's voices aroused me from my thoughts. We trotted up to the main driveway of the Hotel. Looking in through the large window, I glimpsed the lights of a party going on at the hotel bar.

Paying the driver, and adding a tip, I grabbed my stuff, jumped from the carriage, and waved goodbye. He nodded at me with a smile as other potential passengers awaited him.

The doorman held the door open for me as I ran up the steps. "Your friends are waiting for you at the bar," he said.

"Friends?" I couldn't figure out who it could be. I didn't have any friends in the hotel, and I certainly didn't think the likes of Godfrey would be coming over for drinks.

When I walked into the bar, three familiar faces greeted me— Earl, Charlie, and Sam, the traveling salesmen, sitting at their usual places.

Of course, I thought, with a roll of my eyes. I should've guessed it would be these crazy guys. Still, they didn't seem to have noticed me yet.

"Did you guys see the news this morning?" Earl asked, slamming down his drink. "Some scientists are saying they found Noah's Ark. Can you believe it?"

Overhearing what Earl said, I slid onto a barstool alongside the men and startled them right out of their seat.

"Hi guys, what was that you said about the news?"

Earl flinched as he turned to me, nudging Charlie in the side.

"Hey guys, look, it's Clara."

"It's good to see you again," Charlie said, "It's been a while. We were busy drinking to your health."

"Oh, your drinking to my health, yeah, right." I laughed, draping my coat over the back of my chair. "There's nothing like a good excuse to toss one back, right, guys?"

"It's funny you say that," Sam said. "I was just telling Earl here that the only way to better health and a happier life is for him to stop drinking from the well like a poor man and buy himself a quality shot of whiskey!"

"Amen to that!" Charlie laughed.

"Hey, leave him alone," I said half-jokingly. "It's nothing a little exercise won't fix, right, Earl?"

He chuckled at my advice as he took the last of his drink.

"Exercise, did you say, exercise?"

"Yes. Exercise. What are you laughing about, it's the way to better health!"

Earl, as lighthearted as he was, always had a funny joke to answer with.

"Listen, baby girl, I get enough exercise running off at the mouth, flying off the handle, and jumping to conclusions. The last thing a guy like me needs is more exercise!"

They all burst out in laughter, as well did I. Earl shook his head, "You're wrong, Clara. Take Sam here, for instance," he said, slapping Sam around the shoulders. "Yeah, Sam spends his money on top dollar drinks, but what he really needs to buy is a new life and a new attitude!"

"Yeah, and some new shoes too!" Charlie laughed, glancing down at Sam's worn out loafers.

Raising his glass, Charlie gave a toast. "To my best friend Sam, a man whose sole needs changing!" A collective groan ran through the group as Charlie bowed in an exaggerated fashion. "Sole. Get it, s-o-l-e!" Slapping himself on the thigh, he laughed again.

The whole group had been busy drinking and joking and toasting before I noticed it was way past midnight.

"Good grief, it's gotten so late. I have to go, guys."

"Good night, Clara," they said in sloppy unison, heads moving up and down like apples in a bobbing bin.

Before heading up to my room, I went to the doorman and handed him a tip.

"Thanks for pointing me in the right direction when I came in," I said.

He pocketed the bills with a wink and wished me a good night.

There was a small sandwich shop on the other side of the lobby, so I stopped in to grab myself a midnight snack.

The news was on, broadcasting more scenes of wars and famine throughout the world.

"Give me a Turkey and Swiss," I told the cashier as I searched my coat pockets for more cash.

While I waited, I overheard her and one of the servers talking about how beautiful the flowers were. Apparently, they had been delivered earlier that day.

"Someone must be getting married," the cashier speculated as she handed me my sandwich.

"Lucky girl," I gave her the cash.

"Yep. Hopefully, one day, it'll be me," she said with a quirky smile.

Waving goodbye, I headed toward the elevator and took the ride up. Unwrapping my sandwich, I couldn't wait to take the first bite as I kicked the shoes off my tired feet. Ah, a Turkey and Swiss, Chicago style, how I missed the way my life used to be.

The hallways were dim and silent when the elevator doors slid open. I took a big bite and sprawled down the hallway to my room. Approaching the door, I nearly stepped on some rose petals that had fallen on my doormat. *Wow, they must have been delivering those flowers to someone on my floor,* I thought. But when I opened my room door, I noticed those weren't the only ones. Yellow roses adorned my whole room, scattered throughout, filling the room with a lovely scent. By my count, there were seven dozen of them.

So pleasantly surprised, I stood there trying to figure out who the admirer was. Who were they from, the university? Maybe my father's old friend, Dr. Harold. I couldn't believe he would be so generous, as if he hadn't been supportive enough.

There was a small envelope oddly propped on the nightstand beside one of the bouquets. I recognized the handwriting on the cover, even though it was only a one-word inscription, "Congratulations." My stomach churned over the gesture, as I felt it had been long forgotten. I tossed my sandwich in the trash, along with the appetite I thought I had.

Picking up the bouquet, I sat on the floor alongside the bed, grabbing the envelope and noticing there was a card inside. I sat back for a moment before reading it, holding onto those flowers, wondering what I had been doing with my life over the past four years. I knew I had made some difficult choices, some of them not so good for me, but I wasn't ready to resolve all of my issues, considering I had so many other things to do.

As beautiful as the flowers were, I couldn't linger on it anymore. I opened the envelope and took the card out as a strange dread settled in the pit of my stomach. *"I miss you,"* it read in bold letters.

Taking a deep breath, I tried to settle my nerves and calm my rushing heart as the sentiment of those words were about to open a flood gate of emotions inside me.

Maybe a shower will help, I thought, as I got up off the floor. It had gotten late, and I couldn't wait to feel the sensation of hot water hitting my skin, rinsing away the long day I'd gone through. Looking around the room, I thought to put on some soft music, as the flowers had already set a cozy and comfortable mood.

The guys at the bar and their crazy jokes made me chuckle again as I turned the shower on. Earl's words from earlier echoed through my mind as I thought of him teasing Sam. "A new life and a new attitude." Yet even as things changed, some parts of my past refused to let me go.

My thoughts faded into the background as the water heated up, and I stepped in. I thought I had made up my mind that I was dead set on never going back. I had forced myself to keep looking forward, but my heart clearly never got the message.

The towel dropped out of my hand as I leaned against the shower wall, torn between my two realities. I don't know why, but I realized that I had been relating everything in my present to the loss and heartache of my past. I had needed the help I had gotten from that clinic regardless of what the reporters had to say.

After a few minutes, I turned off the water and climbed out. The scent of flowers deepened as I walked out and into my cool bedroom again. So struck by the aroma, I plucked off a few handfuls of petals and pulled back the bedcover. Some fell around me, but most, I held in my hands against my chest.

Tossing the petals in the air, I grabbed my pillows and watched as they all settled around me. Getting in bed and making myself comfortable, I relaxed as the soft music eased my mind and helped me to think clearer. Looking forward was not enough for me anymore but moving forward would be a real step. I loved the yellow roses and what they did to the air, the love and friendship they represented.

It had been a long time, but if I wanted that new life, that new start, I had to do something I hadn't done. Looking over at the nightstand and reading the card once more, as the sentiment of it wouldn't let me go, I picked up the telephone and dialed a number I was well acquainted with. I could feel my heart racing with every ring until there was silence. I managed to say *hello*, then gently placed the phone back on the hook.

23

Writing on the Wall

I LAY THERE in bed for a moment, staring at the phone, wondering if I had done the right thing. There was a time and place for everything, and I had hoped my call wasn't too late. Flicking off the nightstand lamp, and with soft music playing, I retired for the night. The fragrance of the flowers, along with the music, created a tranquil setting as I drifted off to sleep.

The days and weeks crept by at an obnoxious pace, leaving me with more time on my hands than needed. Anxious to fill the void, I decided to take that break in my life and work down at the shelter, serving along with Ms. Jenkins. Helping others meant helping myself, and not once did I feel the urge to visit the hospital again.

Sightseeing was also on the list, as it had been a long time since I had been back in Chicago. Like a tourist, I enjoyed the bike rides through the city, paddle boating down the river, and the outings at parks Joshua and I used to play at. It was all so bittersweet, as I tossed a Frisbee around with kids whose parents looked worn-out from all the fun they were having.

I visited the Christian Institute, studying in its vast and expansive libraries. Those rooms held an extensive collection of books, ancient maps, scribes, and artifacts so exquisite they were placed behind security glass with guards who held the doors.

The soaring marble walls, the mural paintings, the sprawling hallways leading to classrooms in every direction. Yet, they all intersected underneath an enormous rotunda, anchored with three huge granite tablets hanging from its ceilings down into the center of the room. Inscribed on them were the names of the founders. The first one read, "The Honorable, Dr. Clarence Long," the second, "The Honorable, Dr. Robert G. Abbott," and yes, last but not least, "The Honorable, Dr. Michael P. Godfrey." The tablets not only commemorated their names but also memorialized their accolades and life stories. It was how I got to learn more about this Dr. Michael Princeton Godfrey with whom I had become friends with.

I found a way to pass the time, most of all, by filling those days with work that I enjoyed, and with people who were healthy for me. After all, faith without work was dead, and as Ms. Jenkins said before, I wanted to live.

On a crisp Monday morning, and after weeks of waiting, the day had arrived. The Baines Institute had qualified the outcome of its findings and was ready to announce their conclusion. I was in the lobby that morning having a cup of coffee and reading over text messages I'd received from the team, notifying me. All except Mike would be flying in to hear the results.

I also received an email from Dr. Langley—he and his team had finished the decoding of the hieroglyphics and had sent their translations along with a summary back to me.

After six and a half weeks of waiting, our hard work and efforts would be approved.

I couldn't wait for the news. I felt like that spider on the wall at the B&B back in Arizona, repairing her web and re-building her life, and now, so was I. The smell of warm bagels caught my attention for a moment as a light breakfast sounded good. A little cream cheese, a fresh cup of coffee, and a comfortable chair were all I needed to get back to work.

I found a seat in a quiet corner of the lobby and started downloading the summary to my phone. I gave Godfrey a call to go over it with him, but my call went to voicemail each time I tried. He had arrived at the press conference earlier and turned off his phone. Even more reason for me to get there and talk to him in person. After reading over the summation, the alarm on my phone went off, notifying me the event would start in a couple of hours, and it was time for me to get going.

Just as the thought occurred to me, the doorman entered the lobby, calling my name.

"Ms. Hamilton," he greeted me, "Your ride awaits."

"Perfect timing," I said, as I had been waiting for over an hour and was now thrilled my transportation to the university had made it.

Godfrey emailed me just as I was leaving. It was information about the portion of the ark we had tested.

"We've received the Ark back from Baines, and we here at the Christian Institute have cut the big chunk into four remarkable sections and placed them for view. You will be pleasantly surprised. Yours truly, Godfrey."

"Perfect," I messaged back, as I was elated to see the artifact again. To stand in the presence of an unquestionable relic and a monument to a man's tireless efforts in being obedient to God. The world had deliberated and debated over the Ark for weeks, yet on that day, all the world's questions, along with its doubts, would be put to rest.

I headed out the hotel door and jumped in the waiting SUV, buckling in, and making myself comfortable as we hit the expressway fast.

The day couldn't have come soon enough. There were no more questions to ask, not even to me.

After about a forty-five-minute ride, we exited Technology Avenue and continued on the frontage road for about a mile before approaching a stop sign. We made a right turn and cruised Henry Hamilton Lane, a street named after my father for the scientific contributions he had made to the college.

Rows of flags embroidered with the university's mascot lined the streets as the breeze swept over them. It was cool that day, yet sunlight burnished off the hoods of cars, beaming its rays on the faces of the attendants directing the traffic that backed up.

We maneuvered around the bumper to bumper lines and turned down a long winding driveway that cut through the perfectly manicured grounds, leading us to the back doors of the assembly hall. We came to a stop under the atrium, and one of the parking attendants opened the back door where I was sitting and stuck his head in.

"Are you Dr. Hamilton?" he asked, fostering one of the biggest smiles I'd seen.

"Yes, sir, that's me." I flashed a huge smile back at him.

"Great. Right, this way."

I grabbed my sunglasses, snatched up my things, and hopped out of the SUV, prepared to start the day.

Entering the building, I noticed the hallway was littered with students, as classes had let out.

The attendant pointed me toward the entrance of a prevailing oval-shaped hall, with the appearance of a cathedral on the inside and large arched glass doors that invitingly swung open. I stood in the doorway for a minute, craning my neck to see who was in there.

Noting the name tags of everyone in the room, I saw a disproportionate number of Christian bloggers, each tapping away at their iPads and recording their notes.

"A turning point in history," one of them murmured under his breath.

The words of optimism were being circled all over the world as bloggers reported on the events of the day.

National news teams arrived at the scene as well. Some seemed to be arguing, gesturing at the pieces, along with skeptical looks on their faces. But most saddled their chairs, ball caps turned to the back, snapping pictures of our discovery that was now perched on pedestals for full display.

I tiptoed across the marbled floor, hoping not to be seen as I was amongst the last to have entered the room. I strolled to the back of the hall where the equipment men were setting up, hoisting their cameras on tripods, locking them in.

Pam and Sue caught a glimpse of me sneaking in, and they turned and waved, snickering and grinning, catching the attention of everyone sitting behind them. Godfrey tipped his hat, giving me the celebratory wink of the eye, as Chuy and Terry turned with two thumbs-up, fist-bumping, and high-fiving one another.

The only person missing was Mike, who was still recovering. Not seeing him with the others sent a pain through my heart.

I leaned against a cold granite column, one of many that scaled the room, watching other faculty members and grad students file in.

At 10:05, an announcer from the Baines Institute called the conference to order. "Ladies and gentlemen, please welcome the honorable, the astute, Professor Benjamin Baines of the Baines Institute."

A roar of clapping hands filled the room as a short, pudgy gentleman, whom I presumed to be Professor Baines, followed by four men dressed in lab coats, all walked out on stage, glancing around before taking their seat.

"Ladies and gentlemen, I want to thank you all for coming."

Wow, I could tell by the accent the professor was British.

"It is my honor to be here with you, and I will not keep you long."

What? He won't be keeping us long. That was kind of disturbing to me—didn't he realize this was one of the most incredible finds the world had ever seen?

"First, I want to say that even though we've assembled the top experts in the world, it was still a long and arduous analysis. Believe me, we left no stone unturned, we took every painful measure we could take."

Painful measures? I thought as my eyes narrowed. Now, what does he mean by that?

"We have tested and retested again."

Wait a minute. Where's he going with this?

"We are sorry to inform you…"

Oh, my God, no.

"…these are not the remains of *Noah's Ark*."

You've got to be kidding me.

The room erupted into an uproar, as no one could believe the announcement Baines made.

I wrapped my arm around the column to steady myself as the shock of what he said made my knees buckle.

Terry couldn't contain his shock. "That's bull!" he yelled. "Have you lost your mind?"

The dazed look on Pam and Sue's face said it all as they scrambled between aisles, rushing to pull Terry down.

One reporter raised his hand, calling out his question. "Are you telling us this has all been for nothing?"

Baines looked over and said, "We at the Baines Institute believe that by learning from our past, humans have the power to take charge of their future. We took our time to study the artifact through comparisons of the materials to older artifacts and the most advanced methods of carbon dating. From what we can tell, as the dating precedes the Bible's story, it seems to be an ancient shelter, but no evidence points to it being the biblical artifact. It is not what you all wished it to be."

Godfrey and Chuy didn't move, their hands curled into fists, disappointment settling over their faces in slow motion. My head spun. It couldn't be. It just couldn't.

Dr. Baines's pretentious eyes glanced at our team with pity, but not any real empathy.

"I'm sorry, Dr. Godfrey, old chap. I wish things had gone a tad differently."

The sound of wingtip shoes scuffled across the floors as I heard bloggers leave the room in an attempt to retract their prior statements.

I lurched from the shadows of the hall, storming down the aisle, steaming at what I clearly thought was a disconnect from the truth. Dr. Baines turned to me as the clicking of my heels had drawn his attention.

"Excuse me, sir, my name is Dr. Clara Hamilton."

"Yes, I know who you are." He cocked his head back.

"Then, if you know that, sir, you also know I would have a few questions."

"I welcome your queries, Dr. Hamilton. What are your questions?"

"I respect your expertise a great deal, sir, but you do agree this is an ancient treasure. Is this correct?"

"It is." Baines's voice boomed over the microphone.

"The artifact was designed with architecture we've never seen before, right?"

Baines shifted, frowning. "To be frank, I am not sure if I'm following your questions correctly here, Dr. Hamilton. What are you suggesting?"

"You identified it as an ancient shelter, yes?"

"I did."

"But the artifact in question was found with over two thousand hieroglyphics written on its walls, sir. What was the story the hieroglyphics told? Surely this was pertinent to the results of your test."

My foot nervously tapped the floor. The whole auditorium seemed to hold its breath, awaiting an answer. After a brief pause, Baines met my gaze again.

"It appeared to be a story... of redemption," he seethed.

People raised their voices again, questions coming in from every side.

"Who wrote this story of redemption, sir?" I asked. "Did the author write for the people in that shelter, or was it written as a message to the world?"

The crowd exploded again.

Dr. Baines put his hands up. "Everyone, please calm yourselves, calm yourselves."

"Dr. Baines," I said, making sure my voice rose above the chatter. "Maybe, it's the original story. Where Moses got the story from! Maybe it was written and handed down thousands of years before anyone ever called themselves Hebrew. I mean, wouldn't you agree, for it to tell a tale like that, that there might be something sacred about this vessel?"

The frown on Baines's face turned into a full-on scowl. "Dr. Hamilton, I must say I question your professionalism. Turning this argument into a battle of faith versus reality is hardly something a reputable scientist would do. There is no argument here. I'm sorry, but science has spoken, and it disproves your so-called faith."

"Faith is also real."

"How do you know that Dr. Hamilton?" he asked, looking at me with a wary expression.

"Look around you. These sections were made from faith. Can't you see it?"

The crowd shuffled in their seats, twisting around to get a better look at the four samples of the artifact towering behind them in the room. Dr. Baines did not move.

"Faith, Dr. Hamilton?"

"Yes, Dr. Baines. Faith."

"Indeed, faith." He leaned back in his chair. "A neurological deception of the mind. Well, unfortunately, I can't see faith, Dr. Hamilton." Oh wow, he conceded. "But regrettably—neither can you."

"Wait a minute!"

"I'm sorry, Dr. Hamilton, but those thoughts are my last remarks on the subject. This conversation is closed. Good day."

He tipped his hat as my jaw felt like it had hit the floor. He then turned and headed for the door out of that crowded room before anyone could react. The reporters snapped back to themselves soon enough, chasing after him.

In an instant, the mood of the room had changed as the chatter of the crowd drifted out into the hallway. The nervousness in my foot faded, and the tapping—well, it was gone.

Wow, after all we had been through, I thought, shaking my head, and staring at what Baines called a shelter. I couldn't believe what I was going through. Yet the implication of his conclusion was true. It was a shelter. That would take determination and patience to prepare it for the unseen trial it and those aboard would face.

Funny how you notice the smallest of things, especially when you're alone. Particularly when things don't go your way. But like that spider back at the B&B, that had built her web in a higher place, I was also determined to build mine.

CHAPTER

24

Don't Blow It

"DOCTOR, HOW do you feel about their conclusion? You can't be happy with how this turned out?" I heard a reporter ask Godfrey as I walked out into the hallway.

"Of course not, but theirs is not the last word on the subject. We will work further, you can be certain about that. No stone left unturned."

I watched Godfrey handle every question thrown at him from reporters beautifully, as he often did, with a calm and cool manner, always coming off with a quiet but charming confidence. After answering a few more questions, he escaped the crowd, leaving them to draw their own conclusions about the events of the day. The team was upset as if no one appreciated the fight I had put up.

"What in the world was that about, Clara?" Pam asked, sneering.

"I will not let him demean everything we worked for. I had to stand up for us."

She took a deep breath to calm herself, words remaining harsh as ever.

"Have you lost your mind? You're a scientist. I understand your frustration but don't forget where you come from. Be rational!"

"Rational? I don't need you or anyone else to tell me where I came from, or to be rational. That man is wrong, and you know it."

"Clara, don't be stubborn. He said it was an ancient shelter, didn't he? And just look at the architecture. Let's take this as a credit to our careers. At least we can say we found something. We should all be walking out of here with our heads held high."

Sue interrupted, wrenching her face as she glanced at both of us. "I think you should listen to Pam on this one. She might be right. We really have to be rational about this."

I was ready to walk away, but I just couldn't let it go. I turned to her again. "Sue, make up your mind. You're wearing me out with this back and forth. Are you with me or not?"

"Oh, come on, Clara. I just don't want this to turn into a fight or ruin us again, we're all friends, okay? And don't get me wrong, I wanted this to be the ark as well. But who knows? Maybe Baines is right. It could just as well be some petrified thing that ancient people built for shelter."

"My point exactly, Sue. An old petrified thing ancient people built for shelter—from a flood."

"Clara, what are you trying to prove?" Pam tossed her hands out around her. "That there's a God out there? You weren't even a believer."

"Don't you get it? This could be a breakthrough for exactly that. He might be out there, and if He is… that's all we need to know."

"Oh no! Don't you try to bring us into that mess. You're on your own with this one. Maybe you found God—and that's all *you* need to know."

"Chill out, guys."

"No, Sue. Baines is the authority, Clara, and it makes sense that we listen to him."

"You've never wondered why we're here, Pam? Is this not important to you? Even before this all began, I'd considered that. Hadn't everyone?"

"Of course, Clara. Everyone has, it's the human experience. But even with all that, you can't truly see God!"

"Knock it off, you guys," Terry said, coming over and hugging me around the shoulders. "Clara, our careers are important, but who cares about that now. They all think we're a bunch of bums anyway. But you are a fighter. That's why we all love you. Don't stop fighting. If we prove this is Noah's Ark, we might also prove there is something out there bigger than us. Who remembered the hieroglyphics? Hell, I forgot all about them."

"Thank you," I said.

"Clara, my bet is on you." Terry blew over his fist, giving it a quick shake. Opening his arms out, he laid back and said, "I'm rolling my dice on you."

"Okay, Clara," Pam said. "I was trying to tell you to be rational. But go ahead, listen to Terry and make a fool of yourself again."

At that point, Chuy joined us, unaware of our discussion.

"You guys ready to go?" he asked. "I just pulled the car around."

"Oh, Chuy, have you seen Godfrey? I need to talk to him."

His head jerked to the side. "I just saw him walk outside, that way."

I strolled out the back doors of the lobby to look for him. He was standing off in the distance near one of the many sprawling oak trees covering the campus with his eyes closed, head tilted back, allowing the warmth from the sun to spill over him. I took a slow stride over the green grass and crossed the campus grounds, not knowing what to say or where we would go from there.

The oak tree cast its shadow over the lawn as I ambled under its shade, hoping not to disturb Godfrey before he finished. But he must have heard the leaves crushing under my feet, as he opened his eyes and gazed at me, giving me a soft smile.

"Shake the hands of an honest man," he said, reaching out to me.

That time, I brushed his hand away and wrapped my deflated arms around him.

"And you would have hugged a good man, indeed," I told him, putting my twist on the old phrase.

Pulling me up, he looked into my eyes.

"I can tell you're worried."

"Oh really, was it my sparkling look of confidence that gave it away?"

"Clara, what will be, will be."

"I know, Godfrey, but we can't allow Baines to destroy everything."

"Baines is very well-respected in his field. We won't be able to change his mind. But I've been thinking, I don't know, what if we..."

"If we what?" I asked, scrutinizing his pondering gaze.

"I'm not sure, but I've got a thought... I need to go back to the Christian Institute and make some phone calls, but trust me, I will not let Baines bury this. Let's meet later this evening."

"Sure, we can meet at Malley's Pub, around six this evening. It's two miles from the hotel."

He gave me a thumbs-up and abruptly paced off toward the car Chuy had pulled around. I walked back over to the SUV, climbed in, and we drove back to my hotel.

It had been a long day, and my body ached, but I couldn't call it a day yet. Instead, I took a quick halt in the hotel's lobby, distracting myself from my exhausting thoughts with the soothing aroma of warm tea. I remembered the fire in Godfrey's eyes when he said he would not let Baines bury it, and I, for one, hoped he wouldn't.

By now, evening had set in, leaving the sunlit skies that launched the day behind.

It felt cozy for a moment, stretching my legs out on the cushioned couch while facing the crackling fireplace in the hotel's lobby, I wished I could hole up there for some time more, but I had a commitment to fulfill—Godfrey would be waiting for me at the pub. I didn't feel like driving, so I hustled my phone out to call an Uber, and in a jiffy, the driver arrived. Soon, I stood up, unfurled my sleeves, and was back on the road. The day would not end anytime soon.

We zig-zagged our way through the heavy traffic until it all slowed to a halt. Two blocks from the pub, I decided to walk the rest of the way. I didn't want to be late.

Hurrying along the dimly lit sidewalk, I dodged other pedestrians and spotted the old Irish pub. It was hard not to with its neon sign flashing against the packed streets.

I was about to walk in when I saw someone precariously standing at the entrance. My mood soured even further when I noticed who it was. Of all the people, it had to be Peter Prestwick. Great. Simply great.

There he was, standing with those eager eyes, always looking for an opportunity to spice up the day. Before I could consider my next step, I heard him calling out my name.

"Hey there, Clara. Thought you were going the sober and righteous path. What are you doing at a place like this?"

"What do you want now, Peter, and why are you here?" I asked, feeling the life draining from my face.

"I saw the argument between you and Dr. Baines there," he continued. "The guy said your search was a waste of time, didn't he? Must be awful to have someone question your hard work or deem something that you believe in as a futile effort."

"Sure. Can you leave me alone now?" I said, trying to make my way around him.

Yet curiously, he asked, "Have you been watching the news lately? There have been some unbelievable pictures coming from those mountains in Iran, pretty incredible. Just thought you might be interested."

"I know, Peter, I was there," I said, taking a step back. "Why would I need to watch the news to tell me about something that involved me?"

He smirked, "There's been a massive migration of people there. The reports are that they're traveling from all over the world. I think it's about 'that thing' you guys claim to have found." He did air quotes, although his expression sobered up quickly as he folded his arms. "Guess if Dr. Baines can't see faith, maybe he should just try turning on the television. It's all over the news out there."

"Why are you telling me this? I mean, what is this about?"

"I put your story in print, you know, about your daring attempt and the effect a revolutionary discovery like the one you claimed would have on us. For what it would mean to the world."

"Why now?" I asked again. This whole thing, it sounded a little out of character for him.

"I don't know if you remember my wife," he said. "But she always had a fondness for your work."

I watched him as he turned away. The emotion shifted on his face as he spoke about her in the past tense.

"I know Dr. Baines has his opinion," he continued, "but I also heard that Godfrey guy say that theirs wasn't the last opinion on the subject. Seeing that massive migration of people got me to thinking, maybe... just maybe... you got yourself a second chance here. Those people didn't walk all that way for nothing, Dr. Hamilton. Don't blow it."

"I hope not to," I said, yet I couldn't recall his wife, nor anyone named Prestwick apart from him.

"Hey, I gotta go," he said, seeming to have clued in on my thoughts. "Just remember that this isn't personal. I'm paid to bring the news, and that's what I'm about."

Just as Peter disappeared from my line of sight, Godfrey walked around the same shabby corner. Spotting me, he came right over, turning back to glance at Prestwick's retreating figure.

"Who was that guy just now?"

"The reporter who nailed me to the wall that day. You've forgotten already?"

"That guy again?" asked Godfrey, shaking his head. Reaching out, he pulled open the door to the pub. "How about that drink now?" he asked with a half-smile.

Once in the pub, I waved over to the server, getting her attention. "Vodka and orange juice, please," I said, pointing toward an empty table I spotted in the back. Godfrey followed suit, opting for a glass of merlot.

We seated ourselves at the table and the server made her way over, handing us napkins and an empty wine glass. After placing our orders, she tended to others while we waited, scanning the room, and making ourselves comfortable at the little round table I had picked out.

"Oh, look, the game is on," I said, turning to face the big screen above us.

"You seem to be very into the bar scene," Godfrey said.

"I'm not an alcoholic if that's what you're suggesting. I just hate monotony."

"...Doesn't drinking get monotonous?"

"Not if you know what you're doing," I told him.

"If you know what you're doing? Now, what does that mean?"

"Never mind, Godfrey." I smiled a bit, noticing the server was bringing us our cocktails.

"So, what's up with Dr. Benjamin Baines?" I asked, deciding to change the subject. "I heard he's from Cornell."

"You could say that. He was once the president, the one who awarded me my doctorate in astrophysics, in fact. But now he has formed his own research facility."

"So that's how you know him."

"Yes, that's how I know him. It's why I went back to the institute today, to find some information I needed, to make the calls I wanted to make, but I couldn't find anything. I'll have to look further."

"Oh, the institute. I studied there a few weeks ago, it's a treasure of information, isn't it?"

"Yeah, it is, just not what I needed."

The server interrupted us with our drinks.

"Thank you, ma'am," I told her as I continued to Godfrey, "You won't believe the conversation I just had with that reporter."

"I can see how annoyed you are with him."

"I'm more... aggravated with this whole mess. I mean, everyone thinks I'm crazy, trying to defend this as the real Ark. They think I'm trying to prove God's existence, but I just want to prove that our work wasn't in vain."

"You and I are not here as window dressings, Clara. We're here because the work we've done will bless someone."

"Well, that reporter told me about some mass migration, do you know anything about that?"

"We've heard about that as well, the institute is tracking information about it as we speak."

He was fast, but my questions continued. "Are there people out there, marveling over it?"

"Suffering is tough."

"Oh, no kidding! I, for one, know that. But do you think it's okay for us, I mean, for me to question God?"

"Okay? I believe He wants us to. But you have to be prepared for His answers and to trust them."

"Do you think it's okay to doubt Him?"

"Never," he answered without missing a beat.

"Okay, Godfrey, but this has been a rough day."

"I can't disagree with that but remember that everything happening in our lives is not void of God. You have told me a lot about your trials in life, but now what I'm trying to tell you is that your hardships are not without purpose, and that purpose will never be in vain."

"I hope you're right," I said, massaging my neck.

"Do you want to know why I asked Baines about the hieroglyphics?" I asked after a long, poignant pause.

"Yes. Why did you?"

"I sent the pictures to a lab owned by a friend of mine after we got back from Iran."

He looked up at me with surprise. "You knew the answer to the question before even asking Baines."

"Yep! The writing was on the wall," I winked. "I noticed you didn't look so happy when you heard Baines would do the testing. I took it upon myself to do my own research."

A smile spread over Godfrey's face as he fell back into his chair.

"See, Clara, you really are a breath of fresh air. This is why you're a Godsend."

"You might be right about that. Glad to be of service, sir. Cheers!"

We held up our glasses and clinked them, toasting the troubles of our day away.

"It's been interesting these past few months," I confessed. "Something I quite honestly didn't expect, Godfrey. But I hadn't felt that fighter in me for a long time. It's like I have a new sense of awareness. It's like being snapped out of a zombie state of mind."

"Sometimes, Clara, all you need to do is listen to that instinctive gut feeling we all have, pulling and tugging on us, trying to lead us in the right direction."

"Then, Godfrey, let me ask, what does your gut tell you—do you think we found an Ark?"

He turned to me, and without an ounce of joking on his face, he intuitively answered, "Not an ark—the ark."

The bar crowd erupted with cheers at the baseball game as the White Sox hit the game-winning home run. The festive crowd celebrated jubilantly, shouting, and laughing, clashing their mugs of beer together as if they had willed the flight of that ball, which landed in the right-field stands.

Godfrey and I had been talking for hours by that time, and after a few drinks and a couple of high-fives with the crowd, it was time to retire for the night.

He called the bartender over and paid the tab. "I want you to meet me later this week. I have something I need to tell you. You could say that I've gained a new awareness of sorts as well."

It was clear Godfrey had something on his mind. The unmistaken glint in his eyes after the press conference meant something, but I couldn't read him just yet. That was even more intriguing.

"We need to reconsider the facts. Dr. Baines doesn't carry much weight with me. He's been busy backing the Geno seed," Godfrey said as his phone rang. "But I would like to discuss our findings with you at a later time."

"Wait, what's a Geno seed?"

"I'll fill you in later," he said as his phone rang again. "Things aren't over by a long shot, but it's getting late. I have a phone call to take, the one I told you about earlier."

Grabbing his hat, he stood up and started his way out of the bar. I followed him, still full of questions, but when I caught up to him, he was already in the middle of the call, demanding a meeting with someone whose name I couldn't quite catch.

I struggled to read his lips, yet he covered his mouth, turned away, and got into a car that had just pulled up.

There was more to what Godfrey was telling me, and I was willing to wait and find out what it was.

CHAPTER

25

The World Was Changing

UNDER THE dark blue covering of the evening sky, I watched the glowing tail-lights of the vehicle carrying the most intriguing man I had ever met fade away into the shimmering downtown streets.

My mind was in a whirlwind, considering every possible scenario of what Godfrey and I could do as I questioned Baines' conclusion. I wondered what Godfrey's thoughts were for our next move, what he was plotting, and who he was on the phone with. Our conversation had been highjacked by the mysterious caller, leaving so much unsaid. I just couldn't fathom what was going on in his mind. Maybe he just wanted to be proven right.

I felt his passion was strong enough to supersede everyone else's doubts, including mine. The courage Godfrey so eloquently displayed to keep working and seeing this through had given me confidence.

My stomach began to growl just as I spotted a small pizza joint on the corner across the street. 'Luca's Best Chicago Pizza,' the flashing red sign read, making my mouth water. I couldn't resist the smell of fresh mozzarella cheese any longer, so I scurried across the street to pop in for a quick slice.

The bell on the door chimed as I walked into a world of tangy sauces, Italian spices, and savory pies coming out of the oven. I had landed in the right place as I knew I was about to satisfy my hunger. Without much ruckus, I waved for the attention of the short Italian man fiddling with the bills behind the counter.

"One slice of pepperoni pizza, please."

"One slice pepperoni!" he yelled back, grinning.

That was another great thing about locally run small pizzerias—smiling and inviting staff.

Looking around the restaurant, I noticed pictures on the wall of all the celebrities who had eaten there.

"Wow, you've got some history here. Your pizza must be legendary," I said, my stomach growling even louder at the anticipation of something worthwhile.

"Yes, ma'am," said the same kind-faced man from behind the counter. "We've had some of the greatest entertainers in the country walk through those doors. I couldn't be prouder of this place I've got here, it's my baby. You look like you're a woman on a journey. Are you here on business or vacation?"

"Business, although I guess you could say my business has been one crazy journey."

He smiled. "Sometimes, it can be that way. Where are you from?"

"Born in Utah, but raised in Chicago, right here in the Windy City."

"Ah, a Chicago girl."

"Through and through," I said.

"Well, welcome home," said the owner with a big smile on his face and a fresh slice of pizza in his hand.

I paid the man and walked out the door with my pizza. Right before the door closed behind me, the owner spoke up and told me that his brothers were playing jazz music down at the DoubleTree tonight.

"Oh, really? I'm staying there. I'll be sure to stop by and listen for a bit."

"I'm sure you'll enjoy it. Welcome back home."

I waved goodbye, walking out of the restaurant with a big bite of pizza in my mouth. *What a way to end the day*, I thought as the evening appeared to have quieted down. I decided to walk back to my hotel instead of hiring another rideshare, as I could use the time to think.

Everything I'd hoped for had turned against me—Dr. Baines, the results, and, of course, Pam's big mouth. I couldn't believe her. *"Maybe you found God, and that's all you need to know."* Her words recurred in my mind.

Maybe she was right for once. Sometimes people will try and hurt others, but down the road, it ends up helping them. Maybe I had found God, and that was all I needed to know.

Wrapping my scarf around my neck to combat the cold, I spotted the Hotel's sign. I scarfed down the last bite of pizza, relieved to be home. The concierge held the door for me, allowing the sound of music to stream out onto the sidewalk, reviving the night.

I was fueled with a small dose of excitement. The music was just what I needed as I remembered the pizzeria owner saying his brothers would be playing here at the hotel. I walked into the lobby and saw the lounge filled with salsa dancers. It surprised me at first, and I had to take a step back. I thought those three Italian guys would be playing some smooth jazz renditions, not salsa music. Feeling the hot flare of those Mambo horns made my mind want to dodge the mundane routine of going to my room to pour over my work for jamming out to the rhythms of some hot Caribbean music.

Charlie grabbed me by the hand and led the way as soon as I walked in.

"Come on, Clara, dance with me!" he said, showing off his dance moves.

I had no idea where he came from, but for an old guy, he was quick on his feet. Watching him dance, I decided it was about time my six weeks of salsa lessons paid off. Charlie and I danced the life back to a draining day.

We whipped up the dance floor all night until I finally got tired and told him I was going to the bar to order a drink, leaving him to find another willing partner. Which, for Charlie, wasn't going to be a problem, as he was quickly becoming the life of the party.

Brittany was working across the bar, and she motioned me to join her at the end.

"Why are you so far away from all the fun?" she asked. "Come and enjoy the party. Would you like your usual?"

"Yes, please. I need a nightcap to end this long, crazy day."

"You got it," Brittany responded. We chatted for a while as the loud music played. When she turned to tend to other customers, I realized it was getting late. I tossed back my drink, paid my tab, and bid everyone farewell. I was about to walk out when Charlie yelled, "Hey, Clara, it's happy people like you and me that keep this crazy world going 'round." Oh, the irony. I smiled.

"You're right. Happy people do!" Waving goodbye to him, I headed to my room.

Once there, I swiped my key card over the lock and sauntered in, feeling the torture of exhaustion in every cell of my body. Tossing my key card on the table, I welcomed the freedom from the strife of the day.

My bed was a mess, covered in history books and notes. I pushed them all aside, grabbed the remote, and threw myself down with a deep sigh, ready to watch a late-night show.

I got an alert from my phone and noticed that I'd received a lot of emails, but I didn't want to read any of them at the moment as I had heard enough for the day. But I did want to view those pictures of the Ark again.

Scrolling through the photos on my phone, I came across some pictures I had taken of Joshua. There he was, clear as day, his big startling blue eyes, bright red hair, that beautiful smile, just like me. I missed him and all the little moments we'd shared.

I wondered what my own mother would do in this situation. I hadn't thought about her much lately, but for some reason, she came across my mind. Would she just lie in bed alone like this, dwelling on her losses?

I wondered if she had ever prayed, and if so, what did she pray about? I tried to formulate my thoughts. What would my mother say if she tried to pray? Maybe she would say, *"Dear God, I know you don't know me, but I've heard of you. I've seen your picture on the wall without ever having talked to you. I don't know where you are or if you know that I'm here. But I pray to you from the bottom of my heart that if you're listening, please let me know that you're here because I miss my child. Amen."* I thought it would sound something like that.

I figured it was a good time to do some writing. I rolled over, grabbed my pen and notepad from the nightstand, and decided to unload my thoughts. I wondered, did God hear that prayer? I laughed as I thought that might be a ridiculous question. Yet, I hoped He had. But that's when it happened.

I'd only penned a few words when a voice from the television stopped me in my tracks—it was a report from a breaking news event.

"This is a BBN breaking news report! Good evening, viewers!" the reporter said, beaming with excitement.

"This is Christopher Elliott with BBN News, reporting from the remote mountains of Iran."

Oh, wow, that's where we were. I sat up in bed to listen.

"It has been nothing less than an electrifying morning here today. A local man by the name of Mr. Mahdi Fakir, with the help of his brothers, carried his paralyzed wife to what is now considered, holy grounds. Now, for those who don't know, this is what is believed to be the site of Noah's Ark."

Dropping my pen, I focused every ounce of my attention on the screen and the reporter as he gestured toward the relic behind him.

"The energy in the air here is simply stirring! It's quite difficult to describe, but if you've ever been to a World Series game when the last bat is on the line, and the batter hits a home run—that's exactly what it feels like here! Positively electrifying! The men carrying the paralyzed woman I mentioned earlier fought through the crowd, wrestled the hammock up the hill, set her down beside the vessel, and placed her hands against its side. Then, I witnessed—" the reporter grew emotional. "I witnessed a miracle with my own eyes. As I watched, I saw her flinch her legs. And then, her legs began to move. Within moments, the woman stood and began to walk for the first time in, what they tell me, thirty years. Her family began to shout and dance as she walked away from the Ark under her own power."

He paused, looking as if he were overcome with his emotions.

"But it doesn't end there. Before this woman left, she approached another sick man and helped him over to the Ark. When she pressed his hands against it, he regained his strength and his ability to speak again. Some people have walked hundreds of miles across the desert, brought by friends and loved ones, all hoping to find healing. They haven't been disappointed."

He tilted his head and continued thoughtfully, "It all started when a small child by the name of Tumar was healed from lifelong blindness after being drawn to touching the Ark. People have been flocking here from every corner of the earth. The Catholics are blessing the site, the Baptists are baptizing, and the sanctified are dancing and, as you can hear, shouting and praising the name of God. I asked them about their dance, and they say they are doing the dance of David from the Bible."

The reporter took another breath, then added, "It's a lot to take in, but worshipers from all faiths are here by the tens of thousands, every race, creed, and color, representing every kind of religious faction, from Allah to Jehovah to Jehovah gyro, and yes, some just call him Jesus. Jews, Muslims, and Christians, yes, they're all here together, praising what they call *a work of*

God. Governments and politicians are beginning to take notice as the power of the artifact has become a worldwide phenomenon. Diplomats and leaders all over the world are said to be having private meetings on what to do if, in fact, this is proven to be Noah's Ark. Who would have thought that all it would take is an event of this magnitude, an event like this one, along with two daring scientists, Dr. Michael Godfrey, and Dr. Clara Hamilton, pushing the envelope to bring the whole world together! Who would have thought! I'm Christopher Elliott, reporting from the remote mountains of Iran,

Now back to you."

I clasped my hands over my chest, barely able to breathe over what I'd just seen. Thousands of people, maybe even tens of thousands flooding the site.

I was sitting on my bed now, trying to regain my composure, as the astounded look on the news anchor's face was now surging within me. That was my name, our team!

I was struck by that footage onscreen of the huge sea of people in the valley where the fallen portion of the Ark stood. Trying to get a view of it, to touch it, to be near it, and they were not just religious authorities either, not at all. They looked to be an eclectic group of travelers, migrating all that way with nothing much more than what seemed like faith and all that had burdened them.

I couldn't help but be staggered by how many lives the relic had affected—it appeared to be taking on a life of its own.

It seemed almost unreal, but dare I be the one to ask—who's life had been so anguished, mind so tormented, that they would walk miles upon miles, thousands even, to stretch their tired hands out in faith and ask to be healed?

It humbled me, clearing my mind from the fog of problems I called my own as I watched the site of the Ark being rapidly transformed, becoming a place of glorification, prayer, and dare I say… healing. The Jews used it as a wailing wall, the Muslims stood around it in solemn prayer, and masses of followers bowed in unison in honor as the Catholic Church now affirmed the site of the vessel to be hallowed ground.

After all we had done—finding the Ark, bringing it back to the States—I had never even begun to imagine the relic could be a divine artifact that could also cure the sick.

It was an extraordinary sign of faith and had shown me that what we found was, without a doubt, the remains of what we'd so tirelessly searched for.

Tossing the pen and pad on the floor, I logged onto my computer and began searching the web for similar tales of miraculous healings. I read the story of Kirby Grayson, a man who had been given a less than five percent chance of surviving a horrific car accident. But the prayers of his family led to him recovering from a ten-day coma and subsequently walking out of the hospital, restored.

Then there was the story of little Annabel Beam, who had been diagnosed with an incurable digestive disorder. Shortly afterward, she fell thirty feet into the trunk of a tree. Not only did she survive, but her digestive condition was healed. She was quoted as saying that when she was in the tree, Jesus had been with her. These things seemed so unreal before…

On and on, from Gregg Kirk to Jody Osteen, among others, and now these people were saying that whatever impaired them had fallen away, and they too were healed. I had only heard rumors and stories about remarkable recoveries in the past but reading and now seeing these accounts made it clear it happened far more often than I'd assumed.

The phone rang as I surfed the internet for more evidence. The call was from Sue.

"Hi. You have to excuse me, my mind is spinning right now. Is everything okay with Mike?"

"Did you see the news?" she screamed.

"Yes, Sue, yes! You almost burst my eardrum with that one!"

"Clara, I have been up all-night drowning myself in coffee and watching the television—I can't believe it. There's been national and international news coverage of you and Godfrey and what we found!"

"Wait, take your time. Don't you remember what Baines said earlier today?"

"Clara! Open your eyes! They have an agenda of their own, I don't think we can trust anything they say. I've been reading blogger reports about those people walking all that way, some are even barefoot. I saw the pictures, their feet look like they had walked a million miles!"

"Sue! Do you really think this is real?"

"Heck yeah! It's why I said I've been up all night, jacked up on coffee and donuts."

"Are you crazy? You will drink yourself silly, put the coffee down and the donuts away and get some rest."

"After seven cups of coffee, Clara, how can I do that?"

"Go take a cold shower and slow down, we got to chill out!" I told her, but she persisted.

"A child was healed out there when we discovered the artifact. But I don't remember seeing any bolt of lightning, no angels coming from the sky, no one singing hallelujah, not that I recall. Do you remember any kind of healing happening?"

"… Sue, what's gotten into you? And yes, I remember. Godfrey and I talked about that earlier. He said he was working on it."

"You mean this happened back at the site?"

"Oh, yes! I remember a small boy had run through the field, screaming something like, 'I can see.' But I didn't think to write it down because I didn't know what to make of it."

"Well, I do. Just like those people, I think the artifact is divine—I don't think we can argue with the evidence."

"Maybe you're right, Sue, but I don't want us to get ahead of ourselves again, okay? I've been doing some research on faith healing, and apparently, it has happened more often than I thought. It seems that it could all be true."

"Clara, we got to find that kid. He's the nexus behind all this."

"You're right, but let me get in touch with Godfrey on this, Sue. We don't want to shoot ourselves in the foot with this one."

"What in the world are you talking about? The tide is changing, and it's rolling our way. This will be something we tell our grandchildren about, and our great-grandchildren too. This might just be the story of a lifetime!"

"I know, I'm not denying it," I said, now re-inspired. "Do you think we can track him down, though?" I asked.

"I don't know, Clara, but trust me, if he's to be found, I'll find him."

"Call me first when you get more information on his whereabouts, Sue, and I will speak with Godfrey about this."

"Don't worry, Clara, I have your back. Just think, we could have died in those mountains. Mike nearly lost his life."

"You won't hear any argument from me," I told her, "but get you some rest."

"Nope!" she said, with the sassiness of seven coffees in her. "I'm about to call Pam."

"Why?" I asked.

"Because, I've got seven cups of coffee in me, and she likes to talk more than you!" she laughed.

"Thanks, traitor!" I snorted as we ended our call.

What a rush. I thought as I powered my phone down, needing to regain my sanity. I didn't know whether to pinch myself or call Sue again just to check if we really did just have that conversation. I was as thrilled as she was with her liveliness, and, honestly, I couldn't stop laughing.

With no doctors, no hospital room to stay in, that child gained his sight, and now others were doing the same. They were there, living out the same faith Dr. Baines had so brashly mocked me of being blind to.

My mind whirled with possibilities and questions of how those people's journeys began. But like me, only they could answer that.

My fingers circled the screen of my iPhone as I almost dialed Godfrey's number, but stopped myself. It was late, and he was probably sleeping.

Yet, I wanted to let him know I had gotten the news of the events that were happening back at the site, and how I had talked to Sue about finding the child who was healed, how finding him might perk up our argument a bit, brighten the dialogue, or in his words, add to the conversation.

The news was all over it, specifically—a few young journalists and bloggers who had poured onto the site. Bolstering their careers with what they were witnessing, reporting about miracles in the middle of worshipers being showered with prayers, fixating their eyes on what might just be the story of a lifetime.

CHAPTER

26

I Apologize

I HAD WASTED enough breakfasts that I could have fed a
small village. Days had gone by, and I had not been able to
untie the knot of jitters in my stomach.

Every call I'd gotten from Sue was on how she hadn't had much
luck finding any information on the child, Tumar, but she would
keep trying. Even Godfrey was out of pocket, as the Institute
informed me he was in New York leading some delegation but that
he was delighted when he received my message. I wondered what
kind of delegation it was.

I had been out earlier that morning, jogging through the city
by the Lakefront Trail where I was enjoying the water.

After a while of waiting for Sue and Godfrey, exercise had
become my outlet, so I joined my former meditation group and
started to go for runs. It relaxed me but didn't keep my mind from
buzzing over the fact of what we found.

It was unlikely Baines would reexamine our findings, but if we
found the child and brought his story into the public eye, Baines
might buckle under pressure and reconsider his opinion.

I finished my run that day and made it back to the coffee shop near my hotel. I grabbed a cappuccino and a small sandwich, just to have something in my belly.

Still sipping my coffee, I pushed through the hotel doors. I was just about to head for my room when I heard the yap of a friendly voice.

"Hey there, Eagle Eyes!"

I couldn't believe it. When I turned around, standing there with a giant smile on his face was Mike.

"Mike!" I squealed, running over and throwing my arms around him.

"Ouch," he grimaced, reminding me of his injuries.

"Whoa, Clara, you're going to hurt him all over again. Not so tight!"

I looked over to find the source of that souring voice, and just as I guessed, it was Pam. She, along with Mike and Terry, had come to visit me.

"Hey, guys! How are you?" I asked.

"We missed you," Pam said, oddly hugging me. With a hint of hesitation, I hugged her back. *Weren't we on bad terms?* I thought to myself.

Putting his good arm around me, Mike kissed me on the forehead.

"I'm so happy for you," he said in a lighthearted tone.

"It was a group effort. I should be congratulating you instead. But don't tire yourself out, let's sit down."

We retreated to the courtyard just outside the lounge and pulled two tables together to make one big one. Then we talked, and I was the first one to speak.

"Has anyone heard from Sue?"

"Not lately," said Mike, "but a few days ago, she mentioned she was looking for information about that blind boy who regained his sight. I trust you've all seen the wild reports about the Ark. Reporters have been calling me all day long asking for interviews."

"It's all so unbelievable," Pam said. "Since the reports started flooding in, I've been getting job offers to go back and lecture at Texas Tech. I have to say, things aren't going nearly as bad as I imagined." Her tone sounded almost apologetic. I began to understand her sudden change in attitude.

Before I could say anything, my phone rang.

"It's Sue! Sorry, guys, I need to take this."

"Go right ahead, Clara," Mike said, "I'll order us drinks."

"Hey, Sue, where are you?" I asked.

"I just got back from the Iranian embassy. They got word that I was one of the researchers of the discovery, and they informed me there was a package for me to pick up. Well, in that package was a letter the child's father sent to you. Do you want to hear it?"

"Wait, what? Why did he write to me?"

"Just listen, Clara. This is important."

"Fine. Hold on a minute, Sue, the team is here with me. I'll put you on speaker."

After I set the phone up, Sue cleared her throat and began to read.

"I am only a simple man who sought out a simple life. I seek to do what is right but often do what is wrong. I don't know if it's because I cannot help myself, or if it's my lack of faith or the bitterness inside me that drove me away from the light. Every time I try to do right, I fail myself and God. But over the years, I have come to understand that jealousy is a monster that grows in the hearts of those who crave attention. Greed is the loathing of those who can't honor what they already have. But when given the power, I saw those men using their gluttony, robbing others of their dignity. I don't want to die as that kind of man.

I live in one of the most violent places in the world. Writing this letter to you puts my life and my family's lives at stake. But it's all worth it because your discovery might have saved us all. The Ark is a way out from the madness we live in. Police are prepared to persecute me for speaking out, the government has knocked at my door, striking fear in the hearts of my children and wife, but I don't regret anything. I want to help others without demanding anything in return. Such is the way of righteousness. To have the faith is to step out and try again, just for a chance to change.

Therefore, I write to you, Dr. Hamilton. My child was born with an illness that not even doctors could explain. I hated my life as a father until that day, a vision came to me: a woman would come here and heal my child, but I would not appreciate her. Blessed be God, for I have borne witness to my child's healing. Blessed be you, the woman in my vision, the one who came and saved my child.

You might be wondering who I am. I am Lucia Samah, the Iranian guard who arrested you, the same man who sought to punish you, and who hurt your arm. It was God who sent you as an angel into my life to help me change, yet I treated you so cruelly.

After a long day of work, I went home. When I opened the door, my wife was shaking in excitement as she came to me. Before I knew what to make of it, my child leaped into my arms and proclaimed that he could see. My dear child, Tumar. I could not believe it. But now I see just as clearly as he does.

So, as I sit here in my home, alone in my room, I write these words to you. I realize my selfishness made me not only hurtful but hateful. I promise you, Clara, I am learning. My life may be in jeopardy, but I humble myself before you so that I will not die with a hateful word spilled in the same sentence as my name. So, with this letter, on my behalf, and on behalf of those who, for whatever reason, chose not to, I apologize.

If I perish tomorrow, I hope to die uttering the words of my ancestors. Assalamualaikum.

Unto you peace.

Lucia Samah

My heart hammered in my chest as she finished reading the letter he had written to me. "Sue, what happened to him? How did you find him?"

"I didn't. His letter found me. Ten days ago, the Iranian government put him to death after learning about this letter. They claimed that he, writing to you, committed an act of treason."

She waited for me to speak, but my voice was stuck in my throat. I couldn't even breathe.

"Clara, are you still there?"

"Y-yes, I'm here," I stuttered, still stunned by the whole turn of events.

"So, I tried locating the child, but when his father was killed, his family fled and went into hiding. I have no clue where to find them. I've made some phone calls I need to follow up on, so you guys do me a favor, and please keep things under the radar. I don't want to put them in further danger."

"I can barely handle it. How could they be so cruel? Executing a man for sending a letter of apology?"

"Clara, we have to stay focused. Have you heard from Godfrey?"

"He's in New York with a delegation."

"All right," sighed Sue. "We have to do everything in our power to keep this child and his family safe and get them out of there. I know Godfrey can help. But, in the meantime, keep me in the loop, okay?"

"Will do, Sue. Goodbye."

Setting the phone aside, I glanced at my friends. They all looked worried and lost in thought.

"This is so out of bound," Mike said. "We need to go to the media. If we can blow the whistle on the government violating the civil rights of those people, we're obligated to do so."

I sighed. "They'll never respond to the issues of human rights—we are responsible for this. But don't do anything until I consult Godfrey. If anyone can fix things, it's him. I know he would do anything in his power to protect that child and his family."

"You're right." Mike said, "I trust Godfrey. By the way, we're going to need more than this child to prove this is Noah's Ark, although finding the child would be a nice start..."

"I know, and I think I have an idea about how we should do that as well, but I have to sell Godfrey on it first."

Mike stood, wincing, "We need to get going, but call me when you talk to Godfrey."

"I will, and I'll inform him about the letter."

We all stood and hugged goodbye, plastering smiles on our faces because, after all, we were happy to see each other, despite the devastating news about the child's father.

After the team left, I called Godfrey, but there was no answer. Pacing in and out of the lobby, I thought about accepting Baines' results so that maybe it would put an end to the migration. But who was I to crumble under the frustration after knowing a man was killed doing what he believed was the right thing to do. No, that wasn't a viable solution. I had another idea, something Dr. Langley could help us with, but I needed to talk to Godfrey first.

I found a nearby trashcan and dumped my now cold cappuccino and tried phoning again, still with no response. I contacted the Institute and spoke with one of Godfrey's assistants, which led to some good news. Godfrey had made it back, yet he had retired at his parsonage just outside of Rosemont, and the phone reception might be bad out there.

She told me I should try him tomorrow, but I had been trying long enough, and time was of the essence. I just couldn't wait any longer. Given the circumstances, I felt we should protect that child as well as close the door of speculation over what we had unearthed in those mountains. I felt the victory and the gratitude written from that man's heart, the tears he must have shed to God to heal his child, everything.

Given the failures of my own life, how horrible I would feel if I turned back now. His prayers had not gone in vain, nor will the prayers and aspirations of the people who are out there now. I had an idea to run by Godfrey, and although it felt a little reckless, I could only hope that he'd go for it.

27

Who Do You Believe In?

I TRIED CALLING Godfrey several times, but nothing went through. Time and time again, the phone rang, but it just kept going to voicemail.

It had gotten late, and the chipper sound of his voicemail started to grate on my nerves. Ending the call, I began to flip through an address book from the Institute and found the address of the parsonage. Maybe I'd be able to catch him there.

Walking out of the hotel, I got into my rental car and headed toward Godfrey's remote home. The busy streets of Chicago began to fade away, and all I had left was the highway. As I drove, I thought about what an important find Tumar would be to me and how proving this was the Ark was of the highest priority. I needed to tell Godfrey about the letter of apology and how it made my efforts feel worthwhile again. Although it wasn't about me, I needed this.

I pulled off the highway onto a long, winding road hugging the shoreline of a beautiful, moonlit lake. Entering the neighborhood, I drove down the street onto the narrow driveway of the parsonage.

I didn't want to disturb his sleep, but even more than that, I didn't want to go back empty-handed. I just couldn't, not without the answers to as least some of the questions I had.

Balling my hand into a fist, I banged on his door, loud enough to rouse anyone inside. I winced at the noise I was making but pounded again, calling out his name. Finally, the door swung open. Godfrey stood there, thankfully not in his pajamas.

"Why are you banging on my door?" he asked, eyes narrowed.

"I'm sorry, Doctor. You didn't answer my calls."

"I didn't get them."

I winced. "I'm sorry. Were you sleeping?"

"If I was, I'm not anymore." Godfrey opened the screen door. "Come on in."

I obliged, following him into the warm, quaint home. The fireplace heated the floor, casting warmth over my feet. A small lamp in the corner shone dimly within the small, homely room. A chair was pulled back from the table where a child's puzzle lay and a lit cigar smoldered. Seeing it brought back those nights when my had father kicked back in his chair, smoking his cigar, unwinding. I wondered if Godfrey had been relaxing as well, putting together that puzzle?

Handing Godfrey my coat, I looked around the dark room. An eclectic mix of pictures adorned the walls.

"Your lifestyle is so modest," I said, half-jokingly.

"Meager are my means. What's reclusive to some could be solitude for others," he responded. "Have a seat."

The wooden floor creaked as I walked over to the table Godfrey had been working at and sat amidst the coziness of the room. If only I had once had a warm home like this to come back to. Godfrey seemed deep in thought as he sat at the table, taking the next piece of the puzzle in his hand. He was building an Ark.

My admiration for the pictures consumed me, so when he spoke, he startled me a bit, catching me off-guard.

"Clara."

"Oh! Dr. Godfrey, I'm sorry, I guess my appreciation of your artwork captured my attention. But, may I ask, what do they mean?"

"Which one?" he asked, clicking a puzzle piece into place.

"That one… the one to the left, what does that one mean?"

He sat there, studying his puzzle, he never looked up, yet he answered, "That's a picture of the moment man learned to fly."

Oh, is that what that is? I thought as he continued working on the puzzle he had started.

Just as I was about to ask him another question about the artwork, he interrupted me, "Clara, the theory of aerodynamics is just that, a theory, you think?"

"Well, yes, that's true."

He continued, "Although thousands of people watch airplanes fly through the sky every day, we as scientists haven't figured out with certainty, how."

"Well, sounds interesting," I said, watching him click the next piece of his puzzle into place.

"It's the same for buoyancy—just a theory. Thousands of people see ships that are hundreds or thousands of tons, just floating on the waves. But, somehow, a man weighing just two hundred pounds will eventually sink. And we as scientists can't explain why with any sense of certainty"

"Yeah," I agreed. "Unless something else can come along and prove it wrong, it's our working model for the truth. But what's wrong with that?"

He didn't answer but continued with the puzzle he had.

"What is that you have?" I asked.

He turned a piece of the puzzle over in his hand.

"So many people are excited about this Ark that toy manufacturers have built puzzle replicas. Isn't it remarkable?"

"So… you went out and bought one?" I questioned.

Without saying a word, he took that same piece of the puzzle he had in his hand and snapped it into place.

"Just because you can't explain how something happens doesn't mean it can't happen."

"Of course. But, Godfrey, what does that have to do with the puzzle you're playing with?"

Yet again, he gave no reply as he seemed intensely preoccupied with what he was doing. So, I decided to change the subject.

"Godfrey... I wanted to let you know that I was considering going back to Iran."

"Why? To prove that there's a God?" he chuckled.

"No. To find the healed child out there. Tumar."

"Don't worry, the child's safety is of great concern, so the Institute has begun a search for him."

"Well, that's great." I exhaled. "Is that why you led a delegation to New York?"

Godfrey looked over the top of his horn-rimmed glasses and answered, "Yes, among other things."

My concerns about the child were eased for the moment, but other thoughts began to gnaw at me.

"Godfrey, if we find out for a fact this child was healed, it does prove that this relic is divine, doesn't it?"

"We're moving on to talking about divinity now?" he murmured.

"Godfrey, if we don't do all we can to prove we're right, Baines' people will do all they can to prove us wrong. We need to disprove Dr. Baines, and if that means getting to the bottom of this, we need to do that, no matter how hard it is. Carbon dating isn't as reliable as they make it out to be."

Leaving my chair, I wandered around the room for a few seconds but stopped myself. Godfrey's eyes followed me. He looked confused, almost disappointed.

"What are you talking about, Clara?"

"We need to come at this practically," I said. "We've got to convince the world that we're right. I'm going back to Iran. I want to find Tumar so we will have something to substantiate our find."

"That won't prove this is Noah's Ark," he said.

"Well, then, we'll just have to improvise. We need to get a little skittish with our science, like stretch the truth, just a little. I have an idea, maybe I can get Dr. Langley to say the hieroglyphics talked about Noah and—"

"I rebuke that," Godfrey said, cutting me off. "Not under my watch and not under my name," he said as the puzzle piece of the toy ark fell out of his hand. He put out his cigar.

"I understand your concerns," Godfrey said. "You want to continue your father's legacy, and your name is on the line."

"Doctor, I almost lost my life for this."

"But you didn't die. You're here, alive and well."

"How can you not be troubled by all this? And yes, my name is on the line!"

"Lower your voice, Clara," Godfrey said.

"Lower my voice? Because I'm worried out of my mind, you're going to tell me to lower my voice now?"

"Yes," he said, with hard eyes. "I can't hear you when you're shouting."

"Okay," I dropped the tone. "We need to make this happen. If I turn back now, I'll end up right back where I started. All my reasons for working on this—gone."

"Reasons? There's that word again." He shook his head. "What does it even mean, Clara? Do you even know?"

"It's all I can ask for. I don't want to lose anymore, Godfrey. I've lost too much." I sank down in the chair across from him, taking a deep breath to steady myself, trying not to cry. "It's why I left Chicago. I don't ever want to hurt like that again."

Godfrey asked, "What are you in search of, Clara? Is it your name? Is it your past? Is it the life you had with your child, even after God has already said, 'he is with Me?'"

"How could you say that!" I cried out. "Don't you ever talk to me like that again." I tried to counter that statement, but looking into Godfrey's strong eyes, I knew it was true. My child was gone, yet I knew I was not ready to face that. With tears in my eyes, I softly banged on the table with regret.

Godfrey gently placed his hand over mine.

"The ark is God's work. There is no lie to tell the world. The truth is already out there, and there is no way to hide it. Telling lies will only mislead you and me further."

"I… Our credibility is on the line. We might have to pretty up the truth a little bit, that's all I was saying."

"Why are you so worried in the first place? Tell me, Clara, have you ever wondered what it might feel like to have God weave himself into the fabric of your life? Worry or pray, but don't do both. How can you come in here and speak about divinity, and then in the next breath suggest lying? The devil is a liar and a thief, and I've lived long enough to understand that to worry is to be robbed by the same thief that taught us to lie."

"Yes, well—"

Godfrey's chair grated against the floor. "I will never lie about my discoveries. Lies belong to the beast, and I am not in league with him. We can toss the lies around like children on a playground, but give it enough time, and it will turn into a tyrant against us! God gave Satan one power, and one power only—the power to deceive. But he has given mankind an even greater power, and that's the power to decide. Our choice derives either from the truth or the lie. Now, either we live with one or die with the other. Who do you believe in?"

I don't know… I thought to myself, saying nothing to him. I thought I had gained some strength after all I'd gone through. After all that I had seen, and what I knew, there I was behaving as if I didn't trust a letter of God's word…

I drew a circle on the table with the tips of my fingers. I sat there trying to figure out why I was there, trying to convince him to do something I knew he wouldn't. I found no words to explain myself, no words to explain my thoughts on what I believed to be a gainful alternative.

Eyes fixed on his puzzle once more, Godfrey spoke again. "Once, there was a man who walked across the waters. Although we as scientists can't explain how thousands of people claim they saw him do it. My question to you, Clara, is how?"

Wiping the tears from my eyes, I cleared my throat and answered, "Faith, Dr. Godfrey... it's called, the theory of faith."

Godfrey's voice softened, yet his eyes were no less sincere. "God is building himself an ark," he went on to say. "Allow him to finish his work."

Picking up the puzzle piece that had fallen out of his hand, he patiently turned it over, then clicked it into place.

CHAPTER

28

Dr. Kempton's House

THE WEEKEND had arrived, and I had been invited to my secretary Tammy's wedding that Saturday. Beautiful fall leaves blew across the chapel's lawn as the banquet room began to fill with well-wishers. I had arrived late, so, unfortunately, I missed the nuptials. If the wedding was as stunning as the reception, then I missed a wonderful moment. Pictures of the happy couple adorned the entryway, as did an overflowing table of gifts and cards.

A floral centerpiece of purple flowers dressed the table where I sat, quietly watching Tammy's friends and family talk and toast champagne amongst themselves. Dr. Harold was also there, and I did everything I could do to escape his line of sight. He spotted me standing discreetly behind an ice sculpture, which just so happened to be placed near the appetizer table. *Wow, wrong move again, Clara,* I thought, as he gave my name a hefty call, "Clara!"

We talked for a bit, and again, I apologized to him about the Arizona dig and told him how bad I felt about it.

He chuckled, "No big deal, things happen." All I owed him was a dance, and we'd let bygones be bygones.

Twinkling lights hung from the ceiling that evening, as I could only pretend to have a good time dancing with Dr. Harold. The fiasco of an idea I had earlier in the week with Dr. Godfrey was just another one of my many mistakes. What was I thinking? I still hadn't figured it out. And the thought of my child was all too much to handle. As I thought about it, it was not only that he died, but the way he died that I found overwhelming.

Godfrey and I had continued to talk that night, opening up to him even more about what I had been going through. In a small way, it seemed to help the all misdirected ideas I had. I'd even helped finish the puzzle he was working on. He'd given me some of the answers to those mysterious pictures he had hanging on the wall.

He had also told me about the phone calls he had made and the people he had contacted, one of which was a colleague of his, Dr. Darrel Kempton. Dr. Kempton was a prominent chemist in the field of radiocarbon dating, and he might be the one to help us by retesting the Ark, and not the clumsy idea I had devised.

He said Kempton would want to meet with me as he wasn't much of a talker over the phone. I would be all too happy to do so, seeing that I had a chance to get things back on track and regain Godfrey's trust. But until then, at least I had the admiration of Dr. Harold. Although my toes would pay for his terrible footwork in the morning, Tammy's wedding went off easily.

I had made it back from Texas the next morning, and after unpacking, I slipped on my sandals and headed down to the hotel courtyard again. I walked out on the patio, searching for the first seat I could find. The squares of sandstone steps looked a bit damp in the daylight, yet considerably was the green grass growing between the blocks. I slid my feet out of my flip-flops and rubbed my toes over the turf, pondering how pleasant the grass felt under my feet after dancing with Dr. Harold the night before. My phone rang, and I saw it was from an unusual number.

Ah, must be Dr. Kempton. I picked up.

"Hello, is this Dr. Clara Hamilton, daughter of the late, great Dr. Henry Hamilton?" He spoke loudly. "Dr. Godfrey suggested I call you."

"Yes, it's me, sir. How are you? Godfrey told me you were a world-renowned carbon dating expert."

"Well, it is my field of study. I don't dare claim to be world-renowned."

"You're too humble. I'm honored to make your acquaintance, and I must say that I admire your taste in friends. He's a good man. If it weren't for him, I'm not sure where I would be today."

"For sure. How might I help you, Clara?"

"Godfrey talked to me about retesting the sample of the Ark we obtained from Iran. We need an expert to rerun the carbon dating because we suspect there was some sort of error the first time around. Can you help us?"

There was a moment of silence, as if in hesitation.

"Like I told Godfrey if I'm not mistaken, those who originally tested it are, themselves, experts in the field. To second-guess their findings might be questionable to my own reputation. You understand, of course."

"With all due respect, sir, Godfrey wouldn't have asked you to call me if he didn't think you could shine a little more light on the artifact. We need a professional retesting."

When Kempton spoke again, it was with a tone of resistance.

"Pardon me. I feel there's a misunderstanding here. The individuals who tested the Ark are well-known experts. In the event that they weren't the best in the business, they wouldn't have had the chance to test the Ark by any stretch of the imagination. Godfrey suggested they might be wrong about the age of the gopher wood simply because it's an engineered product."

"Yes, sir, that's it. I understand your reluctance when it comes to potentially insulting your colleagues, but a second opinion is always of value when it comes to obtaining the truth. Wouldn't you agree?"

"That's not my biggest concern, Dr. Hamilton. I'm more worried that you'll have gone to a great deal of trouble and expense just to learn that it is, indeed, nothing more than an ancient shelter of unknown origin. In any case, would you be willing to meet with me? You know, I'm not much of a phone talker."

"Sure, Dr. Kempton. I would be honored too."

"Eight o'clock tomorrow morning. Would that work for you?" He asked.

"Yes, sir, send me the address, and I'll see you then."

"See you then." He hung up.

Knowing he was open to suggestions energized me. Returning to my room, I had to get my notes and records together for any questions he had. I called Mike and the rest of the team to tell them that I had talked with Godfrey and what our arrangements were. They were interested to see what Kempton would say as well.

That morning, grabbing a donut from the hotel breakfast bar, I rushed out the front door to the car, googling the address Dr. Kempton gave me.

Less than an hour later, I had arrived at my destination, a small town called Naperville. Ornamental Thanksgiving turkeys dotted neighborhood yards, reminding me of the arrival of the holiday season. I'd been so wrapped up in my work that I had forgotten Christmas would be coming soon.

The rural character of the area made me think of my time as a child in Utah. And yes, my mother again. That was before my father and I left and moved to Chicago. I pulled onto a long, graveled road that led to a large white farmhouse with a wraparound porch and some chickens roaming the grounds. I grabbed my things and headed toward the front door, yet no one answered when I knocked. I tried calling his name.

"Dr. Kempton? Are you home?"

Bang! Bang! Bang!

Finally, from behind the door, a woman shouted, "Hold your horses, hold your horses, I'm coming! Have some patience."

A tall, frowning woman with dark gray hair whipped opened the door. I shrunk beneath her gaze.

"Sorry, ma'am, but I was looking for Dr. Darrell Kempton," I said. "Is this his home?"

"I'm here," a man's voice called from behind her, "Come on in, please."

The woman didn't budge from the doorway. "Before you can speak to my husband, I need to make sure. Are you Dr. Clara Hamilton?"

"Yes, ma'am. I was referred by a friend of your husband's, Dr. Michael Godfrey. I have an appointment."

Clearly unwilling to move, she crossed her arms. "Why are you so testy, child?"

"That's enough," said Dr. Kempton from inside. "Step aside, Darla."

Pushing his way around his wife, Dr. Kempton rolled up to the front door in a wheelchair. He was clean-shaven, with one milky eye that was clearly blind.

Without prompting, his wife said, "Believe it or not, Darrell used to be six foot five. Now, even though he's lost both of his legs, he keeps up such a positive attitude. But as for me, not so much. What are you trying to get from my husband?"

"Oh, get out of here, Darla," said Kempton, waving her away. As she reluctantly left, he offered me his hand. "Pleasure. Come on in and make yourself at home."

We settled in the kitchen, and he wheeled around to face me. "So, tell me. You think you've found Noah's Ark?"

"There's no doubt in my mind," I said, as I watched Darla walk away.

Locking the wheels on his chair, Dr. Kempton spoke again. "Dr. Godfrey and I have known each other for a long time. Perhaps he's failed to mention that we remain at odds when it comes to the issues of science and faith. To be candid, Clara, I have fundamental doubts when it comes to the existence of an Ark. I think it was a metaphor. What about you?"

"Dr. Godfrey is a man of honor. Dr. Kempton, he wouldn't put you on the spot if he didn't think he'd found it," I told him. "And no, I don't think it was a metaphor. At that time, I think it must have been their reality."

"At that time?" he asked.

"Yes, at that time. There is no evidence that at that time, ancient men wrote metaphorically, I believe they actually wrote about what they saw."

"I can tell you are a student of Dr. Godfrey."

"Why is that, sir?"

"Because you're troublesome." He snickered. "Be that as it may," he proceeded, "Godfrey is also a stubborn researcher, especially when he's convinced he's right. He takes great pains in modeling honor and integrity for the next generation, as well do I."

Unlocking his wheelchair, he left the room but soon returned with a huge black bag on his lap. I held my tongue despite my curiosity about what was in the bag.

"As you're aware, Godfrey called and filled me in on the issues you both seem to have run into. He told me all that you had gone through. All I can say is that I'm captivated by your persistence."

"Will you help us retest the sample?" I asked, hope rising in my heart.

He glared. "You're asking me to challenge the findings of one of the foremost researchers in the field."

"Godfrey wouldn't have sent me if he wasn't convinced it was necessary, Dr. Kempton."

"Dr. Hamilton, Baines has years of experience. You're energetic, essentially starting, yet you dare claim there's a flaw in his examination?"

"Possibly," I told him. "Dr. Kempton, Godfrey mentioned this when we spoke previously. I don't believe you can test engineered gopher wood, which may have begun from a wide scope of substances under the same benchmarks you would test other woods. Any test results gained from that system should be seen as suspect."

Unzipping the black bag, Kempton laid some of the contents on the kitchen table. "Dr. Hamilton, to answer your question, I can retest the sample. But, to be frank, I believe it's unlikely my results will differ from what Baines concluded."

"My belief is based on a different premise than his," I said. "The weight and thickness of gopher wood were much greater than anyone might have anticipated, consequently the cause of the fatal crash at the site. We were wrong about the mass of the artifact, just as Baines could be wrong about the age. If retested, the results may be different than first predicted."

"I understand," he said, digging deeper into the bag. "Be that as it may, in light of the fact that you were wrong doesn't mean Baines is. I have faced and conquered many challenges and also failed and made a lot of mistakes."

His sharp look convinced me the subject wasn't yet closed. "Yes, sir, and I have been humbled by mine, trust me. I've learned from my mistakes the hard way. However, the evidentiary facts, the design, the area, the structure itself—"

"Yes. The hard way—" he interrupted me, rummaging through his bag again. Whatever he sought in the bag troubled me, and it seemed to be stuck. Harder, he pulled, his face wrinkled as he let out a slight growl. He tried harder and harder as my curiosity got the better of me. I didn't want to sound out of line, but after I watched him tunneling through his bag all that time, I had to ask him an obvious question.

"Doctor Kempton, may I ask you a question?"

"Of course." He looked up from the bag momentarily. "What is it?"

"What happened to your legs?"

He glanced down and then up again with a look that told me he'd been waiting for the question.

"I'm glad you asked," he said, as Darla sauntered back into the room, turning on the coffee maker. "Would you mind if I tell you my story?"

"No, not at all, sir," I said. "Please, I would like to hear it."

He set the bag aside, placed his hands in his lap, and said, "I became a scientist when I was twenty-eight. I planned things out meticulously and achieved a great deal of progress, making a name for myself in geochemistry and carbon dating. My work was unmatched by any of my colleagues. I worked with some of the most gifted names in the field of chemistry and research, achieving great sought-after acclaims and honors. I had a friend named Warner Shaw. For five years, he and I worked together, discovering ancient artifacts throughout Central Africa. He uncovered them, and I dated them. We were a perfect team."

"Go on."

"Then, one day, he decided it wasn't enough. People were knocking down my door, but barely anyone showed any interest in his work. It's one thing to uncover an ancient artifact, yet something else to confirm the genuineness of the find. Long story short, Shaw wanted to do my work. That's where the big money was, or at least, that's what he thought. On our last mission together, I knew he was sending me out with some rough coordinates."

"If you knew that, why did you still go?"

"I was cocky. I knew I was a jack-of-all-trades and felt like it would be an easy job. I'd done it before, after all, and he was my friend. Before I knew it, I was in the middle of a minefield. He told me everything was okay, that the land mines had been cleared."

Darla came and poured him a cup of coffee. Dr. Kempton continued. "I trusted him. I followed his directions. The next thing I remember was waking up in the hospital, my wife holding on to my hand, telling me my legs had been blown off. Opening my eyes, I could barely see. My friend had set me up to die for his own ambition. The whole thing was sobering. He never called me, never even acknowledged he was there." Kempton kept his voice surprisingly calm as if the events had happened to someone else in another lifetime.

He went on. "He wasn't just my teammate at the time, but my friend as well," he continued. "Someone I may have even called a brother. But it turned out, he was envious and weak, frightened by what the world might think of him for what he'd done, too scared to even get in touch with me again. For years, I hated him. I was depressed, resentful, and angry with myself for trusting him in the first place. But I had to put it away. I learned to live again without legs, and then to walk using prosthetics. Then I taught myself to run. When I had a good pair of legs, I used them to run ten miles four days a week for exercise. Now, I've made running a habit. It taught me a great deal. But through all my hurt and pain, do you know what the hardest lesson I ever had to learn was, Clara?"

I shook my head. "No. What was that?"

"Don't internalize it... I had to get up and learn to let the bitterness go, to be myself again. I even had to learn once more how to love." He reached again into that black bag, and finally pulled out what he had been searching for—two prosthetic limbs. "Yeah, we're all intensely flawed people working our way through life as best we can." He paused. "It's been years now. And I can say that I'm stronger, not because of this ordeal, but despite it." Strapping the limbs on, he stood—a man of six foot five again.

"Doctor Kempton," I had to ask again, stopping him as he headed for the door. "May I ask you one more question, sir?"

"Yes, what is it, Clara?"

"How can you not internalize something that has caused you the worst pain of your life?"

Opening the screen door, he took a deep breath of morning air, then looked back at me, and said, "Forgiveness."

As he turned and stared into the beautiful clear sky, he added, "My team and I will retest the sample in two weeks. Be prepared for the results. I wouldn't have done this for most people, but I must say that I'm impressed with yours and Godfrey's passion, Clara."

I smiled up at him as he towered over me, nearly a foot taller than I was. "Thank you so much, Dr. Kempton." It was clear that our meeting was over.

Taking a moment to stretch, Kempton swung open the front door. I watched him sprint out, starting his ten-mile morning run. Glancing aside, I saw his wife watching him through the window blinds, a proud smile spread across her face.

"Darrell's a resilient man, a great man," she said as he began his morning run. "Every morning, I watched the power of forgiveness sprint out those doors, flourishing in a man who chose not to internalize it, but to let it all go and live his life."

Her words magnified his actions. I could only look into my past and ponder the things I needed to forgive others for, myself as well. The things that still prevented me from moving on as Kempton seemed to have. I thanked her that morning and wandered out the door. Leaving their home, a call from Godfrey disrupted my thoughts. He asked how the meeting went.

"Dr. Kempton is on board," I told him as I drove back to Chicago. "He'll be retesting the sample in two weeks. He said to prepare for the results."

"Great job," Godfrey said. "I wanted to also inform you that I'll be meeting with Dr. Baines in a few days to advise him of our intentions. It was his office that I'd called the other night back at the pub. I insisted on a meeting with him, and with some reluctance, they granted me one."

"Oh great, I had a feeling that's what the call was about."

"Yes, but there is more great news."

"Oh, and?"

"We got the clearances to go back to Iran."

"We did?"

"Yes, there's been a turn of events there—things have gotten bad. People are starving at the site, and there's not enough fresh water, so Iran is looking for volunteers to help. It's how we got the clearances."

"Oh, wow, what about the child?"

"Chuy discovered his location. He's hidden away in some mountain out there. You go find the child, I'll help Chuy and the others."

"Alright, goodness, Godfrey, this is a blessing."

"You're right about that, Clara."

"Oh, and by the way, thank you for introducing me to Dr. Kempton."

"Sure, Clara, and his better half, Darla, she's an exceptional woman, isn't she?"

"That she is, Dr. Godfrey, that she is."

CHAPTER

29

Interlude

Dr. Wilbert "Billy" Baines
(told through the eyes of Dr. Michael Godfrey)

I HAVE BEEN receiving letters for months now from my colleagues, stating that it had become necessary for me and Baines to talk due to the accounts of the miraculous healings that had been multiplying by the day. Clara and I, as well as the Institute, expected more of an explanation for Baines' findings, as well to inform him of the now up-and-coming retest of the Ark.

The mist had settled over I-80 that morning, and I drove through its fog out of Illinois and then toward the Baines Institute in Colorado. Clara had gotten the reassurance I wanted from Dr. Kempton, so, discussing these matters with Dr. Baines face-to-face would seem only appropriate, seeing that we hadn't done it in years. He and I were once old friends, but be that as it may, he needed to know how serious I was about the artifact. I knew how difficult he could be.

It took a full day of driving, a night in a roadside motel, and a few more hours afterward before I saw my destination on the horizon. The Baines institute was one of the finest research facilities on the planet, hidden and tucked away in the woods, located miles away east of Denver. I took the forest-covered route toward the Institute, which later opened up into a broader four-lane road, shielded by stop signs and barricades, requiring me to present my identification at every stop. The multiple checkpoints got me irritated as to why so many were even required.

The sun broke through that morning, shining on the stunning eight-story research facility now in full view. It seemed that Baines had spared no expense, as the structure was plated with huge etched glass windows and mirrored elevators moving passengers along its exterior walls. Yet, for all its supposed transparency, it was surrounded by high-tech security and tall pines. I guess to protect the secrets of Baines' so-called "advanced technology." When I pulled up, I was struck by the herd of deer standing outside the gates of the parking area. Unafraid, sticking their heads between the rails, the herd gazed at the building as if they were trying to see inside. After being buzzed in, the last set of gates pulled open, and I drove in the parking lot, finding a place to park near the front of the building. Exiting my car, I could hear what sounded like bears and other critters clambering in the forest around me.

Quickly finding my way to the entrance of the building, I walked over to the metal detectors, placed my coat and hat on the conveyor belt, and prepared myself for the security guards to search me. Peering over the officers' shoulders, I spotted it. Wow, there it was again, taking my breath away. Resting in a glass-encased room was the primary, portion of the artifact we had submitted for testing. Yet half of it was cut into sections and sent to us. It seemed that the scientists there had taken proper care of God's history, whether they acknowledged it as such or not. Even though the Institute concluded that the artifact's age disqualified it from being the ark, I begged to differ. Another officer greeted me, asking for identification. I held up my credentials for him to scan on his computer. After making a few calls before handing me back my coat and wallet, a gentleman wearing a black suit and white gloves walked out of the back quarters and escorted me to Dr. Baines's office.

When we arrived, my escort stood in the entryway and announced my name.

"Dr. Michael Godfrey, sir," he said, at attention.

Standing behind an old, cluttered, and dusty office desk was a silver-haired gentleman. Staring out of his office windows, he leisurely took a drag from his cigar.

He slowly pulled that cigar away and grumbled my name.

"Godfrey."

I didn't know what to do with that response, so, in all respect, I took my hat off and answered.

"Dr. Wilbert Baines," I began. "It's been some time."

"Yes, it has, professor, please, enter."

Unhurried, I took note that this man's office was full of dust and had fallen away.

"You can stop gawking..." he said.

Wow? Stop gawking? Who does he take me for?

He directed me toward two chairs placed in the center of the room, along with a modest pot of tea set on a small, wooden table.

"Please, have a seat."

I looked over at the chairs placed in the center of the room and wondered why. Although conducive for a pointed conversation, it was such an odd arrangement.

Dr. Baines was an old friend, an intelligent man, but could be unnervingly calculating at times. He had accolades in physics, geography, and radiocarbon dating, to name a few, and it was through this widespread distinction he'd gained his notoriety for being shrewd. It was those accolades that made him rigid and unwilling to bend when challenged as I, for one, often did. He was of much support to those who relied on his research and findings to build their theories and conclusions, but here, lately, he had lost his taste for me.

I watched as he stalled himself, peering out of his eighth-floor window, then rattled for my attention. "You know, professor," he started, tapping the window with a jar he was holding, dumping his ashes in it. "The rumbling sounds of vehicles carrying heavy equipment used to frighten the birds in nearby trees. But now, since I've brought your artifact here, they won't leave. What a bunch of peculiar, dumb animals, wouldn't you agree?"

"Peculiar, yes, sir, but dumb, I'm not so sure," I retorted.

"Really," he stated dryly before dragging his cigar out of the jar. "Are those your thoughts, professor?"

"Well, they absolutely are," I said.

"Would you fathom a cup of tea?" he asked as he slowly strolled over to the chair next to mine.

"No, sir, I'm fine."

As we both sat down, Baines thanked me for coming and began to inform me of his thoughts.

"Professor Godfrey, I've been advised regarding the matters of why you're here," he said, setting his jar of ashes on the table that held the tea set. "And I must say, I'm rather disappointed in you."

"Why?" I pressed.

"Why, you dare to ask, why?" he questioned.

"Dr. Baines, the artifact we've found could prove to be precious to the world—"

"Precious, to the world, Professor?" he asked.

"Sir, I came to let you know that we're retesting the sample—"

Dumping his ashes again, Baines interjected. "The testing we did is complete. I've certified it."

"Sir, we're both very much aware that you, like many other scientists, regularly change their theories. New discoveries change the current paradigm. Scientists have changed their belief system every day and will change them again tomorrow, but there are some things that don't change, and those are the laws written by the Son of Humanity."

"Dr. Godfrey, what goes up, will always come down. There is no Son of Humanity."

"Whatever a man reaped is because of what he sowed, and yes, there is a Son of God."

"Son of God? Why?"

"Love."

"Love? Oh my god," he laughed, slapping his knee.

"Believe me, sir, I wake up every morning, shouting those same words."

He then shuffled his chair around, trying to intimidate me, but there was nothing that could.

"Godfrey, our scientific beliefs are based on new evidence."

"My point exactly, Dr. Baines. Our find is brand new evidence."

"Evidence of what, Godfrey. That the earth once flooded, that there was a man who healed the sick and fed the poor? Turned water into wine?"

"Yes!" I exclaimed. "Maybe it explains why those animals frolic outside your gates." Baines got out of his seat, agitated.

"Godfrey, I've indulged your baseless fantasies for years now. I do not appreciate your attempt to question my credibility. Our science is founded on truth, verified by facts. As for you, you're merely a heretic in the world of research, masquerading as a scientist."

Unable to stand still, Baines paced the length of the office before turning to me again. "Professor, you were once one of the world's most renowned astrophysicists. You understood the cosmos and all that was in it. When we worked together, we uncovered so many answers, made so many discoveries, even hoped to reach the answer to the greatest question mankind has dared ask—that of creation—and now look at you. You've fallen away, giving up all your work to start some Holy Institute."

"Dr. Baines, the Institute has been instrumental in recovering data that substantiate our claims."

"Your claims, professor?" he asked.

"That something transpired in the world in those days, possibly continuing to happen now. Ancient men were not zealots writing about miraculous experiences. They were not just subjects to events passed down, but witnesses to them."

He calmed down, but his tone remained disdainful. "Godfrey, there are scientists around the world discovering new things every day—significant, useful things. There's a French scientist who has found an Earth-like planet, and one based in South America who has found what we believe to be another origin of mankind. And right here, in my institute, we have a scientist who has created the Geno Seed—a corn seed that can grow in the most hostile climates on Earth. It will be able to feed millions, animals as well as humans, no matter if it's in searing desert heat or frigid mountain ranges. Imagine the by-products that can come from it, after which there will be no more need for wars, or conflict, or your particular brand of fiction. So, while you're busy asking your God to bring peace to the earth, mankind will be doing it for himself."

"The Earth will never know peace if it has no love." "No, Godfrey, I believe the opposite is true. The earth will never know love if it has no peace." "Dr. Baines, love begets peace." "You're wrong again, professor." He sighed, "Peace begets love." Sitting down, he asked, "What happened to you, Godfrey? I thought better of you. Putting your faith in fables. Well, let me give you some refreshers here. There was no Jonah to be swallowed by a whale, no David to fight Goliath, and no Noah to build an ark." He sat back, grabbing his cigar as if he had closed the argument, but again, I begged to differ. "Have you ever been so anguished that you felt like you were in the belly of a beast? Have you ever loved someone so much that to protect them, you'd fight a giant? Have you ever lived in a world hurled in such strife, all you could do was trust God?" "Hardly!" snapped Baines. "Well, these men did. And people go through it every day."

Slumping in his chair, Baines sighed. "I'm well acquainted with the plight of mankind, I don't need a lecture from you."

"Dr. Baines, plenty will never bring peace to a joyless world."

"Well pointed, professor, but why must we go through this exercise?"

"Why must we…" I responded.

The look in Baines's eyes was searing, as again, he hated to be questioned.

Grabbing my hat, I dusted the thoughts of swaying Baines out of my head, as he was not to be deterred, but neither was I. But before leaving, I made it a point to reiterate the reason I was there. "Now that I understand your position on the subject, Dr. Baines, I won't trouble you any longer with my presence. But be sure of this—we will retest the artifact. Oh, one more thing. Your mentioning of me being a great scientist who might have figured out how and why the universe was created?" "What about it, professor?" "Well, I did. It's the reason I'm here."

"No, professor. I can't believe you," Baines grunted. "Here we are, looking for the answers to fix and heal a starving world, yet sadly, you're out there a heretic. Searching for God."

Walking out of his office, knowing there would be no way of swaying him, the door closed behind me.

➤┼◆➤•O•◆┼◀

CHAPTER

30

The Quiet Truth

G ODFREY CALLED me earlier that evening, informing
me that his meeting with Dr. Baines did not go as well
as he would have liked.

"Clara, Dr. Baines will be of no help to us," he said, "but the
mission is still on. I will meet you in Iran."

In the middle of the night, I had begun packing my bags.
Finally, we had gotten the clearance. My flight was departing
early that morning, and after the conversation I had with Godfrey,
finding the child had become even more important for me. Sue
had called me as well and told me Terry had already arrived in
Iran and was working with Chuy.

After jumping out of the shower, I noticed the sun had risen.
Hurriedly, I got dressed, grabbed my things, and rushed down to
the hotel lobby, where I saw my old bar friends once more.

"Look, guys, it's Clara!" Charlie pointed.

"Clara!" he shouted. "I didn't know you where famous. I
thought I recognized you on the news. Who'd have known we
were rubbing shoulders with a world-famous scientist!" he said,
flashing a big cheesy grin.

"If we'd known you were the woman in the spotlight, we never would have said all of those crazy things. We would have bowed before you and kissed your hand."

"Yeah right, Charlie," I said, as everyone laughed, giving each other one last hug.

"Listen, Clara," said Earl. "Honestly, we're just grateful to call you our friend."

I smiled. "Truly, I just wanted to thank you. You're a bunch of funny and sincere guys, and I needed that laughter in my life. I'm grateful, but right now, I need to catch a flight."

"We do, too, for a sales convention," Charlie said. "But hopefully, we'll meet again. I don't want to get too mushy, but I'm quite sure I can speak for all of us when I say you're always going to be close to our hearts."

I swallowed, fighting back tears. "Thank you so much for being so kind to me, fellas. I got to go now."

Charlie waved while the others blew kisses to me.

"Stay safe, Clara, stay safe."

I left the hotel, and twenty minutes later, I arrived at the airport. Sue had been waiting for me, and she showed me the government-issued passports Chuy had obtained from the Iranian embassy that would help us get into Iran and through customs. Exchanging a few words filled with compliments, we boarded the plane. After a lengthy eighteen-hour flight included the layover, we landed in Iran again.

Walking out of the tunnel, Chuy, along with two of his helpers, rushed up to the carousel and carried our bags away.

"We've been waiting for you forever," he said. "Come on, we have to go. I have to meet Terry back at the site—you should see what's happening."

"Why, what's happening?"

"Another portion of the Ark has fallen to the ground. The Iranian government has seized it all. They're refusing anyone access to any of it after the huge commotion that happened when the blind child was healed. Now there are thousands of refugees camped around the site, waiting for an opportunity to touch the vessel."

He handed me a slip of paper.

"This is where Tumar might be. You and Sue go find him. Terry and I will wait for Godfrey to arrive. I will call you."

We agreed, and he wished us luck, handing me a satellite phone. Sue and I rushed outside where Muhammed waited in a Jeep, greeting us warmly. We were unfamiliar with the area and even more surprised when the Jeep turned onto an empty, barely-used road that wound up the side of a cliff. We cut through some dense woods and ended at an old church hidden by the forest on the western side of the mountains. Lanterns lit the narrow pathway, guiding us through the church's small courtyard. Cracks scaled its stone walls and nailed over the door was a large wooden cross covered in vines.

"Now, you'll have to wait in front of the church for a moment, ladies," Muhammad said, kicking leaves off the steps.

"Someone will come to get you."

We did as he said, sitting down on the steps. After a while, a priest approached us.

"May I ask who you are and why you are sitting here?"

I stood up. "My name is Dr. Clara Hamilton. I'm one of the scientists who discovered the ark, and I'm looking for the child, Tumar. They said we might find him here. Is that true?"

"Muhammed informed us. Do you have any weapons on you?"

Sue and I answered in tandem, "No, sir."

"Follow me then."

Entering the church, Sue waited in the prayer hall as I followed the priest down a long cold hallway. It led to another hallway beneath the altar, leading us deeper into the back of the church until we stopped at a heavy wooden door. The priest knocked, as in a signal, then opened the door wide enough for us to walk through. The small, dim room seemed empty. But as my eyes adjusted to the candlelight, I saw a woman standing in a dark corner dressed in middle eastern attire.

"Let me introduce you," said the priest. "Dr. Hamilton, this is Quitarre, the mother of the child you seek. The child himself hides behind her."

My heart fluttered, and my mouth trembled, before I could stop myself, I uttered his name, "Tumar?"

I covered my mouth, not wanting to frighten him, nor his mother. The grip around her waist released, and her gown softly opened, and he stepped out from behind her, meeting my gaze with bright, clear eyes. In a hushed voice, he asked in broken English,

"You are the American ... who found the ancient thing I touched? Noah's ark?"

"I am," I said. Tumar quickly retreated shyly behind his mother's robe, but after that, he spoke again.

"Thank you ... for the blessing of my eyesight."

"How did you know that you could see, child?" I asked.

"God... out of love... told him," said Quitarre. She walked out of the corner.

"Was it his father who wrote me that letter?"

She nodded and then said, "And because of that letter, his father... is dead. I fear they want to kill us... for the healing of my child."

"You have my deepest sympathy," I told her.

"Thank you. I also wish to thank you for the joy you've brought to my life in restoring the sight of my son. For there would be no sight in my child's eyes, if there was no God, and there be no sign if there was no you."

Nearly in tears, I sank down onto the rug in front of Quitarre, crossing my legs. For a moment, the candle seemed to flicker brighter, and Tumar emerged again from his hiding place. Standing in front of me with unblinking eyes, he reached out and touched my face, caressing my lips with his hands.

The moment felt magical… But I had to be mindful of the grace that stood there before me.

"I'm so sorry to hear about all that you're going through, but I have the same question as everyone else. How was your child healed?"

Quitarre seemed to stand taller. "You ask how he was healed. I answer you… Without fear. Much like yourself, he was chosen."

Oh my God, the child once again stepped closer to me. He stared deeply into my eyes, whether fascinated by their green color or something else, I couldn't tell.

"He said he did what anyone out there would do. He took one step after another until his hands felt the relic. Before he knew what happened, the world appeared before him," his mother said.

As she spoke, Tumar took my face into his hands. Quitarre pulled him away, yet his eyes remained fixed on mine. She settled him onto the mat beside her. She then sat.

"I do not know exactly how, but he told me it happened when he was without fear, and I trust his words. His father always told him not to fear his enemies, and to never be subservient. But near the end of his own life, he taught Tumar to trust in the one greater than him."

"Who are you referring to?"

"My child's father. Haven't you heard me? But he only learned of it at the end of his life, and that is why he wrote you the letter. After they killed him, they chased us as well until we found refuge in this church. No one out there would think to find us so deep in the forest, not out here. No one can know my true feelings. We must be careful about the words we choose when so much is at stake. Those in control will do whatever it takes to silence anyone who dares speak the truth."

Quitarre took a breath, then continued. "Ma'am, I implore you to speak the truth. Trust in Him. Prove God."

Tears filled my eyes. "But how?"

"God did not create you to solve the world's problems or even your own. He did so for you to have faith that He might have your ear."

"But no one can prove God's existence."

Quitarre grabbed my hands and said, "Through your hope, your generosity, and your courage, ma'am—your faith will prove God's existence, day after day."

"Quitarre, how do you do this?"

"When I hear all the lies, all the killing, and all the wars, I run into my closet, into my quiet place. I close the door, get on my knees, and meditate on God. I block out all the lies anyone has to say, I block out all the fighting they all do and all the noise they all turn out to be. I hear by His love all that I need—the quiet truth. It's the only thing that comforts me. It's the best way to defeat the enemy."

Without warning, the candlelight went out, yet the fireplace still blazed.

Tumar, clutching at his mother's gown, met my gaze.

"Ma'am, are you still afraid?"

"Not anymore," I touched his hand. "Not anymore." Standing up, I turned to Quitarre.

"I came to ask your healed child to reveal himself to the world, to prove the vessel's divinity. But now that I've met you and learned how much is at risk for you to speak out, who am I to demand that of you? I would much rather live with that same truth—"

"The quiet truth," Quitarre, softly added.

"I give you my word that I will not reveal your whereabouts," I told her.

"Thank you," she said, placing a hand on Tumar's head. "I keep you in my heart."

Out of the room, and out of the church, I found Sue again.

"Clara, Terry's on the phone."

"Clara, you need to get down here as fast as you can," Terry said. "Everything is falling apart."

"Wait a minute, I'm on my way. What's wrong?"

"People are dying here around the ark! The Iranian Guard is standing their ground and keeping them away from it."

"Let Godfrey know I'm on my way if he's there."

"Okay, I will. Be safe."

Putting the phone away, I told Muhammed to head to the site immediately. I filled him in on the details, but even so, the ride was long and tedious. I dozed on and off throughout the long night as we traversed the rocky roads. We had reached the hills. Behind them, I knew people were dying, and it made my heart ache. But we needed to press on.

Sue and I jumped out of the jeep and peered below. As the fog began to lift, we saw a vast crowd of people spread as far as the eye could see. Some were alone, and others huddled in groups. All had come after the news of Tumar's healing. Chuy and Godfrey joined us shortly.

"They thought they would be able to touch the Ark and be healed, but the guards never let them have that chance," said Chuy. I could hear the frustration in his voice.

Crowds of people overwhelmed the site, but what looked like makeshift barriers kept them at bay. Within the perimeters of the tape stood the Iranian Guard, forcing them away. Their guns gleamed with a deadly glint in the morning light.

CHAPTER

31

Summoning the Courage to Listen

A S WE headed toward the bottom of the hill, tensions were thickening the air. The crowd seemed to be collectively holding their breath, waiting for something to happen. It could be felt in the air, hanging like a canopy.

Chuy sighed aloud. "I told you we had a problem. The Iranian Guard has cut everyone off from touching the ark."

Before I could respond, I heard my name. "Clara, where in the world, were you?" Terry called out from the bottom of the hill. "We tried calling you, but we got no answer!"

With my voice trembling, I said, "I—I didn't know. I had no idea this was happening." I would have begged for the day people would crowd around a piece of history I had found, but not like this. This was awful.

"Clara, this is real life!" Terry said. "Get your head in the game because they've got guns, and they said the ark belongs to them."

Guns. That was the last thing we needed.

"My God," I looked out at the scene.

It had rained a bit that morning, and the skies were swollen dark gray. Sue and I walked carefully down the slippery hill and into the valley. I could smell death in the air. The people who had pitched tents and camped out there days before had misery written all over their faces. Tears welled in my eyes as I walked among the emaciated bodies of crying children hungering for food. I saw the remains of adults who had died, waiting for the healing that never came. The looming tears had been hanging, but a few fell. There was no way to keep them back.

Taking a long breath and summoning the courage in my heart, I walked through that wet, gloomy scene. My boots stuck in the muddy ground with each painful step, making sounds of suction as I hauled them out. Sue continued to walk beside me, weeping. We came across a small child who sat beside his dying mother, tears streaming down his dirty face. Step by sticky step, I made my way over, kneeling next to him.

He looked me in the eyes and said in Swahili, "*Unwean kuaka mama yang?*"

Muhammed, who stood next to me, quietly translated. "He asked if you could save his mother?" The words seemed to prickle him to ask, yet not as much as how they felt to me.

The woman lay face down in the mud. Sue hesitated but turned her over. Instantly, we both saw she had already died. Reaching out and into the mud, I pulled the boy into my arms, holding him close.

"It's going to be okay, it's going to be okay."

He spoke in a muffled voice, English scarcely decipherable, but the words cut into me. "Never. It hurts, it hurts…"

Painfully shaken, looking through those cloudy skies and holding onto that child, I cried, "God, where are you now?" Taking another breath, I looked over and spotted the fallen vessel in the distance. I held onto the child even tighter. He weighed practically nothing for a boy his age, the obvious reason his mother had brought him there, dying for her efforts. How cruel could it be? I mouthed to Sue and the rest of the team, "I'm taking him to the Ark." They looked at the guards holding their guns, silently swallowing down whatever saliva was left in their mouth through fear and tears. As if on cue, a guard strolled by, growling like a dog at any who dared to walk close.

I made my way through a field of bodies, weaving around some small tents. I walked up a small hill toward the Ark surrounded by uniformed Iranians.

Nearing the police barricade, a guard shouted at me, his tone full of fire. "Halt!"

I kept walking. A single warning shot rang over my head, but that didn't scare me, I only picked up my pace. Carrying the orphaned child in my arms, with his hands clutching the back of my neck, my heart's determination grew even stronger, and my pace grew to a hurry. I guess it was because I didn't care at that moment what the guards might do, but I was not going to allow that child to wither away.

Breaking through the crowd, I came into full view of the fallen vessel. The warning shots rang out over my head once more, this time almost deafening as the whistle of the sound continued long after the bullets had fled by. I flinched, then started running, bursting through the caution tape, and heading straight toward the Ark. The guards trained their guns on me.

"No more warning shots!" One of them shouted. "Halt!"

My pounding heartbeat added to the ringing in my ears. I knew I was in real danger. I darted up the hill, covering the head of the child as best I could, I ducked as the triggers of their guns were pulled. *Boom!*

Shots rang out, bullets shrieked past my ears, and struck the side of the vessel. None of them hit me as I ran as fast as I could.

As the guards took aim once more, Godfrey rushed ahead, standing in front of them.

"Wait, wait, wait! Don't shoot!" He thought he could save us. But the guards only took aim again, as though he wasn't there. I held the child tighter to protect him, knowing they might kill us both. They would if they could.

BOOM! The guns went off again, and the sound echoed throughout the valley. Some bystanders fell to their knees, trying to keep safe. Godfrey ducked to the ground, covering his head.

When the thunder of gunshots faded and the smoke lifted, I was still on my feet. It was impossible, and yet… it was true. Running up the hill, holding onto the child and my love with all my strength, I was pushed toward the Ark by the mercy of God.

The guards cocked their guns again, and still, I kept running. Godfrey and the rest rose, swarming the guards like ants, trying to pull them down to the ground.

Coming up to the side of the Ark, I fell. Thankfully, I managed to place the child in front of me as we both knelt. The guns went off one last time. The bullets ricocheted off the side of the Ark, rebounding all around us. Panic flooded my heart, yet with this child's hands in mine, I took another breath. I slammed our palms together on the side of the vessel, and at that moment, the power of faith rushed through our bodies, just like a flood. It was as if God called it to be. Somehow, someway, the Iranian guards, as well trained as they were, had missed.

It was a shock to my system, like I was struck by a bolt of divine lightning. And it wasn't just my body—my mind tingled, too.

I burst into tears as the child cried out. My faith had pushed me to do something I had never done before. Frightened with every step, not knowing the outcome, yet with the spirit of God, I had run.

No one knew how much I had hurt over the past four years of my life—how I had suffered, how the world I thought I knew had been turned upside down, tossed over like a boat in the storm. Not one person knew of the long, sleepless nights, eyes aching from endless sobbing, and the numbing fear and sadness. Because of the façade I put on, no one knew I was hurting. That day, light rained down on my body and on my soul.

Laying back against the Ark as the child collapsed into my arms, I held him with all my heart. In that moment, I not only prayed to God, I listened. "God, where were you when Joshua died?"

In faith, I felt Him saying, "Right beside you."

I asked, "God, why didn't you take away my pain?"

That voice inside me said, "I gave you my strength. The strength you didn't know you had."

I'd asked Him to heal my broken heart, but instead, with a child in my arms, He made me love again. God had revealed Himself to me, and for that, I was eternally grateful. I had no more questions. The old me faded away, and the new me awoke.

Placing his lips against the side of the Ark, the child kissed it, before he turned and staggered over, kissing me as well. His body trembled, no doubt overcome with the same power I'd felt. Holding him, I found safety, even after all I'd been through. It was the brightness of life, a gift from God.

Standing at the foot of the Ark, gathering my courage and my thoughts, I took a deep breath and spoke. My voice rang out across the valley.

"My name is Dr. Clara Hamilton. I, along with Dr. Michael Godfrey, discovered this vessel. I believe it to be the remains of Noah's Ark. Will you please, please just allow these people to indulge whatever faith they have? To feel, just for a moment, what true love feels like?"

With hesitation, the guards rose, glancing at each other. They moved forward and removed the barriers, dropping their guns. The crowd burst through, rushing to the vessel, each struggling to place their hands on the Ark. The guards didn't try to stop them. Instead, they just watched from the side, their power gone— nothing in the face of faith.

I collapsed to the ground. No strength remained in my body. Helplessly surrendering to God, I wanted nothing more than to rest and catch my breath.

The remainder of the team made their way to us, carrying the child back to his tribe. Dragging myself up, I joined them, and they helped me along, half carrying me back with an arm limp over their shoulders as well. My whole body had been weakened by the transcendent experience, but such a weakness was nothing in comparison to the strength rising in my soul.

For the next few days, the team and I worked, trying to help as many people to the Ark as possible. Before the darkness of night gave way to dawn, I walked back to the camp for a cup of coffee.

Godfrey appeared from the shadows. Together, we sat beside the campfire, sharing the hidden joy we felt. We sighed, almost in unison. Our journey, our lives, had led us to this moment. After a while, Terry joined us in the conversation with Sue by his side.

"You know, my mother tried to tell me about God, but I was hard-headed," Terry said. "She used to tell me, 'Terry, this is real life, get your head in the game.'"

We chuckled before he continued. "I wish my mother got to see in me what I've seen in you, Clara." How could I answer that? Thankfully, Godfrey stepped in.

"We've all done what we could do. Our team has uncovered one of the greatest discoveries of mankind." He clapped Terry on the shoulder. "Our paths have crossed by no coincidence. They've brought us together to this place, and look at how we've grown, in faith, and in everything else.

We've shared something with the world that's bigger than ourselves," he said, with pride glimmering in his eyes, "and I pray that everything we've endured will bring the world love."

He was right. We had done all we could do. We had to let go and allowed others to play their part. It was time for others to make their choices.

Yes, I knew we all prayed, but how often did we listen? I never thought life would bring me here. All the hurt all the pain and all the sadness. Yet, it seemed like when I was at my most vulnerable point, I was also at my strongest. Back at the Ark, sitting there on the ground, I had cried out to God, *"God, please help me."* Yet, in love, He'd lifted me up, and said, *"I'm going to help you—help others."* As if I too, had the strength to do it.

It was as clear as crystal, as resounding as a bell. With the faith he could feel in his heart, the belief he could see within himself, and the strength he may have not known he had—trusting God, Noah had made it through a storm.

Looking into Godfrey's eyes, I felt as though I could see into his soul. There was a kinship there. I knew him, and he knew me. I couldn't explain how it felt to meet a stranger who never felt like one, but that was Godfrey, a stranger, not only fighting for me but with me. He was deep in thought, but I wanted to tell him the rest of my story. It took me a while to summon the courage to speak.

"Godfrey, I'm sorry, but there's something more I have to tell you."

Godfrey smiled. "You don't have to say anything, Clara. I understand." His gentle smile told me all I needed to know. "You owe me no explanation," he said. "God will always love you like nobody can. You have some unfinished business waiting for you at home. Leave Iran and go back to Chicago. It's time you took care of it."

"Thank you, I'll call you when I make it back."

Finishing my coffee, I walked out of the valley, my steps weighed down with heavy thoughts. I told the team I was leaving, that I had more to do back home. Under the midnight moon, I climbed the hill and reached the jeep, calling on Muhammed to drive me away.

On the drive, I wondered how Godfrey knew about the problems I had left back home. What did he really think of me? The thought stayed so long it turned stagnant with every movement on it exhausted. It didn't matter, and I never asked. I was wiser now, stronger too, and knew I had to go. Chicago called with all of the things I'd left undone.

The jeep rocked from side to side as we drove away. I thought about how all of those people had changed my life. How that whole experience had altered everyone. How God had allowed me to play a part in it.

"We're on our way, ma'am. We're on our way," Muhammed yelled out over the rumble of the engine dragging its way over the dirt tracks people in that area called roads.

I smiled when I heard him say that. Leaning back into that moment of reflection, I was humbled by the strength I was given. I thought the answer was to put it all behind me. I thought I would never heal from the love I had lost. But, like Noah, God allowed me to try again, and who was I not to?

"Yes, indeed, Muhammad." I caught his gaze in the rearview mirror. "We're on our way."

32

My Rose Petal Bag

S LOWLY, I lifted my head from the comfort of the pillows. It seemed like minutes since I had drowned myself in their softness. Two days had passed, and there I was on an international airliner, crossing a cloud-covered ocean.

My thoughts churned. The same thoughts I'd expected to last no more than a few moments had extended through the entirety of the flight. The resonant thoughts on things I had done, stark images I recalled, those I saw, and the people I shared time with while they enlightened me on how they won their personal battles—it all played over in my head. That was how I learned what joy was all about.

My depression had snapped, gone out of the way. But it was not in some "Aha!" moment. Not because I saw the sunrise or a moonlit lake or flowers someone had brought me for finding something incredible. No, this journey took time for me, and it all started when someone said a prayer. *Ms. Mattie.* I felt the fight was over. I sat there on the plane in prayer that day, in council with God, finding His strength, listening to His peace.

With the ever-present and welcome voice of Godfrey, counseling me with words that still, on that day, rang in my head.

"Leave Iran and go back to Chicago," he had said, convincingly.

His advice, although thoughtful, was difficult for me. It was a nudge in the right direction, prompting me to kiss the cross hanging around my neck that an elderly lady had given me back at the site of the ark's remains. In all honesty, I'd never imagined myself holding onto a cross, strung with rosary beads and someone's prayers. It felt natural.

"We will land in fifteen minutes," the pilot announced over the intercom. Putting my tray up, I prepared for landing, back to square one for me.

The plane landed gently. I gathered my belongings and shuffled past the family in front of me, making my way out of the airport. A line of cabs was waiting to be hailed, and I was quick to catch one.

"Where to?" the driver asked as I slid into the back seat, the meter ticked on the second I had opened the door.

Normally, I would have gone to my hotel room, but that day, a different location called. I thought about my father and his gravesite. I had some important business to do back there.

Drawing in a deep breath, I told him, "Take me to the Chicago cemetery."

"Okay, ma'am. Buckle up."

We pulled away as I lingered on some hurtful thoughts. I couldn't lie. I was still hurting, but I felt stronger. I spotted a flower shop along the way and asked the cabby to pull over. He waited as I walked into the store. Despite all the impressive arrangements on display, I left with a simple bouquet of two dozen yellow roses.

I apologized to the cabby, and we drove on, though I don't think he minded. Every minute was another dime. With an idle hand, I plucked some yellow petals, turning them in my hand as bittersweet feelings flooded my heart. The loose petals I placed in the bag I had gotten from the store. We arrived at the cemetery, and I briskly got out of the cab, closing the door behind me, with the bag of yellow rose petals in my hands. The sight of gravestones brought the unwelcomed thought of death, but I shrugged it off and focused on where I intended to be.

I finally arrived at my father's grave, where, taking my time, I gently knelt to read the weatherworn headstone with the epitaph, "Here lies Dr. Henry Hamilton. He lived his life well." Wow. It was still hard for me to believe. Slowly, I took note of the surroundings, a combination of well-maintained gray and white granite tombstones reflecting the sunlight.

A short distance away, people were donning black and standing atop freshly mowed grass. They spoke quietly to their loved ones, but I paid no attention as I slipped my hand into my bag to retrieve a handful of the rose petals, tossing them into the air. They caught the wind and swirled delicately through the air as they floated down to the ground around my father's grave.

I sat for some time. I can't say how long. I spoke to him, told him that I loved him, and forgave him for what I used to think was harsh treatment. It wasn't just forgiveness for him, but me as well. My mistakes had taught me how to let go. We're only human, after all—finally, I'd realized that.

I didn't want to cry, despite my eyes welling, but there was another grave beside my father's. I tossed more rose petals into the air, but they fell without softening the ache in my heart. Next to my father was my child, Joshua, slumbered in his grave, at rest forever. I tried and tried again, but the clutch at my chest was too much.

"God, please tell me. Why would you take him away from me?" I cried.

Shaking my head, wiping my face, and slowly drying my tears, I kissed and hugged Joshua's headstone, trying to hold on to him one last time. I thought of his beautiful face, how much I loved him, and how much he meant to me. I reached into my bag again and sprinkled the rest of those petals around the gravesite and along the grounds near the shattered walkways. It was a silent, elegant tribute to all those and to others, including me, who had lost someone. We had all lost people, but it didn't stop it hurting. Time passed, as it always must...

I walked back up the sidewalk and got back in the cab.

"Where to, ma'am?" asked the cabby.

"Take me to 10603 Rebel Street."

"I don't mean to pry, but I wanted to say that I'm sorry for your loss."

I nodded. "I'm okay. Just take me there."

"Whatever you say, ma'am," said the cabby, obviously not wanting to upset me anymore. Again, we drove away, the car pulling me from the sight long before I could let it go. Then again, with wounds like mine, it would take an eternity.

I gazed out the window as we hit the highway and then drove the familiar streets of the neighborhood. It had been years, and until now, I had been so sure I would never come back.

Rebel Street came into view quickly. The cabby drove up and parked. I got out with rushing thoughts. Seeing my nervousness, the cabby stopped me, reached into the backseat, and handed me the bags that I'd forgotten. After handing me my bags, he removed his hat and tossed out his hand for a tip.

"Don't hate, participate!" he said, smiling. I couldn't help but smile back, amused by his grin and his downright cheeky method of asking for a tip. Reaching into my wallet, I handed him a few dollars.

Turning away, I stared at what used to be my home with nervousness.

"Ma'am, I can see you've got a lot on your mind," the cabby said after a long silence, "but I wanted to tell you that God is with you. He is always with us. I just thought you needed to know that."

"How do you know that, sir?" I asked.

"Because that's how good God is." The cabby placed his hat back onto his head and drove away. With that, he was gone, how far or which way was a blur.

The cloudy skies opened up with snow. It was Christmas time in Chicago, and once again, lights were flashing from the houses, and festive ornaments shone from trees in neighboring yards.

How good is God? I thought as I stood in the driveway. The neighborhood was quiet that day, yet I heard the faint sound of chopping wood coming from the backyard.

Searching for my strength, I recalled the last question I had ever asked, Godfrey, "How did Christ walk across the water?" I was curious what a man of science thought of the miracle.

"Clara," Godfrey had answered, gently putting down his cup of coffee. "I don't know, but in faith, I suspect He did it one step at a time."

Taking a deep breath, I grabbed my bags and shoveled my feet up the snowy driveway, one step at a time. I walked onto a sidewalk leading to the backyard. The gate creaked as it swayed open. The sound of chucking wood grew, and my hands clenched around my bags, fingers tightening so that my skin blushed white. Walking through the fenced backyard, I saw him and stopped. Right there was the treehouse he built, and the swing set he'd put together for Joshua.

I watched him for a moment as he chopped away at the wood to put in the fireplace that had kept us warm years ago. The falling snow melted against his shirtless body. He splintered the final log and stopped. Silence fell.

My heart fluttered. I knew he felt my presence as I felt his. He turned around, and my heart tumbled as I saw the hurt in his eyes. The hurt in the eyes of the man I had shared a life with, the man who had shared a life with me. Something else we shared was the pain—he had suffered the same loss I had, and he hurt as I had. He loved Joshua and me the most. It was Joshua's father and my husband. Paul Hill.

The snow fell harder all around us. But through that snow, our eyes found a way to one another, connecting. It had been a long time since we talked. The words our eyes spoke were with sadness.

I didn't know what to say because I knew I had let him down. Apparently, he didn't know what to say either.

We stood in the middle of our backyard, unable to utter a word. Finally, Paul reached across the empty silence between us and found the courage to say, "I'm proud of you."

Off into the wintery mist of that moment, I uttered back to him, "I missed you."

"Clara!" he yelled, slamming his ax into the stump, "I've been waiting four long years to hear those words!"

My God, what had I done? I felt his pain, worries, and love. My senses dulled, so I reached in my pocket for the letter I had written. I didn't realize Paul had closed the gap between us in the time it took to unfold it with shaking hands. Within the flash of a moment, he was holding me, kissing me before I could utter a word.

I bellowed out, wincing in pain, "I'm sorry, I'm sorry, I'm so sorry!"

He held on to me as I collapsed in his arms. The letter in my hand dropped and blew away.

He pulled me away from him slowly, taking a lasting look into my eyes with questions lingering and burning brightly within his. I could see he had been barely holding himself together after seeing me home for the first time since our issues began.

"Why?" he asked softly. "How could you leave me? Did you get any of my letters? How do you think our son would feel if he knew we had fallen apart?"

There came a barrage of questions for which I had no good answers, but holding onto each other, we both cried, our tears falling so hard that droplets dimpled the snow.

"Do you remember the love we shared? Do you remember what brought us together?" his agonized tone cut through everything.

As he ran his fingers through my hair, I remembered how things used to be, how we promised to love one another until the end, never considering the trials life might bring. I remembered our first blind date, how we had connected instantly, and the jokes and the laughter and the priceless conversations. I remembered our spring vacation and our summer wedding. I remembered it all with such clarity, it made my head spin.

I relived every moment of our past. The love we used to share and the fun we used to have. The joy the day I told him I was pregnant, and the anguish in his eyes when the doctor told him Joshua died...

Then I remembered more—the way we isolated ourselves, drowning in pain. How after his passing, I was eaten up by guilt and grief as Paul yelled at me and screamed that it was all my fault.

He and I would fall in and out of arguments, not mentioning Joshua, but fighting about small things we had never argued about before. Paul threw himself into his work and devoted long hours at the office instead of with me. So, I was at home, either living in the past... or living in the present... alone.

Paul and I had drifted apart. He'd often thought out loud, "We never used to be like this."

So young, and so hurt, we didn't know what to do. Our silence together became so loud that it was all I could hear. Paul tried to reach out to me so that we could get help, but his efforts were too late. I was buried down so deep within myself by that time that I didn't recognize the life I had.

Like two strangers, we lay in bed together. We fell asleep next to one another, one last night. The next morning, I walked out of my home—alone. Maybe it was the way we used our emotions, maybe we used them in the wrong way. Instead of using them to draw us closer together, we used them as something to fight about.

I could never shake the feeling that I had let both him and Joshua down. Paul had tried so hard to wake me from the nightmare, from the pain I was living in, from the hurt and the guilt, but he couldn't. It would take an act of God.

On that snowy day, Paul picked up my bags and, with his arm around me, walked me back into our home. For the first time in our lives, my husband and I got on our knees and prayed about our love.

The silence we once shared became our whisper, and that whisper made us listen to each other again. Listening became our conversation, and our conversation became our love, and that love filled the room. We started talking again.

Lighting the fireplace, Paul and I talked about the past four years. Over a hot cup of coffee, we shared our thoughts and feelings. About him and me, about our child, about the love we promised we would share forever, surreal but blessed.

I told him about how I had heard of a self-help guru by the name of Mike Hall in Texas. Paul told me how he had met Godfrey that day on the steps of the hotel where he had asked for my autograph, and that he was the one who told Godfrey where I would be that night. At that chance meeting, Godfrey told Paul about God's research. Paul confided in Godfrey about the difficulties of his and my relationship.

After their meeting, Godfrey would later offer me the most amazing journey of my life that would change my heart and mind and how I thought about life, love, and everything beyond.

Love doesn't internalize the faults of others but forgives. Love does not live in the past, nor does it despair. Love still hopes for today. So much so that it works its fingers down to the bone, feeding people in hope and faith. Because as the Bible says, *"Faith without work is dead."* And I wanted to live.

The word "faith" reminded me of Ms. Mattie and what she taught me. *Faith.* Such an enormous word.

"But faith doesn't start out that way. Not at all." Ms. Mattie had looked so sure. "Faith doesn't start as a giant ready to do battle, but as a mustard seed prepared to conquer all. You have to exercise it. Trust God in the small things and watch Him reveal Himself in the big ones."

The fireplace warmed us as we sat talking all night long. God must have been in the room that night because we could hear in the tone of our voices how enduring love was, how it always hopes, and never fades away. Love is for a lifetime, as the Bible says. That started to reflect in the reunion of Paul and me.

My God, how struggle teaches. But this struggle almost tore my husband and I apart forever. Yet, in that troubled time, God drew us in. We stopped trying to fix everything, and, together, turned our problems over to God. Throughout those days, Paul and I would work on our friendship, allowing God the time to heal our marriage.

No matter what tragic events or mistakes our lives may bring in the future, God will always be there with us, holding us, loving us, and carrying us through. Why? *Because that's how good God is.*

CHAPTER

33

You're Just One of Us

TWO YEARS later, in a small church outside of Chicago, I waited behind the pulpit. I was about to receive an award for my accomplishments, but at that moment, I couldn't help but wonder where my team was. I searched the crowd for them without luck. The pastor announced my name, so I moved up and took to the podium. As the crowd applauded me, I thanked them and began my sermon—I'd titled it, You're Just One of Us.

"For all of those who feel hopeless, you are a child of God. I understand you feel lost and abandoned, as I once felt too. But as I throw my arms around your spirit and hold onto you, I want you to know that life has not forgotten about you, nor has God's faith in you faded, regardless of who you were, who you are, or who you will be. I love you, but more than that, God loves you. You are not alone. Aren't we all going through it?"

I continued. "If you find someone buried in tears, throw your arms around them and call them 'friend.' I know how it feels when life falls apart when you're convinced that you're standing there with no help in sight. But faith is good. You are not alone. You're

one of us." I swallowed a lump in my throat, not afraid to speak
the words but overwhelmed with love as I went on.

"Dear friends, will you allow me to pray for you?"

"Yes!" clamored the crowd. Silence settled among them. They
listened intently as I started my prayer.

My prayer for you:
"I pray that God gives you a peaceful understanding
to know that He is always in control. Even when we
are afraid, sad, and lonely, He is always with us.
I pray that you know how beautiful and strong you are
and that these tough times will not last forever.
"I pray that God guides you in making better decisions
for your life and that you reach your full potential.
I pray that you heal from all the harm that has been
done to you and that you learn that forgiveness will
free your spirit and allow you to elevate in wisdom.
I pray that we meet again someday and that you tell me
about all the wonderful things that have happened in your
life. Your life is your testimony of all you have overcome.
I pray that you continue to pray no matter what
and realize that your words to God are heard.
I pray for your families and everyone connected to you that
they know love and understanding in their own lives.
I pray for your safety and security as you travel
from place to place on your journey.
I pray that you will call someone—a friend, a lover, a stranger—
to talk you through your pain the next time you are in a crisis.
I pray that you understand everything that has
happened in your life is not your fault.
I pray that you have sweet dreams and that you
envision wonderful plans for your future.
I pray that you know how much I pray for you."

The crowd applauded as God's living faith quenched the demons that once were in my head. I ended my prayer with them that day, the crowd clapping as if to say they had been through it too. But that was not how I wanted it to end. There was more I wanted to say, but the words "Amen" reverberated all around.

It was the love God had been sharing with Paul and me over the past few months that gave me strength through love. I stepped out, and from behind the podium, I pulled my robe tightly around my large waist and showed off my stomach to the entire crowd to let them see. I was a full seven months pregnant again. This was a gift from the Lord, a blessing from Him.

I bowed my head in humility and accepted my award. Godfrey did with me as he had always done with his students, he slapped his fedora hat over his head and walked away, leaving me to accept all the credit, ever modest.

My team members showed up, Sue, Terry, my best friend Mike Hall, and a woman I thought to be my adversary but was now his wife, Pamela. I was so happy for them, and they were so happy for me as they smiled at me and what we all had accomplished.

I had achieved what I had been after for a long time—my name. The inscription on the award read, "In honor of Dr. Clara Hamilton, Ph.D. and now Evangelist." I had become a messenger of God. I held the award I was given close to my heart, letting it beat as the magnificent creation of the Lord in gratitude for the opportunity, strengths, and gifts.

"That's how good God is," I told the crowd again as I held up my award in the midst of their applause.

Rubbing my hands across my stomach to soothe the child growing inside me, I walked from the stage and bowed my head in humility, as that door had closed to the bad feelings I once felt, pushed shut with the paternal press of God's fingers.

Walking down the crowd laced steps, I thought about all their stories. There was the story of Ms. Mattie, Ms. Jenkins, and Dr. Kempton, and so many more, each significant. Yet, out of all

those stories, the one I found most humbling was the one God wrote for me.

It wasn't a story of defeat or how I lost it all, but a story of how I gained so much more. A story of victory, a story of triumph, a story of how I too, through Jesus Christ, overcame it all.

It is my story.

The story of Clara Hamilton.

Amen.

EPILOGUE

The Last Report

"**B**REAKING NEWS! This is Christopher Elliott from BBN News. After months of testing by Dr. Kempton and a team of professionals in the field of carbon dating, the vessel found in the mountains of Iran—which some believed to be the remains of Noah's ark—the testing has proven to be inconclusive. A more advanced method of carbon dating has shown that though the vessel appears to fit the Bible claims, there is not enough scientific evidence. It seems scientists may never prove what faithful Christians, Jews, and Muslims have claimed to know and believe about Noah's ark."

The image in the background changed before he continued.

"No matter what faith you come from or what you believe, many ancient societies worldwide recorded a great flood. For Christians, the words Moses wrote in Genesis about God flooding the world was not about God's hatred for mankind but the wickedness of man's ways that God sought to destroy. The Christian faith believes that although God brought about a flood to destroy everything, God loved mankind so much that He allowed man's legacy to carry on through the life of Noah and that His mercy is the real miracle."

He went on. "In Genesis 8:1, the Bible says, 'But God remembered Noah and all the wild animals and the livestock that were with him in the ark, and he sent a wind over the Earth, and the waters receded.' After the conclusion of the flood, which lasted over one year, God promised Noah to never destroy the world with water again." Another image change, showing the specified page followed, letting him pause for the viewer to catch the evidence themselves.

"In later chapters, the prophets tell us that the next time God destroys the world, it will be with fire. It would be some five thousand years later when a young Jewish carpenter by the name of Jesus Christ passionately tells a group of his followers, 'I came to bring fire!' Luke 12:49."

Once more, the passage was shown before the next point was discussed. "Wrapping up the news with my grandmother's favorite quote: 'Whatever problems you have, whatever your pain is, trust in those who love you, but keep your faith in God.'"

He smiled. "This is Christopher Elliott with BBN News. Now back to you."

Printed in the United States
By Bookmasters